I0549345

Also by Joan Byrd
From Indigo Sea Press

The All My Tomorrows Series:
Today, Tomorrow & Forever
A New Beginning
Love Finds a Way

The Box in the Attic

The Good Seed—the Bad Seed, Book 1

indigoseapress.com

The Untold Stories of Jesus

By

Joan Byrd

As Given by the Lord Himself

Deep Indigo Books
Published by Indigo Sea Press
Winston-Salem

Deep Indigo Books
Indigo Sea Press
PO Box 67201
Winston-Salem, NC 27114

First Deep Indigo Books edition published
April, 2019
Deep Indigo Books, Moon Sailor and all production design are trademarks of Indigo Sea Press, used under license.

For information regarding bulk purchases of this book, digital purchase and special discounts, please contact the publisher at indigoseapress@gmail.com

Cover Concept by Joan Byrd
Cover design by Pan Morelli
Manufactured in the United States of America
ISBN 978-1-63066-489-3

I dedicate this book to the followers
of Lord Jesus Christ, our Lord and Savior!
And to all God's children,
as his words say: "Feed my Sheep!"
I give my heartfelt thanks
to my Loving Savior,
who has lit up my
mind, heart and soul
with these inspiring words
to share with his people forever.

—Joan Byrd

Forward

In my daily prayers to Jesus, I prayed that He would reveal to me some of His untold story, when He lived upon the earth. He blessed me with this book, which contains the unfinished stories about some of his hidden years and new revelations of some old familiar stories, all delivered to me by my guardian angel, the source of all my many books!

PREPARE TO BE INSPIRED!

These stories which were told to me did not come from any man or from my own imagination! They came by the revelation of Jesus Christ—just like the apostle Paul's!

The Lord our God has secrets known to no one. We are not accountable for them. But we and our children are accountable forever for all He has revealed to us, so that we may obey all terms of these instructions.

The secret things belong unto the Lord Our God, but those things which are revealed belong unto us and to our children forever, that we may do all the words of the law. Deuteronomy 29:29

THESE WORDS CAME INTO MY VIEW WHEN MY BIBLE FELL OPEN

GOD WILL REVEAL TO YOU ONLY WHAT HE WANTS YOU TO KNOW

Searching the Bible, I have never found these words again! Did Jesus, my Lord, place them there for me to read? The Lord does work in mysterious ways! As soon as I got His permission, the beautiful words started flooding my soul and heart. Read and judge for yourself and if you cannot see the love and beauty that fills each page, then I can only pray that your eyes will be opened and your heart will leap for joy. Through the tears, through the laughter, through the moving words that can only come from our Lord, Jesus!

—Joan Byrd

Joan Byrd

CHAPTER 1

The young man stood quietly in the shadows as he watched the raven-haired girl making her way down the street path. As it always did, his heart seemed filled with butterflies just watching her. Even above the clatter of the noisy merchants who lined the streets of Nazareth, he could hear her bright laughter as she walked along talking to her friend. He raised up on his tiptoes and with dreamy eyes watched her come closer to his shop. As he held his breath and slipped further behind his tooling wall out of view, he thought, *I wonder if she will stop in front of the shop to look for me?* Her footsteps slowed as she looked over at the carpenter's shop. As always, she stopped and placed her hand over her eyes to shield them from the noonday sun.

"Can you see him, Mary?" her friend Dianna teased.

"See who, Dianna?" Mary smiled and pointed to a bird nestled in the big fig tree next to the woodcarver's shop. "It's the same bird I saw before. Such a lovely little creature."

"A bird? Mary, you may stop pretending. I know you are looking for Joseph." Dianna tugged at her light-blue sleeve that hung gracefully down her slim arm. "Joseph is not here, probably gone to deliver some of his fine pieces. Come along or we shall be late getting home."

"Mother won't mind. I've caught up with my chores." Mary glanced once more toward the empty work table of Joseph's and followed her friend on down the dusty street.

Joseph stepped out from the shadows and walked out in front of his shop to see her disappearing around the corner.

"I must be crazy hiding from that young girl," he mumbled as he walked over to retrieve his heavy apron. His dark eyes were drawn back to the empty street. "It seems as though she has grown up overnight. When I look at her…this feeling I am having…can it be..."

"…love, my friend Joseph?" Aaron had slipped up behind his long-time friend and heard his words. "Not that one could blame you. Mary is quite the beauty and if I were not deeply in love with my Dianna, I might snatch the raven-haired girl for my own."

"You shall not be snatching Mary, my friend, now or ever!" Joseph pulled a beautiful trunk off his wooden display shelf and set it gently on his work table. "I have your wedding gift almost finished, Aaron—a fine treasure chest for your betrothal. Does it meet your approval, sir?"

"Your workmanship is far better than any other carpenter in Nazareth, Joseph!" Aaron looked at the skillful delicate carving on top of the trunk: carved butterflies that looked real enough to take flight from the perfect flower pedals they floated above. "My Dianna will love the butterflies! It appears to be finished!"

"Just a few more intimate details, Aaron. Call me picky if you choose, but I strive for perfection in what I make." Joseph watched as his friend squatted down to gaze at a trunk hidden under the carpenter's workbench, made of rich walnut—a heart with two birds surrounding it.

"This, my friend, is the most beautiful treasure trunk I have ever laid my eyes on." Aaron ran his hand over the smooth wood, buffed to a shiny finish. "How much for this one?"

"That one is not for sale." Joseph took a soft cloth and dusted off the piece he was working on.

"Not for sale, huh?" Aaron stood up and looped his arm around his friend's shoulder. "Then tell me, Joseph, if you did not make it to sell, is it for someone very special in your heart?"

"If I tell you, make no joke of it." Joseph stared seriously at his best friend. "Do I have your word, Aaron?"

"This is serious!" Aaron smiled warmly. "By all means, Joseph, speak from your heart. I am first and foremost your good and loyal friend."

"I love her, Aaron." Joseph's eyes looked into the blue afternoon sky. "God help me! Mary is all I think about, day in and day out, first thing in the morning, the last thing at night!"

"Mary is fourteen, is she not?" Aaron pulled his friend down on the workbench and sat down next to him. "Joseph, go to her father; ask him for her hand. It will be a good match!"

"Oh, if it were only that simple, dear friend." Joseph gazed seriously into Aaron's eyes. "JoSiphiah would never allow me to marry his daughter. He has but the one and Mary is very special to her parents. I hear he is looking for someone with wealth and a noble background to be her husband. I have neither of those traits, you must agree."

"I think there is hope for you, my friend." Aaron had a twinkle in his eyes. "If the things my Dianna tells me are true—and I have no cause but to believe my dearest concerning these matters—there is a good chance for your happiness!"

"Speak then, dear friend; tell me of this small amount of hope!" Joseph sat up and took a tight hold on Aaron's shoulders. "Does fair Dianna speak of Mary?"

"She does! She says the girl is fascinated with you, Joseph!" Aaron's eyes twinkled. "Dianna told me that although Mary has never once confessed her true feelings, she knows without a doubt that Mary is totally in love with you, my friend!"

"If it were only true, then"—Joseph stood up and removed his apron—"then maybe there is a life for me and Mary!"

"Finally, home!" Dianna stopped in front of the large dwelling on the edge of town. Mary had another half-mile walk to make before reaching her house and stables on the outskirts of Nazareth. Both cousins were from respectable families with modest wealth. "Mary, I meant to tell you, Aaron is going by Joseph's shop this day to pick up my gift."

"Your wedding gift?" Mary's heart beat wildly at just the mention of Joseph's name. "Is it the trunk you admired so much, the one with the heart and birds? It sounds very beautiful, Dianna, like something I would choose if it were my treasure chest."

"Admit it, Mary, you would like anything Joseph made." Dianna hugged her cousin. "Who knows? Joseph may find the courage to ask you to be his life mate."

"Don't be silly; Joseph doesn't even look at me." Mary kicked at a stone. "He probably thinks I'm still a child."

"Aaron tells me different." Dianna's eyes twinkled with secrets.

"Please keep nothing from me, dearest friend!" Mary's eyes grew wide. "Does your Aaron speak of Joseph's feelings?"

"He does, at least what he can read by his actions concerning you." Dianna laughed softly as Mary drew herself closer, knowing her friend was feeling hope at last. "My Aaron says Joseph walks around like a love-sick goat, whistles when it's raining and watches the streets at certain times of the day."

"Maybe Joseph is love-sick over another." Mary looked down, trying not to get her hopes up just to be disappointed. "It could be any one of the available maidens in Nazareth."

"His eyes light up only at the sound of one name." Dianna grabbed her friend's hand—"Mary!"

"Oh, Dianna, if I could only be certain of his feelings!" Mary once again looked hopeful.

"My Aaron will be coming by this night to bring my gift." She winked at her good friend. "I will find out what he and Joseph spoke about this day and fill you in."

Mary heard a familiar voice call her name so she looped her arms around her friend in a hug.

"'Tis my father calling! He is home early! Let me know if there is any more news of Joseph. Until then, sweet peace!"

"Sweet peace, Mary. Run along." Dianna opened her door as she watched her beautiful cousin dash down the street. "Oh, let there be good news for Mary, dear Lord!"

CHAPTER 2

"Father, you are home early." Mary hugged her smiling father. "What brings such a bright smile upon your lips?"

"News of a visitor coming to our fair town of Nazareth, my beautiful daughter." JoSiphiah beamed. "He is of a noble line and his family has great wealth."

"There is no greater blood line than that of our King David, my father." Mary's thoughts were on Joseph. "Within our people, is that not one of the purest bloodlines, dear father?"

"Why yes, of course, but"—Mary's father hurried about the room picking up things to make the big room look tidy and inviting—"one cannot look down on someone like Alexander, a fine catch!"

"My father, forgive me, but I beg to differ. I find Simon Alexander arrogant and boring." Mary jumped when her father twirled around to face her. "'Tis true, Father, you always taught me to be honest and truthful."

"You only met the lad one time, Mary!" he said loudly. "You cannot judge someone after one short visit!"

"A week in his presence was anything but short, Father"—Mary stood her ground—"and he is anything but a lad, as you called him. He is but a few short years younger than yourself!"

"And, child, that is what you need"—he patted her head playfully—"a mature gentleman who knows his *wheres* and *hows*!"

"This gentleman—and I use the word lightly as he is anything but—cannot give me the one thing I desire." Mary walked over to gaze from the window to avoid looking directly at her father. "He cannot give me the love I need."

"Mary, my beautiful innocent child, Simon is well-experienced in love." Her father forced a laugh. "Has he not had two wives already?"

"Two wives and I am told several mistresses, Father." Mary looked down blushing. "What need have I to marry this man? That is your wish, Father, not mine, is it not—to live a miserable and short life as did his first two wives?"

"My dear, you misjudge Simon Alexander. He is but a gentle man who speaks of his love for you." JoSiphiah turned her around to face him. "It is my wish that you marry well, daughter."

"As it is with me, Father." Mary knew she needed to respect her father's word, but to marry this man instead of Joseph would surely shorten her life and her happiness. "There is another I would gladly marry, Father. He may not have great riches and wealth in material things, but he has so much more: a kind and generous heart, a steady and fulfilling occupation."

"Those are all good traits, child, but it is not enough." His voice grew tender. "I want for you what I could not give your mother."

"And all I want, Father, is the one beautiful thing you did give my mother." Tears laced her beautiful alluring blue eyes. "Love, Father, is the best gift anyone can give someone they care for."

"This love you speak of, Mary, has it already found its way into your heart?" JoSiphiah loved Mary with all his heart. He only wished for her to be happy and never go wanting for anything. Before he could speak another word, a knock came on the door. With quick footsteps, Mary's father walked over and opened it.

"Good day to you, sir." A tall, well-dressed man stood just outside the arched doorway. "I have brought a message from the master of our house to be handed into your hands only."

"You are a servant of Simon Alexander, are you not?" JoSiphiah had seen this same man on previous visits with the rich suitor.

"That I am, sir," was his soft reply. "He wishes an audience with you concerning your daughter. I believe you are aware of his intentions?"

"I was expecting his visit when he arrived in Nazareth." JoSiphiah glanced over his shoulder to see Mary was taking in their conversation. "Tell him he is welcome to the house of JoSiphiah tomorrow eve to sup with us and break bread."

The servant bowed his head politely. "I will inform him of your gracious invitation. Good day, sir." His eyes fell on Mary just inside the door. He nodded his head in greetings, then turned to leave.

"Father, I will have no part of this meeting with Simon Alexander!" Mary watched the slim servant slip around the corner. "I'll arrange a stay over at my friend's house tomorrow eve."

"Mary, what could I do? I had no choice but to invite Simon to come after he made his journey here from Jerusalem just to talk to me." JoSiphiah reached for his daughter's hand. "My child, perhaps I have brought you up unfairly, letting you always think for yourself. In time you will grow to love Simon Alexander."

"Not in the way you speak of, Father." Mary looked thoughtful. "As a faithful servant of the Most-High God, I love everyone, but I only have love in my heart for the one man I would choose to marry."

"Then tell me, girl, who is this very special, very lucky man who has captured our Mary's heart in such a way that she would go against her father's wishes?" JoSiphiah looked deep into his daughter's young eyes and he could see the love he always felt from his only child, not those of a rebellious spoiled child.

"If I told you his name, would it change your mind, Father?" Mary held tightly to his hand. "Would it help to know he is from the house of David, has been a faithful son to his father, dead these past three years, who taught him his trade as a carpenter, one highly sought-after all over Nazareth for his fine work?"

JoSiphiah closed his eyes and smiled. "You speak of Joseph, son of my late friend Heli."

Mary looked down shyly, feeling a sense of butterflies at the very mention of his name. "Yes, Father, my heart belongs to Joseph, although he is yet unaware of my feelings for him."

"And does Joseph have deep feelings for you, Mary? Has he spoken these things to you?" Mary's father felt he was losing his baby girl's heart to another.

"Joseph is too much of a gentleman to openly speak such bold words to my face, Father." She laughed softly. "Much different from the outspoken Alexander."

"What's this, you say?" He looked at her seriously. "Did he say something out of place to you, child?"

"He but told me this summer I was growing into a shapely woman, a very inviting shapely woman who could please him greatly." Mary felt her cheeks blush, just remembering his outspoken comments.

"Why am I just now hearing this, Mary?" JoSiphiah spoke harshly and looked up when his wife Hannah stepped into the room, where she had been listening.

"JoSiphiah, do not scold our Mary, for it was I who told her to keep this conversation of Mr. Alexander from you!" Mary's mother pulled her daughter from her husband's grip. "I merely felt Mary, just thirteen at the time, should not go about repeating the foul man's statement."

"Should I have known, Madam, I would never have insisted on his coming here as a possible match for our Mary!" His eyes softened on his daughter. "I am sorry, child, if I grew upset with you; but this revelation has changed everything where Simon Alexander is concerned."

"JoSiphiah, you are not seriously thinking of asking that carpenter to wed our Mary?" Hannah stood coldly, staring at her husband. "What sort of life would she have with him as the wife of a carpenter?"

"A very happy and love-filled life, Mother!" Mary spoke up. "The same that you share, each of you, with me!"

"But Mary, your father and I have always had big dreams for you, baby." Hannah placed a hand lovingly on Mary's face.

"What about my dreams, Mother? After all, it is my life we are talking about, my happiness, my dreams!" She took both her parents' hands. "I grew up in a home filled with love, not a lot of things that hold no happiness. I too want that kind of home, a love-filled home with Joseph if he loves me and desires the same dream."

CHAPTER 3

Joseph was busy cutting a piece of wood to finish a cabinet he was building, so he hadn't noticed the raven-haired girl stepping in front of him. A sweet fragrant breeze blew across his nose and he closed his eyes, remembering where he had smelled that beautiful aroma. Was she that close, he wondered, or was he merely dreaming again? Joseph jumped when he heard her sweet voice directly in front of him.

"Joseph, my friend, you will never finish that handsome cabinet with your eyes shut!"

"Mary," he spoke softly as he gazed into her blue eyes. His handsome face broke into a smile. "What brings you into town so early?"

She laughed and held up her empty straw basket. "As you can see, my friend, I am on my way to the market. It is a lovely day to be out and about."

"Yes, that it is." He glanced up at the clear blue sky as he laid down his saw, then returned his attention to the girl who had stolen his heart. "So, you just happened to be passing my shop and decided to drop over and say hello."

"And to give you this invitation from my father." Mary produced a folded note and handed it to the man her heart beat for.

Joseph reached over and, brushing his fingers gently across her hand, took the welcome invitation and placed it inside his apron.

"Could you not read it now and give me word of your answer?" Mary quickly looked down, feeling flushed with her sudden outburst. She knew it was an invitation for that eve, the exact time of Simon Alexander's arrival.

"If it would please Mary." Joseph smiled at her blushing cheeks and removed the note to read. His hand swept through his thick black hair as he looked down at his unfinished cabinet. "Mary, this is somewhat short notice and I have several orders I must get completed by week's end."

"I see." Mary's thoughts whirled around quickly as to what she must say to change his mind. Then it dawned on her the statement that could prove Joseph's true intentions where she was concerned. "'Tis a shame you cannot come this eve. That means Simon Alexander will be alone with my parents and me."

"Simon Alexander?" Joseph walked around the work table and looked down at Mary. "Perhaps I can arrange a few hours off this eve. It would be a well-needed break for me."

"Then you can come?" Mary tried to remain calm, even though she wanted to shout for gladness.

"Yes, Mary! Tell your father I gladly except his kind invitation and look forward to my visit with his family." Joseph's eyes held Mary's as they were lost in each other until someone rang a bell in the market and broke their trance.

Mary clutched her basket tightly and slowly backed away. Her voice came just above a whisper, "Tonight then?"

"Tonight!" Joseph could not pull his gaze away from her beautiful face. "I look forward to seeing you, Mary!"

She smiled warmly, then turned to race up the path to the market, her heart beating with total joy.

Hannah and Mary had prepared a fine feast for their guests: roast duck with new potatoes, fresh fruits and goat cheese, crusty round bread and a large jug of rich good wine.

"There! The table is laden with good food and bread." Hannah hugged her daughter. "Now run along and get ready. You will find I have pressed your favorite dress for tonight."

"Thank you, mother, your kindness and support fill my heart with overflowing love!" Mary caught a flash through the window, her friend walking swiftly toward the front door. "I see Dianna is at the door. I will invite her into my bedchamber while I'm getting ready."

"Very good, Mary." Hannah opened the door and waved Mary's friend inside, spoke greetings and walked quickly to her chamber to prepare herself for the evening guests.

Dianna helped Mary with her blue gown, then commenced to drape the matching wraps beautifully around her friend.

"Joseph will be at a loss for words when he lays his eyes on you tonight, Mary!" Dianna picked up a soft brush and ran it through Mary's dark locks. "Will you wear your hair down or would you like me to braid it for you?"

"It will make no difference, Dianna." Mary was anxious to hear about Aaron's visit with Joseph, but her friend seem to be avoiding the subject. Could it be the news was bad? Mary's thoughts ran wild. Could Joseph have no romantic interest in her, after all? Had she misread his eyes when she delivered the invitation or his eagerness to change his mind and accept the invitation to come dine with her family?

"Mary, you seem to be miles away. What is on that mind of yours?" Dianna teased. "But you are right about your hair. Neither gentleman will be able to see your beautiful hair tonight hidden under your head wrap."

"Dianna! You did not come here to pay me a visit just to discuss my clothes or my hair!" Mary stood up to face her friend. "If the news you bring is bad, then it must be told! You cannot change the facts, so tell me, what news of Joseph?"

"Oh, Mary, not to worry! It is with joy I pay you this visit!" Dianna hugged her friend. "Joseph does indeed love you, my cousin! It appears the man thinks of nothing but you, night and day! His coming here this eve only proves my words true!"

"When Joseph read the invitation, he was, at first, concerned about getting his work finished and delivered as he had promised." Mary laughed softly, remembering him walking anxiously around his table to join her. "The mere mention of Simon Alexander coming on this same night, did but change fair Joseph's mind."

"I cannot, for the life of me, understand why your sweet father would even consider Simon Alexander's proposal in the first place!" Dianna shook her blonde head. "It is a shame we women are supposed to remain quiet when it comes to important matters, especially when it affects our entire life!"

"My father has a very open mind where I am concerned, Dianna. He loves me and respects my opinions on many issues, especially when it comes to my happiness." Mary looked out from her small window as the last rays of sun were slipping behind the green hills. She turned to hug her friend. "It grows late, dear friend. Thank you for coming by with such glad news!" Mary took her hand and pulled her to the door. "Now off with you while the streets are yet light."

"Peace be with you this special night, Mary." Dianna kissed her friend's cheek and hurried the half-mile up the dusty path as Mary called lovingly from her doorway.

“Peace and love go with you, dear Dianna!” Then she went back for last-minute preparations before her true love appeared in this house for the first time.

CHAPTER 4

Dressed in his richest robes, Simon Alexander stood smiling in the gathering room of the home of JoSiphiah. He had arrived several minutes before his invitation, his servant accompanying him carrying a golden lamp to light his way. The servant had orders to wait outside until he was ready to return to town.

"I hope my early appearance has not inconvenienced you, my dear Hannah." He spoke with an elegant tone.

"Not at all, sir." Hannah looked around for Mary, who was still in her room. "We shall dine after our other guests have arrived."

"Other guests? Will there be other family members joining us this night?" Alexander looked around the room, small compared to his grand hall but very neat and well-furnished. "Your cousin Elisabeth and her husband, Zacharias, perhaps?"

"Neither will be in attendance, Mr. Alexander. Do you know my cousin Elisabeth and her husband?" Hannah glanced nervously at her husband.

"Just a brief encounter with the older couple when passing through Judaea this trip." He laughed sarcastically to himself. "I was staying with a friend, an overnight layover, when they shared with me a most unusual story concerning your cousin."

"And what might that be, Simon?" JoSiphian checked the hourglass. Joseph would be coming any minute.

"My friends told me about this very old couple, way beyond childbearing years, who found themselves with a child!" The rude man sat down laughing. "It was told that Zacharias, the husband, is one of the priests and after finding out his wife was expecting a baby, he went completely mute, unable to utter one word! I can imagine that old man's shock! Where he found the strength to lie down with the old woman in the first place is...ridiculous!" Simon got up and walked around, still laughing. "I had to go and see this old couple for myself, just to see if it were true. That is when I found out she was kin to you, Hannah."

"If Elisabeth is indeed with child, as you say, Simon Alexander, then it is a gift from God Himself!" Mary had been listening to the vile man speak ill of her favorite cousin. "You must never make a jest out of an act of God the Almighty!"

"Sweet Mary speaks her mind." Alexander admired the beautiful girl standing next to her mother. "The only thing required of such a beautiful flower as you, Mary, is to please your husband and restrain from giving any opinions. Men make all the decisions in a family, my dear. I am sure your father knows the scriptures referring to this very topic."

The knock came softly on the door, interrupting the arrogant man's winded speech. Mary walked quickly to answer it while calling over her shoulder, "I shall see to our special guest, Father."

Simon Alexander's eyes grew dark when he saw who waited outside the door, holding a simple tin lantern. Tall and handsome in his fresh clean robe, Joseph stood smiling down at the face he loved. "I hope I have not arrived too late."

"Joseph, you are exactly on time, son!" JoSiphiah motioned the carpenter inside. "Besides, it takes a working man longer to complete his daily routine before he can prepare himself for a dinner invitation."

"I have brought you a small gift of thanks for asking me to dine with your family." Joseph handed Mary's father a beautifully-carved pipe. "Here, sir, I noticed yours had a small crack in the stim."

"So it does!" JoSiphiah laughed as he held up his old pipe and took the new one, carved by the expert hands of Joseph. He admired the gift. "It's almost too handsome to use, but"—he tossed the old pipe down and replaced it with Joseph's—"I know my smokes will taste so much better now."

From his shirt, Joseph took out a small wooden box with flowers carved on the top and handed it to Mary's mother. "A small thank-you for all the love that went into the meal we are about to enjoy at your beautiful table, Hannah."

Hannah could not resist the smile that graced her lips after receiving the elegant box from the handsome carpenter.

"It is truly the loveliest trinket box I have ever seen, Joseph." Her fingers laid it gently in her daughter's hands. "Mary darling, would you lay this carefully on top of my wooden chest?"

"Yes, Mother." Mary smiled at Joseph for thinking to bring her parents such lovely gifts. "The pipe and the trinket box are exquisite,

Joseph. I know my parents will cherish them and the time you spent carving them."

"I too have gifts!" Alexander stepped up close to Mary, as if she were already his possession. "A solid gold jewelry box for your mother and a ruby topping a golden tobacco tin for your father!"

"Tell me, sir, did you make these gifts yourself?" Mary knew the rich man had not.

"My dear Mary, when you have wealth as I have, you purchase fine gifts from a gifted artist, not some inexperienced carpenter." Simon's eyebrow went up as he turned his nose up at the gifts Joseph had brought. "I suppose one must make his own gifts when he cannot afford to buy fine works of art!"

"There is no pipe or trinket box in any market as beautiful and as well-made as these Joseph made!" Mary smiled over at her father. "Would you not agree, Father?"

"Indeed, I would, child!" He patted Joseph's back. "Your smooth wooden pipe will be so much warmer than a solid gold one!"

"And a gift made personal, just for one person, is far better than one bought in the market's many duplicates." Hannah motioned the group toward the table after Mary returned. "Shall we partake of the meal?"

"Hannah, it smells heavenly." Joseph made a space for her to sit. "Is this seat alright for you?"

"Not only talented in wood but an excellent choice for seating." She smiled up at Joseph.

Simon Alexander started to sit at the head of the table when Joseph stepped up next to him.

"Sir, the head of this house sits there, not you." Joseph's eyes twinkled at the frowning ones of Simon. "Would you not agree with me, Mr. Alexander?"

"I beg your pardon, JoSiphiah." Simon bowed slightly to Mary's father. "I shall take my seat next to you, sir." He glanced over at the carpenter with eyebrows arched. "Does that meet your approval?"

"You should ask the host, Alexander, not I." Joseph looked down to keep from laughing. "Where would you like me to sit, JoSiphiah?"

"Joseph, at the other end of the table. Simon, you are fine next to me and my dear wife has her usual spot." Mary's father winked at the carpenter. "Mary, you may sit next to your mother."

"Excuse me, sir, could not fair Mary sit next to me?" Simon spoke to his host, but his attention was on Mary sitting next to this Joseph instead of himself.

"The places have been chosen, my friend." JoSiphian smiled at his happy daughter, then turned to the angry Simon. "Perhaps you would do us the honor of giving grace before partaking of this wonderful food."

"If you don't mind, I'd rather not." Simon Alexander felt his face flush with embarrassment, knowing he had never said a blessing in his life. "It is my throat, sir. It appears to have a slight tickle."

"Permit me to say grace, JoSiphiah." Joseph bowed his head and reaching under the table, took hold of Mary's hand. "Our most loving Heavenly Jehovah, bless the house of JoSiphiah and for the food and fellowship we are about to share. We thank you, Holy One. Amen."

"Amen and amen!" Mary's father cut slices of the fat duck and laid a piece on each plate. After all the serving bowls were passed around the table, the small group ate in silence.

Mary smiled down at her plate, happily remembering how Joseph had taken her hand under the table and held it throughout his prayer, then squeezed it lightly before releasing it. After everyone had eaten, the men returned to the gathering room and joined in conversation, much to-do about the high taxes put upon them by Rome and how Herod demanded much from the people.

Mary and Hannah stayed behind to clean the table and put away the remaining food. In the cool outer room where meals were prepared and bottles of new wine lined the shelves, the women made up a tray with wine glasses filled with red wine to toast an engagement that would be coming shortly. The talk between the men turned to Mary.

"JoSiphiah, enough small talk." Simon Alexander leaned forward. "You know my intentions for coming this night. I have come to ask for the hand of Mary, your daughter."

Joseph straightened up. "Sir, I have come to your house for two reasons: first as a guest, both for dining and in fellowship. Lastly but most important"—Joseph stood up—"I have come because my heart belongs to Mary. I love her very much and ask for her hand in marriage."

"You"—Simon stood up laughing—"a poor carpenter?"

"A man of modest means, true, but I am a God-fearing, honest man!" Joseph held his own against this arrogant snob. "And yes, sir, a carpenter, hard- working! Taught by the best man I have ever known, my dear departed father!"

Simon turned to Mary's father. "Surely you are not considering this…this poor carpenter? I can give your daughter everything she wants!"

"Can you give my Mary happiness, Simon Alexander?" JoSiphiah could not understand what he had ever seen in this man standing over him.

"Girls like pretty things! I can buy her anything!" Simon's voice grew tense. "She will be happy. I will see to it, by God!"

"Tell me, Alexander, can you stay loyal to Mary?" Joseph stepped up beside him, towering over the well-dressed man, remembering seeing this very man in the streets outside his shop making over prostitutes.

"I beg your worthless pardon!" he sneered. "How dare you question my faithfulness where Mary is concerned!"

"I too have heard rumors about many ladies, Simon." JoSiphiah was relieved Joseph had mentioned the man's adulterous acts.

"False reports, I grant you!" Simon Alexander was angry, and his hate for the outspoken carpenter showed clearly as he turned on Joseph, venom dripping from his lips. "You smear a good man's name because you attempt to cover up your own evil acts, sir!"

"It is you, Simon Alexander, who is giving a false report about a decent man just to cover your own guilt!" Mary could not control herself any longer. "There is nothing you can give me that will bring me happiness!"

"Woman, one so sweet should not be so outspoken on such matters." Simon stared coldly down at Mary. "I shall have to break you from this habit of yours when you are my wife!"

"She is not yours, Simon Alexander!" Joseph's voice grew strong. "If I am blessed to have Mary as my wife, I welcome her ideas, no matter how large or small!"

"Well-said, Joseph! Mary has a good head for thinking!" JoSiphiah put his arm around his daughter.

"JoSiphiah, this decision is not up to your daughter! You, sir, have the last word about Mary's husband." Simon tried to stay calm.

"Will you pick me, a man of means and of noble blood. I can give Mary everything while this poor carpenter has little to offer."

"'Tis true, I have the last word." JoSiphiah looked at both men. "I have weighed the difference. You,

Simon, can indeed offer my daughter a fine home and many things." The arrogant man smiled mockingly at Joseph. "Yet, Joseph is rich in the things that make for a happy marriage, a warm home with well-built furnishings and lots of love."

"Love? And do not I love Mary?" Simon began to sweat with worry.

"The love you offer is through possessions, rich costly things, Simon Alexander. The love I seek cannot be purchased; it already lives in my heart." Mary smiled up at the man she loved.

"Can you not hear, woman! It is not your choice!" Simon shouted, never having had a woman talk back to him. "I traveled all the way from Jerusalem for you! You will be mine!"

"The choice is then made." Mary's father opened the front door. "Joseph, you stay! Simon Alexander, you may take your leave."

"Your choice is this…this carpenter, a worthless nobody!" Simon's eyes shot fire.

"This fine carpenter will make my Mary the happiest girl in all of Nazareth!" JoSiphiah waved for the waiting servant and gently pushed the fancy-dressed man over the threshold. "Good day, sir!"

"You will regret this decision, sir!" Simon Alexander turned and stormed up the hill, his servant struggling to keep up.

As Mary's father shut the door laughing, Joseph stepped up to him.

"JoSiphiah, sir, I promise I will love and honor Mary for as long as I live." Joseph had never felt such happiness. "I will give her a good home and lots of children for you and Hannah to spoil!"

"Joseph, my son, I know you will be good to Mary. Let's share a glass in celebration of your engagement!" After Hannah had handed the glasses of wine around, they were held up for the blessing, then drunk down. "Hannah and I will leave you and Mary so that farewells can be spoken."

After the older couple slipped behind their door, Joseph took Mary's soft hands in his working hands. Mary did not notice his rough skin for all she felt was his love coming through his manly fingers. She tilted her head in thought.

"Is my Mary rethinking her choice?" His voice came soft as they gazed in each other's eyes.

"My heart is filled with complete joy over our engagement, Joseph." Mary gently squeezed his hand. "I was thinking about what Father said about your making me the happiest girl in all of Nazareth."

"And he was wrong about this?" Joseph looked puzzled.

"I'm not just the happiest girl in Nazareth, dear Joseph, but the happiest girl in all of God's earth!"

"Then I am indeed blessed!" Joseph looked at her perfect lips and longed to kiss them but thought it may be too soon for such a passionate act. "My Mary, you have made me the happiest man since our forefather Adam, now and forever more!" He ran his fingertips over her lips. "I will call on you tomorrow, with your permission."

"Granted." Mary watched him turn and open the door. "Joseph?"

He turned to face her, a warm smile on his lips. "Yes, my love?"

"Could you not give me a kiss of farewell?" Mary glanced down at her hands. "Even good friends deserve a farewell kiss, do they not?"

"You are far more than a good friend, Mary." Joseph lifted her face, his eyes falling on her warm beautiful lips, the lips he had dreamed so often about feeling in a kiss. "I am your betrothed, Mary. I am sure one kiss will please us both."

"I am quite certain, Joseph." Mary closed her eyes as she tilted up her head for Joseph to lower his until their lips met. He parted his lips tenderly over Mary's for their very first kiss. It was far better than the kisses in their dreams.

If there had been any doubts about their feelings for one another—which there weren't—this kiss would indeed seal their hearts as one. Mary and Joseph declared their love for one another, and they were engaged to become husband and wife.

CHAPTER 5

Early April, The Year: 01 BC

Joseph came by early the next evening to bring Mary the first of many wedding presents. He knew she had admired this one in his shop, never knowing he was making it for her and her alone. Mary opened the front door to see Joseph, standing on the threshold, smiling broadly. In his hands he held the cherished chest, now with two hearts joined, carved beautifully in the middle of the top, flanked by two white doves.

"Oh, Joseph! The chest!" Mary's eyes grew wide with surprised joy. "You made this beautiful chest for me?"

"You and you alone, sweet Mary." Joseph carried it inside and placed it gently on the floor. "You may keep your favorite treasures in here."

"I see you have your traveling bags ready to depart to Cana." Mary got down on her knees and ran her hands lovingly over the chest. She looked up happily into Joseph's eyes. "Father has been excited that he finally has a son to go with him to the spring festival."

"I find it an honor that he should ask me to go with him." Joseph squatted down beside his true love. "I hear your mother has gone to visit your cousin in the hillside town of Judaea, leaving you alone."

"Alone? Not quite, my love." Mary laughed softly. "Have I not the sheep, cow and chickens to keep me busy?"

"Not to mention the house and the garden that needs constant attention!" JoSiphiah had overheard their conversation as he made his way across the gathering room carrying his travel bags. "Not to worry about the girl being alone, Joseph. Our Mary will keep as busy as a busy bee!"

"While my two favorite men are checking out the latest tools, livestock, seed and new carriages to pull the finest horses should you be able to afford one such luxury!" Mary smiled brightly, happy to see her father and her fiancé getting along so well.

"At least we shall be traveling in style, right, Father?" Joseph opened the door and led Mary and her father outside to see the fine cart and donkey standing in the yard. I finished it only this morning. I knew my Mary and I would need one when we set off on our Passover trip to Jerusalem after we have wed."

"It is a handsome cart, if ever I saw one!" Mary's father beamed as he handed Joseph his luggage to place in the back next to his own. "Well, kiss the girl goodbye, Joseph. Time is moving on and I would like to reach Cana before nightfall."

"Father, with this fine cart, you will arrive the short distance to Cana way before nightfall." Mary smiled shyly up at Joseph, who stood staring down at her perfect lips. "You heard Father, Joseph, kiss the girl goodbye and hurry back home so you may kiss me hello!"

"I happily oblige, my dearest love, to give sweet Mary a kiss." With tender passion, Joseph kissed his girl goodbye.

"Alright, little sheep, go to sleep. You have been well-fed, my darlings"—Mary patted the milk cow— "and you, dear lady, have had your grain and have given me the milk I need for tomorrow. I see all my precious chickens have found your roosts so I bid you all good night!"

Mary lifted the lantern off the stable hook and walked out into the starry night, shutting the big wooden door securely. As she reached the back of the house, a light in the stable drew her attention.

"Now that's funny!" Mary looked at the lantern in her hand, still lit but not nearly as bright as the light glowing inside the barn. "I just this moment left that stable! Could it be the moon shining through beyond the other side?" she talked softly to herself as she retraced her footsteps. Mary looked into the night sky as her hand rested on the door latch. Just above her, the moon crept out from behind a cloud.

Mary trembled as she opened the door slowly. She had to shield her eyes from the bright light which took her breath away. Mary tried to reason with herself as to where the light was coming from. Surely, she thought, the stable had not caught fire; she could smell no smoke and the light remained calm, not flickering as flames would. Then out of the light Mary heard a soft comforting voice,

"Greetings to you, Mary, O favored one! The Lord be with you!"

Mary was deeply perturbed at these words and wondered what

such a greeting could possibly mean. The bright glow began to dim so her eyes could see who was speaking to her. Mary had never seen an angel before, but in her pure heart she knew she was in the presence of one of God's messenger angels.

The angel's smile was radiant as he continued to speak to her, "Do not be afraid, Mary. God loves you dearly. You are going to be the mother of a son and you shall call him Jesus. He will be great and will be known as the Son of the Most-High! The Lord Jehovah will give Him the throne of His forefather David, and He will be king over the people of Jacob forever! His reign shall never end!"

Mary's heart pounded as she found her voice to speak to the magnificent angel standing before her. "How can this be? I am not yet married!"

The angel gazed at Mary with tender loving eyes as he spoke,

"I am Gabriel. I sit at God's left hand. Listen, child, the Holy Spirit will come upon you! The power of the Most-High will overshadow you! Your child will therefore be called Holy, the Son of God! Your cousin Elisabeth has also conceived a son, old as she is, indeed, this is the sixth month for her, a woman who was called barren. For no promise of God can fail to be fulfilled. Mary, the time has come! The Messiah is coming and you are to be His mother, blessed one!"

Mary fell to her knees and held out her hand. "I belong to the Lord, body and soul. Let it happen as you say."

"Be ready this night, sweet Mary, for He will arrive!" With those words, the angel departed from her, leaving the stable once again dark, except for the lantern still clutched in her hand.

Mary lay quietly gazing out of the window into the starry night. She didn't know what to expect; she only knew the prophets had spoken of a virgin conceiving the Son of God, and Mary was a virgin. Her thoughts drifted to Joseph. How would he take this revelation that the great Jehovah had chosen her over every woman ever born to have His Son? Then she started to question herself. "Am I truly worthy to be the mother of my Lord?" Mary grew silent when she felt a presence in her room.

"You are truly worthy, Mary. Do you question the choice I have made? Does your God ever make a mistake? Mary, you are loved!" Mary could see the form of a man appear out of a bright light.

Surprisingly, she was not afraid of the vision standing over her.

His eyes were the most intense, most beautiful blue-green she had ever seen. His rich dark-brown hair seemed to dance in waves and touched his shoulders. The beard was full, yet well-trimmed. It was the most handsome face Mary had ever looked upon; even her beloved Joseph could not compare to this heavenly spirit.

"Do not be afraid, Mary," came His soft loving voice. "We are going to make a son. You will be his mother! I will be his Father, just as the angel Gabriel has told you." He came down softly on her. "You will feel only beautiful joy, Mary, unlike anything ever known. You are my first! You are my last! When you have conceived my Son, you will remain a virgin. By my word. All is possible!"

God's overpowering love invaded Mary's body that starry night in early spring. It would always be locked away in her heart for all eternity.

CHAPTER 6

Mary could not bring herself to tell Joseph yet. Every time they were together, he was so happy talking about the addition he was building onto his house for them. They had plans to marry that summer.

Bursting inside, she knew the only person she could turn to who would understand was her cousin Elisabeth, so Mary set out for the hillside town of Judaea where Elisabeth and Zacharias lived. When Mary arrived, she could hear her cousin singing just inside their house. Taking a deep breath, Mary walked quickly inside to greet Elisabeth, "Greetings, dear cousin!"

When Elisabeth heard Mary's voice, the unborn child which had been still stirred inside her and she herself was filled with the Holy Spirit as she cried out, "Blessed are you among women, and blessed is your child!" Elisabeth jumped up and grabbed Mary's hands firmly in her own. "What an honor it is to have the mother of my Lord come to see me! Why, as soon as your greeting reached my ears, the child within me jumped for joy! Oh, how happy is the women who believes in God, for He does make His promises to her come true!"

"Then…then you know!" Mary's eyes were filled with light. "My heart is overflowing with praise of my Lord; my soul is full of joy in God my Savior! For He has deigned to notice me, His humble servant! After this, all the people who shall ever be will call me the happiest of women!"

Mary laughed happily. "The one who can do all things has done a great thing in me! Oh, holy is His name! Truly His mercy rests on those who fear Him in every generation!"

She danced around the room. "He has shown strength of His arm. He has swept away the high and mighty. He has set kings down from their thrones and lifted up the humble!"

She raced over to Elisabeth and threw her arms around her. "He has satisfied the hungry with good things and sent the rich away with empty hands. Yes!" she laughed out. "He has helped Israel, His child. He has remembered the mercy He promised to our forefathers, to Abraham and his sons forever more!" She stopped and took a deep breath. "And He chose me, a poor humble girl, to bear His only son, Jesus, my Lord and Savior."

Mary and Elisabeth held each other as they let the love of God radiate down on them.

After spending a month with Elisabeth, Mary knew she must return home to Nazareth and Joseph.

"Dear cousin, how can I tell Joseph? What words can I say?" Mary clutched her stomach which had not yet begun to show the special baby growing inside her.

"Mary, sweet child, you must tell Joseph the truth. The words the angel Gabriel spoke to you and how you are the chosen one of Jehovah Himself." Elisabeth held Mary in her arms. "Mary, your Joseph is a good honorable man. It may take time, but he will come around to believing this wonderful news!"

"Dear cousin, what if he does not believe me? What if Joseph casts me aside, a fallen woman?" Mary felt the tears falling down her beautiful face. "The law for this is to be stoned to death!"

"Mary, Mary, you must never forget God Almighty Himself is watching over you." Elisabeth let her hand move down Mary's hair. "Joseph loves you, Mary. Give him a little time to sort things out for himself. God will not let you down. I feel it was God Himself who brought you and Joseph together. I feel certain that He will send his angel Gabriel to your Joseph and help him know the truth of your words."

"Joseph is such a loving patient man; never once has he tried to be intimate with me like some men who think they have the right as a betrothed." Mary gathered her things for traveling. "He told me I would remain a virgin, sweet and pure, until our wedding night."

"'Tis a rare and good man, your Joseph." Elisabeth walked her young cousin to the door. "After thinking things through, he will do what is right, perhaps with the aid of an angel's word."

"Then I'm off to tell him. I must not keep such news from the man I love a moment longer." Mary forced a weak smile, feeling apprehensive about the task that lay ahead. "If Joseph accepts the truth and we wed as planned, then my heart shall leap with complete joy! But it is the will of God, the great Jehovah that comes first, above everything!"

"Peace go with you, Mary, blessed one." Elisabeth kissed her cousin. "All will be well, you shall see."

"My heart says you are right, dear Elisabeth. I shall put my full trust in the Father of my baby." Mary returned her kiss. "Then I shall take my leave and say sweet peace to you, dear Elisabeth." With a wave of farewell, Mary started down the long road back to Joseph.

CHAPTER 7

"Mary, you are back!" Joseph walked quickly from his workbench and hugged his betrothed. "I have longed for your return, sweet one."

Mary's smile trembled as she looked up at Joseph's bright smile. "I came straight here, my Joseph, so forgive my appearance. The road was long and dry, so that should explain my dusty clothes."

"Yet you look as bright and fresh as a wildflower, one that grows on the desert byway and still holds its colorful beauty despite its surroundings!" Joseph took her hand. "I have made a drawing of what the addition to our home will look like. There must be room for many children, would you not agree?"

"I love children, dear Joseph. My love, before you share with me this beautiful plan, I must speak to you about an important matter." Mary looked down at their hands, held together in love.

"Dearest Mary, you but worry me." Joseph looked suddenly concerned. "Are you ill? Is that why you made such haste to spend time with your cousin?"

"Ill? No, Joseph, I am very healthy." Mary glanced up into his worried eyes. "It is a matter of great importance that I need to reveal."

"Come, let us sit down." Joseph led her to his bench. "Mary, please do not tell me you have changed your mind about us or that there is someone else."

"Never would I tell you that, my love." Mary took his strong hand. "'Tis you and you alone I love, Joseph. I live for the day that I am your devoted wife."

"Then tell me, Mary, what is this thing that you keep from me?"

"Joseph, I know you are well-learned in the scriptures and the words written by our forefathers, the prophets." He nodded his head. "Isaiah said, 'Therefore the Lord himself shall give you a sign. Behold, a virgin shall conceive and bear a son and shall call His name Immanuel, God with us.'"

"Oh, I get it! That is why you went to see your cousin

Elisabeth!" Joseph smiled, thinking he had solved the mystery. "The miracle of her being with child. She is the chosen one! No wonder you are so filled with overwhelming happiness and total amazement!"

"Joseph, darling, Isaiah firmly states a virgin shall conceive and bear a son." Mary did not know whether to laugh or cry. "Cousin Elisabeth has been married for many years, and she and Zacharias have tried many times to have children, but she was barren and could not."

Joseph's heart began to beat faster as he gazed down at the girl he loved most in the world. "Mary, what…are you trying to tell me?"

"Joseph, the eve that you and Father left for Cana, I was visited"—Mary held tightly to his hand—"by God's angel, Gabriel."

"An angel?" Joseph blinked his eyes nervously. "Mary, it was but a dream."

"Dearest Joseph, I was as much awake as I am at this very moment. It was far more than a dream!" She sat up. "I had just fed the animals and saw they were bedded down for the night. I took the lantern, secured the stable door and was about to enter the back of the house when I noticed a bright light coming from the very stable I had just left.

"I went back, thinking at first it was probably a full moon shining through the back side of the stable. But looking up into the sky, I saw the moon come out from behind a cloud. I then thought the stable must be on fire, but the blinding bright light did not flicker like a fire does, neither was there smoke or a burning smell. As the light began to fade, I heard him speak. Then I saw him, a very tall angel who glowed brightly. He told me I had been chosen by God to bear His one and only son. I asked him how this was possible because I was not yet married. He told me the Holy Spirit would come to me and overshadow me. Then he said, 'Your child will therefore be called Holy, the Son of God.'"

Joseph released her hands and stood up on trembling legs, then made his way over to his workbench in a daze. He bent over and gripped the sides of the big table, his eyes downcast. Mary stood up and walked up behind the man she loved.

"The Holy One, the Holy Spirit, did come to me that very night,

Joseph, and come this winter, I will deliver the Son of God!" She swallowed when Joseph remained silent, head down.

"Say something, Joseph. You know I would never lie to you. Perhaps you are thinking the same thing as I, that I am not worthy enough to be the Holy One's mother."

"Mary," Joseph whispered, "Never has there been another girl born any more appropriate for that honor than yourself." He turned to face her. "But Mary, you cannot be, not now! The Messiah?"

"It is true, Joseph. As humble as I am, the great Jehovah has chosen me. I am the chosen one!" Tears filled Mary's eyes. "You must believe me!"

"Mary, if you were raped, say someone slipped inside your home while you were alone…" His words choked, "If you are with child…I…"

"Dear Joseph, never would I lie to you! Search your heart!" Mary touched his tear-stained face. "It was as I said. God himself came to me in the form of a man through the Holy Spirit. He stood over me in a bright light, just like the angel Gabriel had done. Never have I felt more love than He bestowed upon me. Not from my parents and forgive me, my love, not even from you. The joy and complete happiness I felt when I received His son from Him was unexplainable. No such feeling has ever been felt between man and woman since the birth of our earth. The Lord filled me with overwhelming love!"

"Mary, my head is spinning! I must ask you to leave, so I can think." Joseph could not control his tears. "I…I must sort things out so I can come to a decision as to what to do."

"Very well, Joseph. I understand this revelation must be more than anyone can accept." Mary turned to leave. "Earlier you said I cannot be the chosen one, not now! Why not, Joseph? God does not make mistakes! Have not our people longed for and waited for the coming of the Messiah?"

Joseph turned his back and stared down at his workbench as Mary lifted up her skirt and raced down the path in tears.

Slowly Joseph turned to see Mary disappear around the corner. He fell to the ground and wept.

CHAPTER 8

Joseph paced back and forth in his room trying to make a decision. The only reality he knew was that Mary was pregnant and he was not the father. Joseph had deliberately fought his emotions when it came to making love to her before their wedding as many men have done once they were engaged to be married. He reasoned with himself wondering if he had made love to Mary, he would not be going through this hell.

If he let it be known publicly, it would surely mean death for Mary. He could never subject her to that; his love for her was too great. The only solution was to break off the engagement quietly because he did not wish to see the one he loved disgraced. Joseph also knew this meant sending Mary away and never being able to see her beautiful face again.

Joseph felt as though he were dying inside. The happiness he had felt a few short hours earlier seemed to be fading quickly from his mind. What would happen to him after she was gone? Would he pour himself into his work with the largest part of his heart gone forever?

Joseph fell exhausted into his bed and, after tossing and turning, finally drifted off into a restless sleep.

"Joseph, son of David," came a strong yet loving voice out of a bright light. Shielding his eyes from the brilliant light, Joseph could recall Mary's description of a similar light. Then the light began to fade away and he saw a majestic angel, standing tall over him. Was he dreaming? he wondered. The angel smiled as though he could read Joseph's thoughts. Then he continued to speak, "Do not be afraid to take Mary as your wife. What she has conceived is conceived through the Holy Spirit and she shall give birth to a son, whom you shall call Jesus, the Savior! For it is He who will save His people from their sins!"

"Art thou Gabriel?" Joseph knew his spirit was speaking to this holy messenger sent by the great Jehovah.

"The same! I am Gabriel, the messenger archangel! I sit at the Almighty God's left hand!" The massive angel held out his hand.

"Mary is God's chosen one, the virgin who will be blessed throughout all generations! All of this has happened to fulfill what the Lord has said through the prophet. Joseph, you know this prophecy! You learned it as a child! Have you not read it many times yourself and felt hope for yourself and your people of Israel?"

"Behold, the virgin shall be with child and shall bring forth a son, and they shall call his name Immanuel." Joseph was sure he had just spoken these words aloud to the angel.

"You are to marry Mary as soon as possible!" A twinkle came into the angel's eyes. "And, Joseph, you shall have no intercourse with her until she has given birth to God's only son, even until after the child is weaned from his mother's milk."

Joseph woke from his dream and sat up, a smile spread across his lips. He knew just as soon as the sun kissed the morning sky, he would be waiting outside Mary's door. Then Joseph recalled the last words given to him by the angel Gabriel and the hint of mischief in his strong powerful voice. Joseph could not help but chuckle to himself as he climbed out of bed to get ready for his Mary.

"Mary, you have a handsome visitor, child." Hannah called just outside her bedchamber.

Mary had been up and dressed way before dawn in hopes Joseph had come to some kind of decision. No matter what he had decided, she knew the waiting and wondering was far worse than knowing. When she saw his face lit up with joy, her heart beat with complete happiness. "You believe now, Joseph, my words?"

"And would I doubt the words of God's own messenger!" Joseph fell down on his knees in front of the girl his heart belonged to. "Sweet dearest Mary, can you find it in your heart to forgive me for doubting your words?"

"Joseph darling, could any man hear his betrothed confess this astounding news and accept it outright?" Mary got down to face him. "Joseph, how long have our people been waiting for His arrival? Do you think I was prepared for this?" She laughed softly. "Never, my love, in one million years—had I that long to live—would I dream that I, Mary, keeper of sheep, chickens and a cow from the little town of Nazareth, would be the mother of my Lord, our Lord!"

"Nazareth?" Joseph helped her to her feet. "Does not the

prophet say, 'He shall be called a Nazarene'?"

"My love, you and I can see God's prophecy's being fulfilled!" Mary touched his face lovingly. "Did Gabriel tell you His name? The holy baby growing inside me?"

"He did!" Joseph's eyes sparkled. "Gabriel said…name him"—he stopped so Mary could say it with him—"Jesus!" they both said softly and with reverence.

"Mary, we must wed right away. We cannot wait until summer as planned."

"Our marriage cannot come soon enough, my love, for I shall be showing soon." Mary could not stop smiling. Never had she felt so much joy, and she knew her Joseph shared the same joy.

"Knowing this child is the son of God, I must restrain myself from wanting you completely, my dearest." Joseph felt flushed as he continued, "It was a direct order from Gabriel himself that I must wait to make love to you until after the boy has been weaned from…your breast."

"And when we do make love, dear Joseph, I will come to you still a virgin, untouched by man!' Mary looped her arms around his neck.

"Mary, I will not question how you will be a virgin still, but then you are the only girl who has made a baby with the Holy Creator, the great Jehovah himself!"

"'Tis true! The Lord said—and I quote—'You are my first! You are my last! When you have conceived my son, you will still be a virgin, sweet Mary!'" She laughed as she pulled her Joseph inside the gathering room to plan a quick marriage.

CHAPTER 9

Late November, Year: 01 BC

"Joseph, this boy will be coming soon." Mary rubbed her stomach. "It's incredible the love I feel growing inside me!" She went back to her job, darning the holes in Joseph's robe.

"You are the prettiest girl in the world, Mary, even fat!" Joseph teased as he watched a courier making his way down the village street, stopping at each house along the way.

Joseph turned his attention back on the woman he loved. Even close to delivery, she was still the prettiest girl he had ever seen. He watched her as she concentrated on her needlework, his mind going back to their wedding day.

It had been quickly decided that it would take place in Mary's parents' large backyard. Just a few friends and family members from Mary's side. Joseph's only brother had failed to come, too busy with his business to break away and take time for his younger brother. It did not disappoint Joseph that he had not come; their relationship was strained and neither enjoyed the other's company.

Aaron, on the other hand, was Joseph's childhood friend. He was the first to greet him when he'd moved to Nazareth at ten years of age with his family from the town of Bethlehem in Judaea.

After the wedding vows, Aaron got Joseph to one side as everyone enjoyed wine in the happy celebration. He bent in close to Joseph's ear and whispered, "Your Mary is indeed an angel. Confess, my friend, you dream of sweeping her off to your bedchamber and finally get to know her completely!"

"I must admit, my friend, I do long to lie down next to her and hold her in my arms at last." Joseph took a sip of his wine, knowing the meaning behind his friend's cunning remarks. Joseph knew he could not have any personal relations with Mary until after God's holy son was born and weaned from his mother, so he had to guard his words and choose them wisely.

Aaron laughed softly as he drank his wine and held his goblet up for the server to refill.

"'Tis a most enjoyable pleasure that awaits you, dear friend, to finally make love to the woman you love." Aaron looked dreamily at his wife, Dianna, who sat next to Mary, chatting. "Having the village wenches is no fair comparison to having a pure maiden, still a virgin, in your bed to warm your manly desires."

"Unlike you, Aaron, I will gladly give my Mary that honor as well." Joseph stood up, tired of the conversation and wanting only that the night would end so he could take Mary to his bed and hold her, to steal a kiss or two before drifting off in each other's embrace.

"You claim to be a virgin, Joseph?" Aaron spoke louder than he had intended, as those sitting near the bridegroom looked his way smiling. "I am truly sorry for my outburst, Joseph. I must admit, I am feeling the effects of this great wine!" He tried to compose himself. "I could not help but remember the two occasions you accompanied me to the red-lantern district, where the harlots sell for your pleasure."

"I did accompany you to town, Aaron, and as soon as you would shamefully go in with a harlot, I would take my leave and return home." Joseph's eyes were fixed on Mary, who was also looking at him, hoping the guests would soon depart. "I am glad I saved myself for the only girl I have ever loved. Though the waiting is hard, the reward will be greater still." Joseph knew in his heart this statement had a two-way meaning—not just the fact that he would finally feel Mary one day, but the greater reward was to be the first to look into the eyes of God.

"Joseph, where is your mind? You seem to be a thousand miles away!" Mary smiled when he snapped back. He could hear a wild dog barking somewhere down the street. Joseph smiled at Mary, then glanced out at the courier drawing near to their house.

"I am sorry for letting my mind wander, sweet one. I was remembering back to our wedding day, my love. Such happy memories." Joseph looked out again and could finally make out a scroll in the man's hands as he stopped at the house nearest them. He had to be a man with authority because two Roman soldiers were escorting him.

"What is out there, Joseph? That poor dog has not let up its bark and you cannot keep your eyes off the open window." Mary put away her needles and watched her husband closely.

"Some sort of courier, I would say, sent by the good King Caesar himself." Joseph's attention remained on the well-dressed man as he watched him roll up the scroll. "I would guess, more taxes!"

"More taxes?" Mary sat up. "Has he not taxed the citizens of Israel beyond their limit?"

"Perhaps he has had a change of heart." Joseph tried to joke about the dire situation. "Good King Caesar has decided to reduce our taxes instead." He watched as the three Romans walked swiftly toward their door. "We shall soon know the reason for their visit." Standing up, Joseph smiled down at Mary, then walked over to open the door wide, so Mary could hear all that was said.

"Good citizen of Nazareth, I have a proclamation which was made by our own Caesar Augustus!" Boldly the courier opened the scroll and began reading, "All those who inhabit the world should be registered. This is the first census made by Cyrenius, the governor of Syria, so that all the world should be taxed. Everyone must go to the town of his birth to be registered! This order must be carried out at once and all who are in your household"—the stern man glanced inside the house at Mary and noticed she was far long into her pregnancy—"all who are in your household must travel with you to be registered under your name." His dark eyes met Joseph's. "All who fail this decree will face Roman punishment for total disobedience against his majesty, Caesar Augustus!"

The arrogant man rolled up the scroll, then turned to leave as Joseph stepped from the door to his side.

"Sir, my wife, she is due any day now. I must travel to Bethlehem, the town of my birth. The journey is far, much too far for one in her condition. Could not my wife remain here and let me register for us both? We have no children as of yet, so there will only be the two."

"I cannot change Caesar's decree to suit one man! This God your people serve and worship, perhaps He will show you mercy!" The rude man faked a smile. "I serve Caesar and my royal majesty will not show you or your wife mercy if you do not obey his command! It appears the Roman punishment would extend to this unborn Jew as well!"

"Joseph"—Mary walked up beside her husband—"did not Micah say our baby would be born in Bethlehem?"

"Micah's prophecy, of course!" Joseph looked into Mary's eyes, knowing the hard-hearted Roman knew nothing of their scriptures.

Mary's smile was genuine when she looked into the eyes of the stony-faced courier. "You were quite right, sir, to say our loving God would show us mercy, and He will protect us on our journey to Bethlehem."

The Roman courier stood staring at the beautiful girl. There was no doubting the fact that this child she was carrying could come any moment, yet her faith in her God was written on her glowing face. He felt admiration for this brave, outspoken girl. Most women would break down weeping at the thought of traveling so far in that condition. There was a spark of concern in his voice when he finally broke out of his trance, "Then, dear lady, may this God you trust so much keep you safe." His lips broke into a real smile. "I admire your bravery, young one." The Roman finally turned to Joseph, who had been observing his mood change closely. "Take a lesson from your wife, though it is true we men think we can arrive at the best decisions. Your travel will be slow. I will inform all my Roman soldiers guarding the roads and bordering towns to give you a free pass. You will be among the last to arrive in Bethlehem, so finding a room will be very difficult. I cannot help you there, but something tells me you shall be safe."

The courier reached inside his pouch, got out a pass card and handed it to Joseph as one of the soldiers with him whispered something in his ear. "Yes, I know the day is winding down and I have to finish my rounds." He took the scroll and rolled it up, then turned to leave.

"Thank you, sir, for your words of encouragement and the guard pass." Joseph took Mary's hand. "We shall never forget your kindness."

"Sweet peace and may our God keep you safe." Mary added and noticed a tear appear in the courier's once-steely eyes as he turned without a word and walked quickly down the street to the next house.

Joseph shut the door and pulled Mary over to join him on the bench he had built from olive wood.

"Never would I have believed a hard-hearted Roman would melt at your radiant face and pure words."

"My dearest Joseph, when God lives in our hearts, He will shine through us!" Mary laughed happily. "Caesar made a decree. God chose the time so His word could be fulfilled."

"But thou Bethlehem, thou be little among the thousands in Judah, yet out of thee shall He come forth unto me that is to be the ruler in all Israel!" Joseph joyfully lifted Mary up, laughing, "Bethlehem, home of King David, we come to you so the real King shall be born there, just as prophecy was foretold!"

CHAPTER 10

"Joseph, my son, take things slow and easy on the road to Bethlehem." JoSiphiah helped his son-in-law tie their clothing, supplies and food on the sides of the donkey. "It is a shame you had to sell your fine cart to raise the money needed for your wedding. I wanted to give it to you as a wedding gift."

"I was the happy bridegroom, Father JoSiphiah." Joseph looked up when he saw Mary walking next to her mother. "I wanted to give my Mary a beautiful wedding as well as a grand party. The rest of my holdings are tied up in our home and the carpentry shop."

"The cart would have been nice." Hannah looked at the donkey standing strong despite his heavy load. She reached out and patted the humble beast. "Come to think of it, though the cart was convenient and roomier, those big wheels would bump along jarring your insides. But this small donkey is sure-footed if led properly and will take you on a fairly smooth ride."

"This precious little donkey will be gentle all the way to Bethlehem, Mother." Mary patted the small donkey and handed Joseph a small bundle. "The baby's swaddling clothes, along with birthing cloths and a sharp knife to separate mother from son." Mary beamed. "Only flesh from flesh, never from my heart and arms."

Joseph opened a large bundle that had been tied securely on the donkey's hip and gently placed the baby items inside. After Mary kissed and hugged her parents farewell, Joseph helped her get comfortable on the donkey's back, which had been covered in a soft thick cloth. He waved at his in-laws and started leading the small donkey up the hill of Nazareth.

As they traveled slowly, many other people passed them, some on donkeys or oxen, many riding on carts and carriages. As each group of travelers passed, they would quickly disappear from view as the donkey's slow steps made it impossible to keep up. Joseph could see the first day quickly coming to an end as the sun began to set behind the steep hills of Galilee.

"Mary, we shall have to stop soon. It grows dark." Joseph kept silently praying that other travelers had stopped ahead to rest for the night. Sleeping by the side of the road alone could prove dangerous. Coming over a small ridge, Joseph noticed campfire smoke drifting up into the growing darkness.

"God be praised! A campsite ahead! We need not be alone on this highway tonight." Joseph headed the small donkey toward the fire's glow. An older couple sat huddled near the flames, wooden bowls of steaming stew in their hands. They smiled at the young couple, a look of relief on their faces. Joseph held tightly to the rope as he spoke,

"Do you mind if we rest here tonight near you?" Joseph felt if he did not sit down soon, he might give way to exhaustion.

"It would be our pleasure." The old gentleman seemed calm and not the least bit afraid. "Put your bedrolls near the fire and have some stew. Mother makes a good stew." His eyes twinkled in the moonlight as he smiled at the old woman next to him, "And there's always more than enough."

"If you are sure. We wouldn't wish to be a burden." Mary stretched her stiff muscles. She knew Joseph had to be tired from walking all day so patiently so as not to rush the donkey.

"We welcome the company, my dear." The kindness of the woman radiated as she got up to get two more wooden bowls and spoons. "Where are you children traveling to?" She dipped two full bowls of the good-smelling stew and handed them over to them while her husband got up, retrieved some grain and fed the donkey.

Joseph nodded a thank-you to both the man and the sweet woman. "We must register in Bethlehem in Judaea. Our journey started at dawn this day from Nazareth and we have only taken a few short breaks along the way. I am sure there are many more miles ahead." His eyes fell lovingly on Mary. "As you see, we must move with care."

"Yes, I did notice your wife seems to be very close to having this baby." The older woman's eyes seem to light up in the fire's glow. "You will make it to Bethlehem, child. Do not be afraid."

Mary felt a sense of peace and assurance. Had not the angel said those same words she spoke in the stable when he announced she would have the Son of God.

After everyone had finished their meal, the woman retrieved the bowls and spoons. "I will wash these things. You must get your rest, children. The road is long, but God will see you safely to Bethlehem."

The same peaceful feeling, Mary thought as she stretched out. Unable to keep her eyes open, she said sleepily, "Thank you both for your kindness. May God bless you and be with you as well."

"Oh, He is, Mary; now sleep." The old man stood over the tired couple as Joseph snuggled near his wife and, unable to stay awake, drifted off to sleep as the kind strangers covered them with a warm spread. "Sleep well now, Mary and Joseph, for soon the heavens will reveal the glory of God!"

The first rays of sunlight dawned on another beautiful day as Mary and Joseph sat up and looked around, expecting to see the friendly couple. There was no sign of them, except for the fire that was still lit and two bowls of hot morning porridge waiting near the warm flame.

"Let it be said that there are still friendly, giving strangers on God's good earth!" Joseph helped his wife up and found a private place behind some bushes for them to relieve themselves before eating.

"They were so quiet when they left, I did not hear a sound from them." Mary ate the honey-sweet porridge like a child. "Never have I tasted porridge this good!"

"I must admit the stew last evening was beyond any I have ever tasted"—Joseph winked at Mary—"but yours is a close second, my dearest."

Mary laughed. "'Tis true, her cooking is the very best! There is some special spice I could not place in her stew. It made it taste…well…heavenly."

They both grew silent for a moment, as though Mary's statement made sense to both of them for some unknown reason. The blessed couple set the bowls aside to wash later after they had packed their bed clothes. Mary held out the big spread the old man had placed over them.

"That dear couple—I failed to ask their names—should have woken us so they could pack their spread and bowls. These things are far too nice to leave behind for strangers."

"Nonetheless, they did leave them. We cannot leave them here, hoping they will return to pick it up on their return trip. Some highway thief would probably steal them for themselves."

"Yes, of course you are right, Joseph." Mary turned to get the bowls and spoons and instantly all she saw was an empty cold spot. "Joseph?" she whispered to get his attention. Thinking she saw some sort of danger, he glanced slowly her way.

"Did you hear something, Mary? See anything?"

"That is the problem, husband!" Her eyes remained frozen on the spot. "I see nothing and I hear no crackling fire! Everything has vanished as though it had never been here!"

Joseph slung his head around to see the fire, along with the bowls and wooden spoons, no longer there. Walking over for a closer inspection, Joseph also noticed that the ground where they had set up their tent had not been disturbed. There were no signs of the cart wheels or the horse hooves anywhere either. It was as if they were never there.

"Mary, I do not understand what happened, unless the wind blew in after they left and..."

"Then explain the fire and bowls disappearing, Joseph!" Mary took his hand. "Do not think me crazy, but I sensed something last night from both the man and the woman." Mary's eyes sparkled. "They both knew our names. I remember hearing them say them as we drifted off to sleep. We never told them our names, and the words they spoke brought peace to my soul. They were angels sent by God, Joseph."

"I do not think you are crazy, my love. I too felt the peace and love that radiated from them." Joseph helped Mary on the donkey. "God will make sure His son will be safe, and I can stop worrying about stopping alone after dark for we are never alone."

From that time on, Joseph did not worry when others would pass. He knew they would arrive in Bethlehem and there would be a warm, safe place set aside for them where Mary would deliver her son.

It had been a long journey, and Joseph was very tired when they finally reached the streets of Bethlehem. Things had not changed much since he had left as a child, except for a few more inns thrown up in haste for the influx of people coming to register in Caesar's ordered census.

By the calmness of the crowds on the streets, he knew they must all have a place to rest. He and Mary were the last to arrive and found the first three inns full. They made their way to the oldest inn at the edge of town. The innkeeper stepped outside to speak to Joseph, for the noise inside from the many guest made it hard to communicate.

"My good sir, I have not an inch left inside the inn." His eyes grew accustomed to the moonlight so he could plainly see the carpenter holding the reins of a weary donkey. "Never have I seen Bethlehem so busy. Even our personal apartment on the top floor is filled with strangers, even the halls and lobby."

"Is there nowhere we can go?" Joseph took Mary's cold hand. "Any shelter, dry and somewhat warm?"

The innkeeper rubbed his chin in thought. "I have a small stable behind the inn. It is dry and fairly warm from the animals fastened in their stalls. The floors have a thick blanket of straw so it is clean enough."

"That will do fine, kind sir." Joseph closed his eyes thankfully. "Is there room for our donkey as well?"

"Plenty of room." He looked toward the inn, well-lit with lanterns. "I will go and inform my wife. She will get you the things you might need. Then I shall return to take you there myself."

"Our thanks, good innkeeper." Joseph took a deep breath. "We need not bother your wife. We brought what we need. We would not want to worry you or your wife with such a full house to care for."

"Are you not a guest as well?" The friendly man smiled at Mary. "Hold on there, little mother. Soon you may lie down and rest."

Mary laughed softly, thinking, *There will be no rest for me until this fine baby boy has arrived.* The stable was warm and dry as promised, with only one cow, one lamb and one small horse safe inside their stalls. Their tired donkey happily ate the grain the innkeeper's servant supplied while the innkeeper's wife busied herself preparing for the baby's birth.

Joseph was relieved that he did not have to perform the delivery; but he knew that if he had been alone with his Mary, with God's help he would somehow manage.

"It won't be long now, child." The friendly woman smiled at Mary's radiant face. "This is your first?"

"It is and he is ready to come out and see his world." Mary clutched Joseph's hand.

"You said 'he'? Are you hoping for a boy?" The woman winked at a nervous Joseph.

"Jesus has patiently waited until his mother arrived in Bethlehem." Joseph patted the innkeeper's wife on her back when she stared up confused.

"Jesus? That will be his name?" She admired the beauty of the expectant mother.

"That is his name, gracious woman, and I can feel him moving, ready to come out." Mary shut her eyes to block out the pains that had begun. "He…he comes…even now!" Mary cried out loudly as the wife of the innkeeper instructed her servant girl to quickly sterilize the knife in the flames coming from a stone firebox her husband had brought in to warm them. Mary gave birth to her first-born son quickly. The small perfect baby was wrapped in swaddling clothes and placed in his mother's arms.

"Oh Joseph, see how perfect he is!" Mary gently lifted up a tiny hand and kissed it. Baby Jesus had a beautiful sweet smell, the perfect sweetness from heaven. She slowly pulled the cloth up over his small feet and ran her hand gently over his toes. "My son, your mother loves you so very much."

The newborn kicked his feet as he watched his mother with his bright blue-green eyes. Jesus' tiny fingers took hold of Mary's hand as a smile fell on his sweet lips. It was indeed the first love he had seen since leaving Paradise.

CHAPTER 11

Joseph made sure the firebox was safe before blowing out the oil lamp. Just before he could settle down to rest, he noticed a bright light that filtered in through the rafters over the loft. Mary opened her eyes and realized she could make out even small details in the barn. Had the night gone by so quickly, she wondered until she noticed the darkness just outside.

"Joseph, where does that light come from?"

"I have never known the moon to be that bright." Joseph did not need to relight the oil lamp to find his way to the stable door. "This I have to see!"

"Be careful out there, my love." Mary watched and waited for her husband's return. When he finally came back, he was practically beaming with joy. "Joseph, tell me the wonderous thing you have seen."

"'Tis the biggest, most magnificent star that has ever shone in the eastern sky, Mary!" His voice grew excited as he described it. "It shines right over this humble stable as though God Himself is sending his light down to tell the world, 'My Son is born!'"

"Oh, dearest Joseph, how blessed we are to be his chosen parents!" Mary sang and looked down at her baby boy. His striking eyes were fixed on something invisible to Mary and Joseph. Jesus' hand reached up as if to touch a being standing near him. "Even now, Jesus sees what we cannot. Just a baby, yet in his wisdom he can communicate with"—Mary took a deep breath—"with angels!"

"Can you see them, Mary?" Joseph looked around at the empty spaces beside and above the holy child. "Can you hear them speak to him?"

"No, I cannot but he can hear their words." Mary remembered how the baby's eyes had taken her breath away when she'd gazed at him for the first time and his blue-green eyes met hers. "Joseph?"

"Yes, Mary, there is something important weighing on your mind." Joseph got up and took her hands. "It shows on your face. What worries you, my Mary?"

"It is not a worry that has me mystified, Joseph. It is his eyes, his heavenly eyes." Closing her eyes, Mary could see the Holy Spirit standing over her, his penetrating blue-green eyes pouring out love like no other. "Joseph, Jesus' eyes are exactly like His Father's!"

While everyone in Bethlehem rested in slumber, the shepherds on the Judaea hillside had to stay alert. Their job was to keep watch over their flock, and the night watch was the most critical in a shepherd's life. The wild animals that roamed the hillsides in the cloak of darkness to plunder for food could destroy one's livelihood if the shepherds were not watchful.

This night was no different from any other night for these shepherds who kept the fires going to stay warm on a cold winter night such as this one and, more important still, to frighten away the hungry wild dogs or cats waiting for a time to strike. The small newborn lambs were always their main targets.

Samuel, a young boy, a son of the head shepherd, walked up next to the fire carrying a newborn lamb that shook from the cold of the winter winds coming over the hills.

"What have you there, Samuel?" Ethan, the boy's father, said as he put more wood on the blazing fire. "Found you an orphan, have you?"

"Yes, Father. No ewe would accept the poor little thing." Samuel squatted by the fire to warm the white ball of fur. "See how it calms down with a bit of care and rubbing."

"And do you intend to feed this one lamb yourself?" A young teen smiled down on the six-year-old.

"I intend to fetch the stillborn lamb and cut away its skin, then put its skin on this small orphan and hope its mother accepts him for her own."

"I have seen others try to do that and failed, Sammy boy." The outspoken young man did not feel pity for this helpless baby lamb. He had witnessed far too many dying in his years as a shepherd. "What makes you think your trying that will be a success, Samuel?"

"Because it was my very father who taught me this miracle." Young Samuel was filled with child-like faith, some more than others. "I know our Heavenly Father will hear my prayers and make it work!"

"With that much faith and prayer, son, this little fellow should be sucking a nice warm tit very soon." Ethan patted his son's head playfully. "Come, let us find that sad ewe and make her glad within."

Shortly father and son came back to the fire. "Never have I seen a hungrier lamb!" The father laughed but stopped when he sensed how still everything had grown. The constant baaing of the sheep died away. What had they felt? Perhaps a dangerous wild beast creeping into the group?

Ethan lit his lantern and walked back out to the sheep. He gasped when he saw every single sheep in his flock gazing up into the eastern sky as though they were mystified. If he thought the sheep were acting unusual, Ethan's own breath was taken away for a moment when he looked up into the sky. The other shepherds had noticed the bright star shining down near Bethlehem. Samuel hugged his father's waist as his young eyes stayed fixed on the bright star whose beams seemed to point down to earth.

"Father, what is it?" The six-year-old shook.

"It appears to be some sort of giant star!" Ethan and the other shepherds were trying to figure out the celestial happening when the clouds opened like a curtain and a magnificent angel appeared over them.

From fear, the group of men dropped to their knees, but their eyes were transfixed on the beautiful, yet handsome, male angel who suddenly appeared by their side. The splendor of the Lord blazed around them which made them terror-stricken. The angel smiled brightly, then said unto them,

"Fear not: for behold, I bring you glorious news of great joy, which shall be to all people!" The shining angel waved his hand toward Bethlehem. "For unto you is born this day in the city of David, a Savior, which is Christ the Lord"—his rich blue eyes shone on them with total love—"and this shall be a sign unto you, you shall find the baby wrapped in swaddling clothes and lying in a manger!"

Suddenly there was a multitude of heavenly angels beside the messenger angel. The heavenly host began praising God and saying in unison,

"Glory to God in the highest, and on earth peace, good will toward men!"

When the angels left them and went back into heaven, the shepherds stood up slowly and started speaking all at once. Ethan stepped forward, his face turned toward the small town below them. "Let us go now to Bethlehem and see this thing which the Lord has made known to us!" Without hesitation, he began to walk when the young teen shepherd asked about leaving their sheep unattended. The stars and the moon suddenly filled the night sky and shone down upon the sleeping sheep.

The head shepherd smiled as he spoke calmly, "My heart tells me no harm will come to our sheep this holy night, young one." Ethan touched the lad's arm. "Our people have long waited for the coming of the Messiah! He is here, Nathan! The angels chose to tell us this glorious news—poor shepherds, not rich kings or nobles!"

"Then let us make haste, wise one!" Nathan laughed with joy. "Just down those hills we shall find Him! A baby lying in a manger! Our God! Our Messiah!"

"Our Savior!" Six-year-old Samuel raced off behind his father. The angels had told them the good news. Now they would be the first to see the Son of God!

CHAPTER 12

Late December, Year: 01 BC

"Joseph, wake up!" Mary had been awakened by voices just outside the stable.

"What is it, Mary?" He sat up and tried to focus on her.

"There is someone just outside the stable door. I heard their quiet talking," she whispered and could tell by Joseph's rising that he had heard them as well. He reached for the oil lamp and lit it, although the bright star still shone through the cracks of the old stable.

"I will go and see what they want. Do not be afraid, Mary, God will not let any harm come to us or this baby." Joseph stepped outside into the cold night air, the warmth of the stable quickly fading. He immediately noticed the small group huddled together, trying to stay warm.

"Friends, are you waiting for some purpose?" Joseph could see they were shepherds by their clothes and the staffs they carried, but there was no sign of their sheep.

"Sir, we are looking for a baby, one who is lying in a manger, newborn, wrapped in swaddling clothes." Ethan stepped from the group. "Do not think us mad, but we have been visited by angels on the Judaea hillside where we tend our sheep! They told us we would find the Christ child, our long-awaited Messiah, somewhere in the city of David! A manger could only mean a stable or a barn, an unlikely place for a king to be born, yet the brilliant star shines directly over this stable. Is it…?"

"Come inside, out of the cold." Joseph opened the door as the shepherds looked inside. First, they saw Mary sitting next to a manger. Then their gaze fell on the baby, awake and smiling. "This is the child the angel told you to seek."

Ethan looked at Mary, who seemed to be glowing. "Blessed are you to be His mother, fair one."

"God has sent you to see His Son. Come, see Him whom you seek." Mary's voice was soft and filled with love.

Young Samuel fell down next to the manger and gazed at the

happy baby. "Look how good he is, Father! He does not cry at the sight of strangers!" The six-year-old reached over to take his small hand, wanting to touch him. The small fingers of Jesus wrapped around the boy's index finger and with words only Samuel could hear, Jesus spoke to the boy,

"Samuel, my name is Jesus. I love you! Know this, you will look upon my face again when you become a man." Samuel could feel the tiny fingers squeeze his finger as he stared amazed into the blue-green eyes of his Savior. Finding his voice, Samuel spoke up happily,

"Father, did you hear him? He spoke to me!"

"My son, it is the joy you feel and all the excitement from seeing the angels that make you hear this." Ethan helped the boy up off the stable floor. "Forgive my son, but he feels such joy in seeing our King."

Samuel could not control his tears as he looked first at Mary, then Joseph. With pleading eyes, he drew close to them. "Please, he did speak to me! Perhaps in a way that only a child could hear, but he told me I would look upon His face again when I become a man!"

"What else did he say, lad?" Joseph knew that children who still had a child-like faith could hear words spoken in spirit. He also knew children could have big imaginations.

"He spoke my name. He called me Samuel! He knew who I am!" His eyes looked into Mary's. "He said, 'My name is Jesus and I love you!'"

"Son, son, such things are from your mind. You must not bother these good people with your childhood fantasies." Ethan took his son's hand and pulled him beside him.

"Your son speaks the truth, good shepherd." Mary reached out her hands for the boy and hugged him. "We never told you His name. His name is Jesus and He did speak to you, son, from His heart to yours."

Samuel smiled. Never had he felt so much joy. He did not care if anyone else believed his words. Jesus' mother knew and to his delight, so did his father and his fellow shepherds. They all left the stable with glad hearts, for they had seen the face of God!

Samuel's Story Jumps Forward, the Year: 31 AD

Years later the words Jesus spoke to the shepherd boy in the

Bethlehem stable would be brought to full circle. Ethan had become an old man, forgetful about many things, but he still took care of his son Samuel, now thirty-six-years-old. After they had moved to Capernaum some years back to live with relatives, Samuel had found a job in a tannery and some dyes had spilled into his eyes, rendering him completely blind.

The old father went to the streets every day, except the Sabbath, to beg for money with which to feed him and his son. Memory loss had erased all the miracles he had witnessed over thirty years ago in Bethlehem and on the hillside where he tended his flock.

"It is He!" someone in town called out. "It is Jesus of Nazareth!"

Ethan had heard about the healing this man had done for others, but would his old legs be able to keep up with the excited crowd as they rushed down the street to see the rabbi? Trying to keep up, Ethan stumbled and fell into a crumbled heap. He sat up slowly, tears forming in his once-bright eyes. "It is no use! These old legs cannot move as fast as they once did when I was…" His eyes grew blank as he tried to remember. Scratching his head in defeat, he mumbled, "What was it I used to do?" He talked to himself. Everyone else had moved on to see Jesus.

"You were a shepherd, Ethan, on the Judaea hillside near the town of Bethlehem," came the soothing voice of the tall man standing above him who stretched out his hand and lifted the old man to his feet. "You could not keep up with the crowd to see Jesus."

Ethan looked up into the blue-green eyes of the handsome stranger. There was something about those penetrating eyes. Had he not seen this man before?"

"I believe I should know you, kind sir. You look so familiar, but my mind…it's not working as it should." Ethan could not take his eyes off of the man, how his dark-brown hair moved around his face in waves, not very long, not short, barely touching his shoulders.

"Ethan"—Jesus placed his palm on the old man's brow—"I have come to keep a promise made to a six-year-old friend."

Moving his hand away, Ethan took a deep breath as his memory flooded his mind. "The baby in a stable, of course! Those eyes, those beautiful heavenly eyes!" Tears fell down his cheeks. "I remember you now! You are Jesus, the one everyone has been longing to see and hear!"

"It is for your son I have come. I made a promise; now it will be fulfilled!" Jesus took Ethan's shaking hand and he calmed down. "Take me to Samuel."

"Samuel, I have brought an old friend to see you, son." Ethan winked at Jesus, who returned it smiling.

"Samuel, my friend." Jesus sat down next to him.

"I know that voice. I heard it as a child…" Samuel choked up. "Jesus."

Jesus gently placed his hand over Samuel's eyes and spoke softly, "I made you a promise. I have come to deliver it to you. Do you remember what it was, Samuel?"

"I do. It is something I could never forget." Samuel could feel something strange happening under the warm hands of Jesus. Tears started to collect and dance down his thin cheeks as he kept his eyes closed. "You said that when I was a grown man, I would…" Jesus removed his hand and Samuel opened his eyes. The face of Jesus came into focus, clearer than he had ever seen before. "You said…I would look…upon…your face again!" Samuel could not control his tears, his laughter, his joy as he leaped up, hugging the good shepherd. "I can see again! Praise be to God on High!" Falling down on his knees at the feet of the promised one, he said, "Jesus, my Lord and my Savior!"

"No promise of God can fail to be fulfilled!" came the angelic voice above their heads.

CHAPTER 13

The weeks passed by quickly for Mary and Joseph. Word had spread as the shepherds went about telling everyone about Jesus. Those who heard them were amazed at what they said. Many people went to see for themselves this glorious baby. Some brought small gifts. Others brought food for the couple in the stable.

Finally, the shepherds had to return to the hillside to tend their sheep, but as they walked along, they glorified and sang praises to God for everything they had heard and seen, which happened just as they had been told by the angel.

On the eighth day the time came for circumcising the child Jesus. When the purification time, stipulated by the law of Moses, was completed, Joseph and Mary took Jesus and the things they needed to Jerusalem to present him to the Lord, another law that was to be fulfilled.

"Mary, wait here while I purchase two turtle doves to offer for his sacrifice." Joseph walked quickly to buy the offering, then returned to continue on to the temple.

Just inside the temple stood an old man, whose bright eyes watched the entrance. The Holy Spirit had led him to the temple to fulfill his one wish—that before he died, he would see the Lord's Christ. His old eyes caught the sight of Mary and Joseph as they brought in the child. Simeon took the child, lifted him up in his arms, blessed God and rejoiced, "At last, my Lord, you can dismiss your servant in peace, as you promised! For my eyes have seen your salvation, which you have made ready for every people, a light to show truth to the gentiles and bring glory to your people Israel!"

Mary and Joseph turned to one another in amazement at what this man said about Jesus. After Simeon gave them a blessing, his eyes fell solemnly on Mary.

"This child is destined to make many fall and many rise in Israel and set up a standard which many will attack, for he will expose the secret thoughts of many hearts." His eyes grew sad as he took Mary's hand. "And you, dear girl, your very soul will be pierced by a sword."

Mary felt her hand tremble in his as she wondered what he could mean. She noticed a very old woman walking toward them, her eyes alight with wonder and joy.

"People of Jerusalem"—she looked around at those in the temple—"I am Anna, a prophetess of God. My whole life, I have spent in the temple, worshipping God night and day with fasting and prayers." She fastened her eyes on Jesus. "This child is for all in Jerusalem who are expecting redemption!"

After they had completed all the requirements of the law, Joseph, Mary and Jesus returned to Bethlehem and the stable until Mary and her small son could travel to Nazareth.

Late Winter, the Year: 01 AD

Mary had just finished feeding Jesus when she heard a strange sound just outside the stable. Joseph had heard it as well, for he looked up from milking the innkeeper's cow.

"What strange noise is that, Joseph?" Mary wrapped Jesus warmly and laid him in the manger.

"I have not heard a camel since I left Bethlehem when I was a child." Joseph looked at the door. "I will go and inquire what they doing here."

When he opened the stable door, he noticed three camels, richly dressed in head tassels and fancy gold saddles. Three very distinguished men, resembling royalty, sat astride the animals while dark-skinned servants held onto the reins. A small caravan of donkeys carried what appeared to be supplies on their stout backs.

"Gentlemen, what brings you to Bethlehem this night and here at a humble stable?" Joseph had never seen so much wealth.

The servants lowered the camels to the ground so the men could easily get off. One dressed in rich red silk bowed his head in respect. "We are Magi. We have traveled a far distance from our home in Persia. We are priestly astrologers and we predict events which arise by the stars."

"You traveled all this distance because of the great star that shines overhead?" Joseph had never seen real astrologers before, but he could understand why this star would be of interest.

"We study the stars, when an old one vanishes and a new one appears." The second Magi stepped up, dressed in a royal blue robe with matching cloak. "We have seen His star in the east and know that a child has been born. A child to be King of the Jews."

"On our way through Jerusalem, we stopped to ask where might this king be born and Herod, the king, overheard our conversation." The third Magi came forward, dressed in green and rich purple. "Herod asked us to return after we had found this king to tell him where he could go and worship him also."

"King Herod, worship another king?" Joseph opened the door. "Very unlikely! But you may come in and see for yourself this king, whose star led you all this way."

The three Magi entered slowly and reverently bowed down at the manger and gazed into the young child's penetrating eyes. They instantly knew, each royal king, that they were looking at a Holy face.

With care, each man pulled out a gift, all richly placed in beautiful boxes or jars: gold, frankincense and myrrh. The small stable became alive with the fragrance as the three Magi rose slowly to their feet. "We must leave now, for we travel at night, guided by the stars."

Joseph followed the three men back outside into the night's chill. The man in the red silk robes placed his hand on Joseph's shoulder, "Take heed, my friend, this king, this Herod, is an evil man! I was warned in a dream by God Himself that we should return not to Herod, so we will travel in another direction."

"Thank you for the warning and for the gifts given the child." Joseph watched as the servants lowered the camels but before the last Magi climbed on, he stepped up next to Joseph.

"Please take my camel for your travel home. I shall give you one of my servants to assist you."

"That is most kind, but our donkey is more than enough to see us safely home." Joseph felt warmed by this unexpected offer. "Your distance is far greater than ours, so please ride your fine animal."

"It is the least I can do for my Savior, Joseph." Tears came into his warm eyes. "I would gladly walk all the way back to Persia for Him!"

"What great love you have." Joseph patted the Magi's back. "The thought is sufficient. Go in peace and may God keep you safe." He glanced up at the other two Magi whose heads were dropped, their eyes sparkling with tears. Raising his hands in farewell toward them, he smiled. "May God keep your trip home safe as well, good friends. Go in peace!"

That night Joseph was in a deep sleep when he heard the familiar voice of the angel Gabriel, "Arise! Take the young child and his mother and flee into Egypt! Stay there until I bring you word of when to leave. Herod will seek the young child to destroy him!"

Joseph sat up, breathing rapidly as he remembered the warning from the angel. He quickly awoke Mary. "My love, we must pack at once and leave Bethlehem! I have been warned in a dream by God's own angel to leave for Egypt this night!" Joseph helped his wife up off the straw-covered earth floor. "King Herod wants to kill Jesus! There is no time to waste! We must leave at once!"

"The innkeeper will expect to get his pay, Joseph!" Mary quickly started packing their things. "If you wish to run to the inn and pay, I can finish here."

"There is no need, Mary." Joseph got the donkey out of its stall. "No more rest for you, good fellow."

"Joseph, did you pay the innkeeper already?" Mary handed her husband the first bundle.

"After the wise men asked me to beware of Herod, I thought we should be ready to leave quickly, so I spoke to the innkeeper this morning." Joseph couldn't help but smile, remembering his conversation with the friendly man. "He said we owed him nothing! First, the stable had never been rented out so there was no reason to start now. Second, he regretted having to put us in his stable to begin with. Last, this was his gift to God's son. Not much of a royal palace for the King of Kings, but Jesus's radiance would light up any place he lived!"

After placing Mary and Jesus on the small donkey, Joseph slipped out of Bethlehem under the cover of night while everyone else slept, unaware what was soon to happen in their quiet streets.

As they traveled toward Egypt, Mary and Joseph noticed a wagon had stopped up ahead. Two men were quickly replacing a tire rim that had rolled off without warning. Joseph stopped to listen to their conversation and thought he recognized familiar voices.

"I cannot imagine what made the stupid thing come loose!" the taller man grunted, out of breath as he tightened the wooden peg. "Did I not just check the devil a few short hours ago?"

"I say divine intervention, Hezekiah." The shorter man wiped his brow. "God has halted our travel!"

"You have quite the imagination, Ram." Hezekiah stood up when the couple came to a stop next to them. As he got closer to them, Joseph recognized both men. They were workers for his friend Aaron on their way somewhere to buy, sell or trade goods from his friend's huge supply shop.

"Hezekiah, Ram! What a surprise to see both of you on the same road we are traveling!"

"Joseph? It is Joseph!" Ram noticed the young child in Mary's arms. "Did you get turned around, Joseph? This is not the way to Nazareth."

"We had a warning from God. We head to Egypt." Joseph noticed the two men exchanged wide-eyed glances at one another as they recalled Ram's remarks about God halting their travel.

"We too are on our way to Egypt on business, Joseph, just as soon as I get this loose wheel fixed."

"Loose wheel? It looks fine to me, Hezekiah." Joseph pointed to the wheel sitting straight, tight and secure.

Hezekiah stared down at the wheel, in place like new. "Now how did that happen?" He glanced up nervously at the young couple until his attention rested on Jesus. "Come along with us, Joseph. We know the way well and can get you there safely."

As they traveled along the way, Joseph told the two men he would remain in Egypt until the danger had passed and God would bring them word so they could return home to Nazareth.

CHAPTER 14

Joseph pulled the tired donkey down the crowded streets of Cairo, looking for employment as he passed the many shops. The Egyptians stared at the strangers in curiosity. The shop near the end of town had a big wanted sign in the dusty window. It read: *Needed, A Head Carpenter. Apply Inside!*

"Mary, God has supplied our needs." Joseph pointed at the sign. "Stay with the donkey. I will tie her securely and return as quickly as possible."

"We shall be alright here, Joseph." Mary's smile was radiant as she stroked Jesus's soft curls. "And do not worry, you will easily get the job."

He winked at her and walked inside the shop. Immediately Joseph felt at home among the smells of new lumber and sawdust. A short stout man with wavy white hair dashed from the back room, looking anxious, and said, "Tell me you are here for the carpenter's job and not as a customer!"

Joseph laughed softly. "I have indeed come in hopes of the job. To let you know, sir, my father was the best carpenter in all Nazareth and he taught me everything he knew. Now that my father has departed, I run my own shop. Circumstances have brought me and my family to Egypt and I seek temporary employment. I assure you, I will work hard for you."

"Can you start right away?" The man moved about nervously. "I have an order for a big chest and my head carpenter up and died, through no fault of his own, leaving me in a pickle."

"I have a wife and a child just outside. First let me find shelter for us; then I will return." Joseph did not like to keep Mary waiting. "My name is Joseph."

"I am Pharez, my son." He pulled off his apron and walked toward the door. "Joseph, I will pay you a fair wage and supply a house for you to live in. I shall take you there now so we can return and see an example of your work."

The shopkeeper looked at Joseph's family as they were introduced. Never had the old Egyptian seen so much radiance on the faces of a mother and a child. He nodded his head politely as he spoke to Joseph, "Such a fair maiden, and your son is a fine boy truly, Joseph."

"Your kindness to strangers will not go unrewarded, Pharez." Mary walked inside the spacious house. "You will find my husband's work is some of the finest ever known."

"The wisdom of women can prove dangerous." He teased with a wink. "But this young one, I have a feeling, is very correct. You will start with something small. A chest in which to keep trinkets or small treasures." Pharez smiled at Mary, already feeling love for this young family and trying to block out Joseph's statement about the job being temporary. "I won't keep him long this first day, Mary, as the evening shadows will soon appear. After he has shown me a simple example of his work, I will send him home to you with food for your evening meal."

"My Joseph will make you proud, Pharez." Mary waved from the door. "Sweet peace!"

In two hours Joseph returned to the shop. "It is finished, sir." Joseph stepped to one side to reveal his work, a carving of the legendary phoenix, its wings stretching across the lid in a splendid display.

"Joseph!" Pharez stared wide-eyed at the beautiful piece that only took the young carpenter less than two hours to make. "Such craftmanship! It is indeed the most beautiful, handsome chest I have ever seen! Your dear sweet wife was absolutely right!"

"I'm glad you like it, Pharez." Joseph brushed the wood shavings off his apron onto the floor.

"Like it? I adore it, Joseph, and so will Zerub, my richest customer, who just happens to be the client waiting for the large chest." Pharez rubbed his chin. "He claims he has all the small chests he needs. I grant you, Joseph, he will change his mind when he sees this one."

"I am happy my work pleases you, Pharez." Joseph briefly looked over the plans for the larger storage chest. There were three great pyramids sketched across the top. The drawing detailed palm trees flanking the smaller pyramids on either end, with the higher, grander pyramid dominating the center. "This detailed carving requires a very smooth, very strong wood. I shall see what lumber you have in stock first thing in the morning." Joseph waited for his employer to dismiss him.

Pharez smiled knowingly. "Then run along home, Joseph. My servant is waiting at the shop entrance to follow you with your evening meal." The owner continued to admire the small chest. "I will see you first thing in the morning."

"Yes, thank you." Joseph walked out the door to meet the servant waiting with a large basket.

Joseph settled into his job nicely. All his customers were overjoyed with his work and, true to Pharez's word, his rich customer, Zerub, was not only delighted with his large chest, but also bought the first small one Joseph had made and gave many of his old ones away.

Joseph walked around with a big smile on his face all day. It was not because he was doing the one job he loved most; it was the fact that he and Mary had started making love. It had been even better than the joyful groom had dreamed it would be.

Two years had passed since Mary and Joseph had taken Jesus and left Bethlehem, and they felt sure God had kept Mary from having another child until they were safely back in Nazareth.

Joseph had convinced his employer that he would work twice as hard on the first six days of the week, but the seventh day was the Sabbath, God's holy day, when no Jew worked. That was no problem for Pharez so he willingly gave him the day off. He thought Joseph already did twice the amount of work any of his other carpenters did and even better work.

Having no Jewish temple to attend in Egypt, Joseph would recite the Holy Scriptures inside his adopted home with Mary and Jesus listening. As he spoke them, they would repeat his words. To Mary and Joseph's surprise, the two-year-old Jesus would quote the next chapter even before Joseph could say it.

As always, their sabbath was peaceful until a loud knock came on their door, along with shouts of news. "Joseph! Good news! It has just arrived! King Herod is dead!" Opening the door, Joseph saw Aaron's helpers had returned with the news they had been waiting for. "Get your things together, my friend. We leave for Nazareth first thing in the morning!" Ram looked past Joseph and noticed the packed bundles next to the door. "You are packed? You know already? How?"

"An angel told me last night in a dream." Joseph smiled into their confused faces. "These are the words he spoke: 'Arise and take the young child and his mother and go into the land of Galilee, the land of Israel, for they are dead which tried to kill the young child."

"And he certainly would have, Joseph, had you stayed in Bethlehem." Hezekiah swallowed, remembering the horrible details. "Herod had his soldiers ride into Bethlehem and kill all the children, even in the coast nearby, from two years of age and under, according to the time he had spoken to the Magi when they'd come through Jerusalem on their way to Bethlehem!"

"Oh, Joseph, I can almost hear those mothers weeping in great mourning." Mary lifted Jesus up in her arms and held him tightly. "What an evil sick man Herod was! His heart was as cold as stone!"

"It is a sad tragic affair, Mary. That is why the angel insisted we leave at once and go far away into Egypt." Joseph patted Hezekiah's arm and smiled at Ram. "Since I would never travel on the Sabbath, I was leaving for home tomorrow morning anyway after I inform my employer."

"Then we shall be ready to depart with you." With that, both men drove their wagon of goods to their customer's warehouse to unload it after the close of God's Holy Day.

CHAPTER 15

Saying goodbye to his boss and good friend did not come easily for Joseph. The poor man was beside himself as he paced the wooden floor.

"Never could I replace you, Joseph." Pharez looked around at all the extra pieces Joseph had built just for this day. They were to hold his employer over until he could find a replacement. "I do not know where you had all these fine chests and beautiful furniture hidden, but thank the gods you did."

"And you may thank the one and only true God for what I am about to say." Joseph showed him his calloused hands. "It came to me in a dream. That is how our God speaks to us sometimes. Some followers are gifted with visions, but I dream and this dream from God had to do with you, my friend."

"Oh, do tell me, Joseph! I have come to believe in this God of yours. The old man had tears in his eyes, both from his broken heart that he might never see this wonderful carpenter or his beautiful family again and from his feeling the power of the real God within him. "Joseph, I believe because I can see his love through you and your Mary. But mostly in your boy, Jesus! What a special love he radiates and at such a tender age! Yes, I know He is very special!"

"Jesus is closer to God than anyone I know." Joseph was glad that this Egyptian believed in the one true God and recognized His Son was special.

"This dream you had about me…was it a good dream?" Pharez swallowed, nervous at the thought that he was being singled out by the Almighty.

"I think you will find it very good, Pharez." Joseph smiled as he patted Pharez's back. "I have a good friend who lives in Nazareth. His name is Aaron and he has a big trading business there. Aaron sends his trade goods to Egypt a lot. If you would like to send me orders, I could continue to build for you, then ship them to you in Aaron's big wagon."

The white-haired man chuckled out loud. "Happy day! Yes, Joseph! Yes, yes, yes!"

The small group of travelers journeyed toward the land of Israel. The evening grew late, so they pulled off the road to set up camp. Other travelers sometimes stopped to join them and would head in the opposite direction when morning came.

"We just came through Judaea and heard the news that Archelaus is reigning as king in Judaea in place of his father Herod." The tall friendly stranger chewed on his cooked meat as though it were hot. "I hear that he is as bad as his evil father was."

"It could be dangerous if we enter the country." Joseph was suddenly afraid to go anywhere near that new king.

"Let us rest for the night, Joseph." Hezekiah pulled out his bedding. "Perhaps you will be visited again this night by that angel to help with our decision."

"Perhaps. Goodnight, Hezekiah." Joseph did not wish to explain everything to these strangers. He was tired from the long walk and needed to rest. God willing, a little help from Gabriel would be welcome.

As Joseph lay sleeping, the angel came in a dream and said, "Joseph, turn aside into the district of Galilee. Get thee around Jerusalem and stay on the outskirts of Judaea until you safely reach Nazareth!

With each passing day, Jesus grew and became strong and full of wisdom. God's blessings were upon him. A day never went by that Jesus did not go up on the hill behind their house, where He would talk to His Father at length. He was well-studied in the holy scriptures and knew them all by heart.

When Jesus was ten, new neighbors moved in down their street. Their family had come to Nazareth to live with the widow Ruth, a cousin of Mary's. Her daughter's name was Anna, the mother of two children. They would soon become Jesus' best friends. Samuel, the oldest, was also ten and his younger sister was Joanna.

The new family walked up the dusty street to meet the carpenter's family and to place an order with Joseph for two beds and a storage chest in which to store their linens.

"My, such a big family you have, Mary." Anna looked over at the six handsome children, four boys and two girls. "It is good your husband is such a fine woodworker he can afford this big group."

"We have a happy, lively home, Anna." Mary smiled over at the two shy children. "There is yet one more, Jesus. He would be about Samuel's age. Jesus is our firstborn and helps his father in the shop."

"Then your other sons, James, Jo'ses, Simon and Judas are not yet old enough to help in the shop?" Samuel spoke as he looked around the small house, wondering how they all fit into such a small space.

"Jo'ses and I help sometimes," James spoke softly. "Father is beginning to train us in simple skills, the same as he did our brother Jesus. Jesus can build things now almost as good as Father. He is a quick learner in everything."

"Jesus sounds interesting. I should like to meet him." Samuel looked over at his quiet sister. "Little Joanna is very shy around strangers, at least until she knows you better."

"When can we meet Jesus?" came her sweet voice.

"My dear child, we cannot disturb him now, but why not come back for the evening meal with us at six and bring our cousin Ruth." Mary stood up when Anna rose to leave.

"If it would be no problem for you, Mary. You have so many already to feed." Anna was grateful for the kind invitation and a chance to meet the famous carpenter who would be building her furniture. "I count nine of you. Are you sure you have room for four more?"

"There is always room in our home, Anna. Besides, it is a lovely evening. I will have the boys set up the long table in the backyard. Joseph built it and made it plenty long enough for friends and family." Mary's smile was warm and bright as she walked them to the door. "We shall put torches up for light. It will be a pleasing fellowship."

"Then I insist on bringing a couple of dishes. I consider myself a fairly good cook and Mother is wonderful." Anna and her two children walked across the threshold. "We will see you at six."

After everyone was seated at the long table, filled with simple, but good-smelling food, Joseph asked Jesus to give the blessing. His words flowed beautifully from his lips and the visitors thought he sounded years older than he actually was. Samuel admired the young man and hoped to be his friend. Five-year-old Joanna felt butterflies just looking at him and his beautiful eyes whenever he gazed at her. Even at five-years-of-age, Joanna knew her heart belonged to Jesus.

Whenever Jesus had spare time, he would spend it with his new best friends. Jesus liked going fishing with Samuel and he enjoyed long walks with Joanna. They always ended up at what they called their special place. It was a quiet path that ran alongside a lazy brook. Joanna would pick wildflowers while she listened to Jesus teaching her about the prophets. When he explained the meaning behind their words, even at six she could understand.

Some days Jesus and Joanna would sit under a big shade tree as he told her stories, which he called parables. Jesus explained to her that a parable was an earthly story with a heavenly meaning.

"There once was a baby lamb that came down from heaven. God sent the lamb to save all the other lambs on the earth that had gotten lost and could not find their way home. The earthly lambs did not know how to save themselves, so God's only lamb had to save all of them."

"Jesus, how did the baby lamb save so many lambs?" Joanna's eyes were big and filled with questions. "Was it because he was the lamb of God, so he was good?"

"That is a very good answer, Joanna." Jesus stood up and pulled her to her feet. "In a sense, it was His goodness that saved them!"

The young girl smiled happily for the statement she made was very good. Joanna loved being with Jesus more than anything and she was glad they were friends.

"Are you excited about going to Jerusalem, Jesus?" Samuel threw his line into the water, hoping to catch at least one fish to his friend's ten.

"I have longed to go there for years." Jesus pulled out his eleventh catch. "I have not seen the temple since I was a baby in my mother's arms."

"Surely you do not remember it, my friend." Samuel watched as Jesus threw his line back into the water. "I do not get it! I never catch one fish and we sit at the same fishing hole and use the same bait!"

"Here, let me check your pole." Jesus took his friend's fishing pole and closed his eyes, then handed it back "Throw it back in, Samuel. You shall catch fish!"

"Sure, whatever you say," Samuel mumbled as he tossed the bait back in the same place thinking it was a waste of time. "Hey

Jesus, you never did say about remembering the temple as a baby. I am sure it is because your parents told you all about it, right?"

"My parents never spoke of it and yet I can even remember the way it smelled. There was this old man name Simeon who blessed me, then spoke to my parents. There was a woman filled with the Spirit named Anna, the same as your mother, only she was very old." Jesus noticed the tug on his friend's pole. "Samuel, you have a catch!"

"Holy leaping frogs! That must be one big fish!" Samuel stood up for a better grip. He breathed in a big gulp of air as he pulled. "It is too heavy for me!"

Jesus threw down his pole to help. With one strong pull, the line came up out of the water revealing twelve perfect-sized fish. Samuel stared at his catch, then at Jesus.

"It…it is…a…"

"A gift from God, my friend!" Jesus gathered his fish. "Mother is waiting for supper and now you can deliver supper to your mother as well." He turned to leave. "And to answer your first question, Samuel, I am overjoyed about going to Jerusalem! I am sorry you must wait till next Passover."

"Yes, one week kept me from my twelfth birthday!" Samuel held up his fish laughing. "You can tell me all about it when you return!"

CHAPTER 16

The Passover was drawing near and as always, Mary and Joseph prepared for the long journey from Nazareth to the Holy City of Jerusalem. The difference this time was that twelve-year-old Jesus was also traveling with them. He had mixed emotions about the trip: first, complete joy, and second, the deep dark fact that he knew his last breath would be taken in that very city some twenty-one years later.

They arrived in the busy streets where many pilgrims were coming into Jerusalem from all parts of the surrounding cities and towns. Unlike Nazareth, the streets were free of dust due to the fact they had been paved with flat stones by the Romans. He and his family marveled at the large city within tall walls as they walked through the crowds. Their footsteps were deliberately slow as Mary's parents, getting up in years, had made the long trip from Nazareth with them.

Mary and Joseph's six other children had remained behind in Nazareth with relatives unable to make the long tiresome journey. JoSiphiah had felt this might be his last Passover in the Holy City so, despite his failing health and tiredness, he had insisted on coming.

Joseph looked at the map in his hand. He knew the walk to the tent area would take a few hours, and then their two tents would need to be set up. Always the thoughtful son-in-law, Joseph could tell his father-in-law was exhausted from the trip so he pulled the family aside out of the foot traffic.

"JoSiphiah, the temple is only a few steps to our right." Joseph clutched Mary's hand as he gazed up at the massive temple. "If you and Hannah would watch Jesus for us, it would be a big help. I will return to get you after we have found our resting spot and put up our tents."

"Joseph is right, Father. Perhaps you could take Jesus inside the temple to hear the teachers speaking." Mary rubbed her son's head. "Would you like that, son?"

"It would please me greatly, Mother." Jesus' smile was radiant as he gently took his grandparents' hands. "Grandmother, you can wait outside on a bench that sits under a beautiful juniper tree."

Everyone in the family knew not to question how Jesus knew things without first seeing them. They merely accepted his words as gospel.

Jesus led his grandfather into the cool interior of the high-walled temple. Several men in fancy robes were gathered around, some speaking, some listening to the scriptures being discussed. After helping the older man find a seat, Jesus turned to a middle-aged man sitting next to an empty space.

"Excuse me, is this space taken, Joseph?" Jesus asked politely as the stranger stared back with curiosity. "My name is Jesus. This is my grandfather JoSiphiah, the father of my beloved mother."

"It is good to know you, young Jesus." Joseph of Arimathea smiled over at the older man. "Tell me, JoSiphiah, is your grandson a wizard?"

"Never, sir! Jesus is a special gift from God!" Mary's father chuckled softly as the stranger's eyes went back to Jesus. "He has been gifted with special gifts. That is how he knows your name."

Another gentleman stepped inside the large room and looked around for his friend Joseph. When he saw him, he smiled at him when he waved for him to come over to him. He took the seat on the opposite side of Joseph of Arimathea and glanced over to the young lad sitting next to his friend.

"You are a young one to be here listening to the likes of old men when you could be playing with your friends or exploring our big city." His smile was warm and friendly as he spoke to Jesus. "Tell me, were you forced to sit and listen to a bunch of grown men speak of their beliefs about the holy word?"

"Me forced? Oh no, sir. 'Tis a joy for me to be here among all you fine teachers, to listen to your understanding of my Father's word and to offer my own true facts!"

The two teachers glanced at one another in astonishment; then Joseph winked at the child. "And can you tell me what my friend's name is, young Jesus?"

"It is an honor to meet you, Nicodemus." Jesus smiled at his surprised expression. "Shall we discuss some prophecy, gentlemen?"

"But…of course." Nicodemus whispered into Joseph's ear,

"You told the lad my name, did you not?"

Joseph shook his head. "No, my friend, I did not. The boy is a gift from God Himself. Let us put young Jesus to the test."

"Yes, let's." Nicodemus smiled at the youth. "Young one, I have a question for you. When sister Eve ate from the tree of knowledge and gave one of the fruits to her husband, they heard God coming through the garden and they hid themselves. Was this the first sin, young Jesus?" Nicodemus placed a crooked finger over his lips as he waited for the child to answer. He was not prepared for the answer he was to receive, along with the rest of the room. All had grown silent to hear the twelve-year-old.

"If you consider the fact that the first sin started in heaven, even before the Father of all creation created this beautiful earth where humans dwell, then no, friend Nicodemus. Lucifer was a strong and powerful angel, loved by the Father, as was every angel who dwelt in heaven. Lucifer's beauty was far greater than that of any other angel that God, the father, created. He became powerful and was convinced that with his great power he could take over God's throne, with the backing of one-third of the Father's holy angels.

"Michael was just as powerful as Lucifer, as were the warrior angels. The battle in heaven took place until Lucifer and his followers were defeated and thrown out of heaven into the deep that would become earth.

"It was that evil serpent that tempted sister Eve to eat the forbidden fruit and sin against God and heaven. I can still feel the great sadness the Father felt when He walked in the garden calling out their names and found them hiding from Him." Tears came into Jesus' eyes. "So the sin of Adam and Eve fell among the children of the earth and not one would be saved. So God would send down a lamb without sin to save those who would believe."

There was complete silence in the grand room as every eye was on young Jesus. They had expected to hear the words of a young boy; instead, they received words from heaven.

"Come along, Jesus, we must get back to Hannah." JoSiphiah stood up and took the boy's hand as he smiled at the astonished group of teachers. "Thank you for allowing us to join in your discussion."

Joseph of Arimathea snapped out of his trance. "Yes, of course. It was our pleasure having such a brilliant student among us this evening."

"Although I am not certain who was the teacher and who was the student, my friend." Nicodemus stood up and stretched. "Perhaps if you have the time, you may join us again before your return trip."

"I think our day tomorrow is quite full, Lord Nicodemus." The child's grandfather noticed the disappointment written on their faces. "If we can spare the time, we may drop by for a short time before we depart the day after tomorrow." With those words, JoSiphiah ushered Jesus from the temple and made his way to where Hannah was waiting and watching all the activities going on around her.

Jesus caught a glimpse of the sacrificial altar and the smoke rising up. He had a sudden feeling of sadness knowing that some innocent lamb, dove or turtle dove would take its last breath for someone's sins. Jesus felt a strong hand take a hold of his shoulder.

"We shall be up there tomorrow, my son." Joseph had come back to collect his family. "But for now, your mother is preparing our evening meal. Then we will rest from our long journey so we may be bright and alert for all tomorrow's activities."

"Yes, Father. We must not keep Mother waiting." Jesus helped his grandmother from the bench and held her hand all the way to the tent site.

The sun came up bright over the Holy City as many pilgrims made their way around the crowded streets. Joseph and Mary had gotten up early to prepare the morning meal and noticed their son some distance away. He had awakened before daybreak to climb up a small hill where he knelt in morning prayer. It was a ritual Jesus carried out every morning, no matter where he was.

"How do you think Jesus will take the innocent animals and birds being given in sacrifice today, Joseph?" Mary stirred the good-smelling porridge in a pot hanging over the fire Joseph had made. Her eyes followed Jesus as he walked toward them.

"Not to worry your pretty head, my dearest. Jesus will make us proud." Joseph smiled at the handsome lad as he stepped up next to his mother and kissed her in greetings.

"Bless you, Mother! Food to nourish the body as we start a new day."

"And are you ready for a new adventure, the one you will be

experiencing this day?" Joseph dished out the hot porridge in the wooden bowls he had made for the trip and handed them out.

"Yes, father Joseph, it is a day I have looked forward to, to reach the age of twelve and become a man."

Jesus looked around to see everyone was ready to pray. He bowed his head and gazed up at his earthly father who was watching his special son with a warm smile. "Permit me, Father Joseph. Our Heavenly Father, for this food, we give thee thanks. Help us to know your will for us this day to listen and to obey. Amen."

"Amen!" Joseph dipped his spoon into the thick porridge and ate it. He turned to wink his approval at his beautiful wife. "Mary, this is wonderful, as always! Food eaten outdoors tastes extra good!" He looked around and saw the rest of the family was enjoying their morning meal. "Our first stop will be the altar. The lines will grow long as the day if we leave it until later. I will buy a lamb for me and Mary. Father JoSiphiah, you can get whatever you feel appropriate for you and Hannah." His eyes fell on Jesus. "Son, I will get you a dove to take up."

"Can I take it up myself, Father Joseph?" Jesus knew he was clean of sin, and for any of His Father's creation to die for him was unfavorable.

"You are twelve, Jesus, and considered a man by our laws"—Joseph smiled when Mary breathed out in annoyance—"except your mother would disagree the matter. You are still her little boy," he teased.

"Joseph, just eat your porridge before you find yourself wearing it!" Mary gazed down at her bowl smiling at the idea.

Her father laughed, "Tell me, Joseph, my son, do you think our Mary should have her own lamb to sacrifice instead of sharing yours?"

"If I have committed a great sin for wanting my son to remain a child a while longer or wishing that my husband would spill his morning meal over himself for suggesting that our son was a man already, then by all means, make it a heifer or a bull!" Mary winked at Jesus when he laughed softly.

"Mother, you really need nothing this year." Jesus reached for her empty bowl and stacked it with his. "Father Joseph, very little. Perhaps a small bird for words he let slip when he hit his thumb instead of the peg." His eyes rose up to the temple standing high in the distance. "Now the Scribes and the Pharisees, along with the High Priest, could use something big to burn on the altar!" Remaining calm, he continued to stare upward. "But they only judge those coming to offer burnt sacrifices for sins committed, when many of them will commit the biggest sin of all!"

CHAPTER 17

Even early in the morning, the lines were long, but Jesus found himself walking up holding a white dove. The priest sized him up as he arched his eyebrow.

"I take it you are twelve, son." The priest noticed Jesus clutching tightly to the beautiful bird. "It will not feel a thing, son. You need not worry."

"Yes, I know." Jesus looked over at the last offering as it went up in smoke. "This beautiful creature made by God will soar to greater heights this day!"

"That is one way of putting it, young man." The priest held out his left hand while his right clutched the bloody knife. "The smoke this small bird will create will indeed climb upward."

"Sir, I speak of its flying up, a living breathing dove." Jesus trained his attention on the priest who was growing impatient with this outspoken boy. "For you see, I have no sin to place upon this innocent creature."

"Young one, you are misguided. All sin, one way or the other." The priest spotted his parents standing nearby. "Surely you have been taught this, boy!"

"I beg your pardon, sir, but our son has been taught all the scriptures." Joseph stepped up next to Jesus trying to calm the angry priest. "Our son knows the scriptures far better than most grown men. He can quote them, word for word! If he says he is without sin, then he speaks the truth! Never have I seen one so loving and giving as Jesus."

The priest turned back to Jesus. "You say you have not sinned, so this sacrifice you hold will simply fly away?" His eyebrow shot back up. "I must perform my rites! It is my duty to cut the dove's throat so his blood can be poured on the altar. This sacrifice has been passed down from generation to generation!"

"I know our laws well. Did not Abel give God the best of his lambs while his brother Cain cheated the Heavenly Father with less than the best of his wheat." Jesus held out the dove. "Take it as the law requires. Cut its throat, then hand it to me to place upon the altar."

"This cannot be! It is the custom that the priest must perform the sacrificial offering, not the poor sinner." The priest reached for the bird but was unable to take it.

"Forgive me, sir, but if you put the dove upon the altar, it will be your sins that are placed upon him." Jesus knew an angel was holding the dove so the priest could not lift it out of his outstretched hands.

"My sins, you say?" His voice grew loud as his attention focused on the waiting crowd. "I am a man of God! There is no sin in me!"

"Forgive me, but all men sin and fall short of salvation!" Jesus placed the dove in his hand.

"You say all men sin, yet you claim you are without sin!" The priest felt a hand on his shoulder and turned to see the serious faces of Nicodemus and Joseph of Arimathea.

"What harm could it do to hand the bleeding dove to the young lad so he can lay it on the altar for himself? It could perhaps prove your point to him, that he is just like everyone else."

Joseph of Arimathea leaned in close to the priest's ear. "Or just maybe we can all learn a lesson from this one small boy, Haran. Is not God the true judge of sin? Let Him decide the fate of the dove."

With a strong thrust, the sharp blade slid across the beautiful white neck and red blood spilled out. The arrogant priest laid the dying bird in the young hands of Jesus. "Then you put it on the hot fire and wait for your miracle!" A sneer fell on his lips.

Jesus tenderly held the still bird over the hot flames and spoke softly, "Father, you know my words are true. Let those who cannot believe truth, believe as I do!" He laid the helpless dove, now covered red in its own blood, gently on the altar.

Smoke rose up and out of the smoke flew the white dove and it landed on Jesus' shoulder. A soft voice came from the dove in a whisper, "My Son!" Then it took flight and soared up into the heavens.

Everyone watching stood speechless as Jesus walked slowly back to his mother, who hugged him in her protecting arms. Joseph carried the lamb he had chosen for him and Mary and held it up for the priest, whose eyes had not left Jesus. Clearing his throat, Joseph focused attention on himself. With shaky fingers, the priest took the lamb offered and the sacrificial offerings continued.

An uncle of Joseph's walked up to the group of weary people. The Passover had been packed with so much to do and see. The Passover meal had been eaten as the tired family sat around discussing their plans for returning home to Nazareth the following morning.

Their uncle sat smiling at something he had just seen. "It was the funniest thing! A most talented little monkey that dances to his master's tambourine! Quite the sight!" He looked around at the young boys listening to his words. "I was thinking, tomorrow morning right after our meal, I could take the young lads out of your hair while you take down your tents and pack up." His eyes were bright with the idea of entertaining the boys. "I will see to my things this night so we can catch you on the road out!"

Joseph looked around at some of the boys noisily picking at each other. He thought to have them out of his hair while packing might prove helpful. He scratched his head and gazed at his uncle. "Are you planning on taking the boys to see the monkey's tricks, Uncle Ishod?" Joseph sat with his arm around Mary's shoulders. "Will he be performing for an audience early in the morning?"

"I asked the man that very question, Joseph," Ishod chuckled. "His said for a few pennies he would be there. It is his livelihood, and before caging the monkey he added that performing for children always made his monkey Sacar perform extra well. The spirited creature enjoys their laughter and giggles!"

"Then it is settled. Take the young lads out of our hair and be sure to meet us on the road at nine sharp!" Joseph stood up and stretched. Taking Mary's hands, he lifted her off the ground. "Uncle, be sure all the boys are accounted for. We would not want to leave one behind."

"Never would I forget my duty, nephew." Uncle Ishod smiled, "We shall stick together and enjoy the funny dancing monkey! Then at nine sharp, we will join our group traveling back to Nazareth!

CHAPTER 18

The boys stood in a large group watching the funny monkey. True to its owner's words, the louder they laughed, the sillier the monkey became.

Jesus' attention was not on the silly monkey. To him it was kids' stuff. He had his attention focused on a group of teachers and leaders walking toward the temple. He noticed his new friends, Nicodemus and Joseph of Arimathea, had spotted him among the boys interested in the monkey's dance. They waved him over to them and he nodded as he turned to the nearest boy, caught up in the monkey's antics.

"Judah, tell Uncle Ishod I have gone off with a couple of friends. I'm tired of watching the silly monkey. I have more important things to do before I leave for home."

Judah, trying not to miss anything the creature did, nodded yes and waved him away so he could give the monkey his full attention.

There was a fever of activity in God's house as word had gotten out about the bright young boy whose knowledge for the word astounded all who heard him.

Jesus entered the temple with his new friends where they all joined in discussions relating to the holy scriptures. Many of those present asked Jesus questions, and his answers seemed to flow from the heights of heaven. With all the attention and excitement while discussing God's holy word, Jesus lost all track of time. He was in His Father's house. He felt safe and He was doing His Father's will.

Uncle Ishod rode up next to Joseph's small group when they had traveled several miles out of Jerusalem. Joseph looked around and behind the smiling man.

"There you are, Uncle. Where is Jesus? Is he not still with you?"

"Young Jesus chose to go back with other friends of our group. I think he tired quickly of the monkey's antics." Ishod chuckled as he remembered looking around at the excited youth and found all but Jesus were paying attention to the furry creature. "I can assure you that Jesus is fine, Joseph. He is a smart lad. He spoke to Judah before he left our group and told him he was going back with friends."

"I wonder who he could have seen in the street, Joseph?" Mary walked slowly with her head down to avoid any rocks in the road. "I thought only the boys and Uncle Ishod left the campsite this morning."

"I suppose some of our large group could have finished with their packing earlier with one tent to take down instead of two like us." Joseph tried to reassure his wife of Jesus's safety. "Jesus is a smart and clever boy. I am sure he is among our friends, Mary."

"Jesus is our responsibility to watch and keep safe, Joseph," Mary spoke softly. "You know his importance."

"I also know even if Jesus were alone, he would be safe, Mary." Joseph took her hand as they walked. "God is always with him." He could tell she was still worried and uncertain of where he was. "Listen, dearest, as soon as we stop for the night, I will search for our son and bring him to his worried mother."

"Thank you, my love. I would feel better knowing he was among us." Mary finally smiled as she continued to put distance between them and the temple in Jerusalem.

"This is an all-night stay, young Jesus. It is but one of our many traditions held after Passover," Joseph said as he passed the wine cup to Jesus, who took a drink, then passed the wine to Nicodemus. "If you need your rest, we could see you safely home."

"I am home, my dear friend Joseph. Sleep does not come to one who is alive with questions and answers!" Jesus's smile was bright as he looked at his friends. "I could speak all through the night and yet find strength to continue into tomorrow!"

"Then it is a delight to have you stay among us, my young friend." Nicodemus handed him some bread and cheese. "Eat now; then we shall get back to the book of Isaiah."

"I tell you, he is not here! We have searched twice from front to back! No one has seen or heard from Jesus since he was last seen by the boys and Uncle Ishod when they were watching that silly monkey!" Joseph sat down, weary from the long search. He looked up at his father-in-law with concern. "What could have become of him, Father? How do I tell Mary Jesus is missing?"

"Have you spoken to Judah, Joseph? He was the last boy to speak to my grandson." Mary's father felt bad for the young boy's parents, thinking he was safe among relatives only to find him gone.

"Young Judah said he was too interested in the monkey to even notice who Jesus went off with. But he swears Jesus said they were friends." Joseph stood up nervously. "I must tell Mary. It will not be easy, but it must be done. Mary and I need to turn around and go back to Jerusalem. Jesus has to be there!"

"So, Jesus is gone!" Mary stepped out of the shadows. "There will be no rest for us tonight, Joseph! Not until we find him, even if it means traveling all night!"

"Mary, my child, it is not safe to travel this road at night in the dark!" JoSiphiah took his daughter's hand. "There are great dangers beyond this resting point! Thieves, highwaymen out to rob and kill! Stay here this night; then at the first rays of light set out for Jerusalem riding donkeys, mine for one. I can make it on foot two days, and it might even do me good to move my old legs instead of dangling them!"

"But, Father, our son could be in danger!" Mary was afraid. "I cannot rest till he is safe in my arms."

"And he will be, Mary, soon, I promise. We will find Jesus tomorrow." Joseph pulled her into his protecting arms and held her close. "But your father is right, dear one. We cannot help find Jesus if we meet up with danger on that road in the dark. We can make good time starting at first light and riding on two donkeys. Uncle Ishod has two donkeys and taking one to help find Jesus will ease his guilty conscience." Joseph could tell Mary was still upset as he stroked her hair and spoke softly, "I too love Jesus. I know God has trusted us with him and I know how special he is, Mary. We will find him."

"Yes, my love, if it takes all the morrow! I will walk, crawl or run through every nook and cranny until we find our son!" Mary held tightly to her carpenter.

After returning to Jerusalem, Mary and Joseph began their long search. They started at the Sheep Gate, wandered through the Mount of Olives and Gethsemane Garden, turned back to the suburbs, the lower city, then the upper city and turned around at the pool of Siloam, then rested at the steps of the Sanhedrin. The weary couple walked slowly to the temple and heard Jesus speaking, clear and unafraid,

"Surely He hath borne our griefs and carried our sorrows. Yet we did esteem Him stricken, smitten of God and afflicted. But He was wounded for our transgressions. He was bruised for our iniquities; the chastisement of our peace was upon Him. With His stripes we are healed. All we like sheep have gone astray; we have turned everyone to his own way, and the Lord hath laid on Him the iniquity of us all."

Mary and Joseph stepped inside the cool temple, filled with the leaders of the Sanhedrin, doctors, teachers and one twelve-year-old boy.

Jesus was standing in the center, quoting from the book of Isaiah. He held no scroll in his hands for He was speaking from memory, words He had heard for many generations.

There was silence inside the large room, as every man was listening eagerly to the young evangelist speak. No one noticed the young couple until Mary dashed up and grabbed her son.

"Jesus! Why have you treated us like this, my son? Here have your father and I been very worried, looking for you everywhere!"

"But why were you looking everywhere for me, Mother?" Jesus took her trembling hands. "Did you not know that I must be in my Father's house and come straight here?"

Mary turned to look at Joseph, confused by their son's reply. She could see from Joseph's expression that he too did not understand. Joseph reached over to stroke his soft hair, falling in perfect waves.

"Come, son, we are going home to Nazareth." Joseph waited by the big open doors for Mary and Jesus.

"Very well, Father Joseph." Jesus smiled lovingly at his earthly father and walked over to tell his two friends goodbye. "My good friends"—he took a hand of each—"Joseph and Nicodemus, we will meet again after my thirtieth birthday. Until then, God's peace to you both."

The two leaders watched as Jesus left with his parents, then gazed at each other tensely, unsure of the strange feelings they felt for this young man and the strange manner in which he left them.

"Not until now have I wished time would take flight and pass quickly." Nicodemus spoke just above a whisper, "To be in his presence after he reaches manhood will bring even more revelations about what he spoke of this day."

"My good friend Nicodemus, we shall have eighteen short years to reflect on the words our young Jesus spoke from his heart and he quoted every word correctly. The joy I felt in my own heart when I listened was pure and even more, holy." As Joseph looked at his friend, tears filled both their eyes. "Did not we feel his love leap upon us when he spoke our names?"

With that, the two friends got up to leave—to think, to pray, and to ponder about who this gifted child was or, deep down inside, did they already know?

CHAPTER 19

The years flew by for Jesus and he found himself eighteen years of age. His friend Samuel was in love with Ester, Jesus' sister. He could not wait until they were married, just as soon as she reached fifteen.

Joanna had become a pretty thirteen-year-old and had grown quite bold in asking Jesus questions while they were together. Her love for him had only grown, and it proved to her what she felt wasn't just a young girl's crush but the real thing. Deep down in Joanna's heart she had hopes of becoming Jesus's wife one day. It did not appear he had eyes for another.

"Jesus, do not you think it is romantic that my brother and your sister have fallen in love and plan marriage?" Joanna glanced up at him, only to find his attention was on something down the path. She was not certain he had even heard her when he spoke.

"They make a beautiful couple, Joanna." He smiled to himself. "I told Samuel only yesterday, their children would be fair to look upon, despite his looks."

"Jesus? You big tease!" Joanna laughed. "You did not hurt my poor brother's feelings now, did you?"

"Samuel's laugh was even bigger and brighter than your own, my friend." Jesus stopped when they reached their favorite spot and sat down. "I have not long to visit with you, Joanna. I promised Father Joseph I would help in the shop later today."

Joanna joined him on the grassy knoll. "I never grow tired of coming here with you, Jesus. It is so quiet and peaceful." She placed her hand on Jesus' arm and could feel great love in her touch. She gazed up into his blue-green eyes. "Nor do I grow tired of our walks together."

"There is a prophecy of Isaiah that weighs heavily on your mind, Joanna." Jesus took her hand resting on his arm and held it as she looked at him perplexed for a brief moment before giving him an answer.

"Why yes, there is! I know not why I'm so surprised you knew this thought from me, Jesus. You always seem to know what I'm thinking, feeling, or…wanting." She glanced down shyly, wondering if Jesus knew her thoughts about being in love with him.

"Friends learn to know their friends by their actions." He smiled warmly. "Now, what is it you wish to know about Isaiah's words?"

"Isaiah did foretell this: 'Therefore, the Lord Himself shall give you a sign: behold, a virgin shall conceive and bear a son, and shall call Him Immanuel.'" When she looked up, Jesus was watching her closely. "Someday some girl, like me"—her faced flushed with embarrassment—"you know, a virgin. She will be the chosen one, the mother of God's Son." Joanna's face lit up in wonder. "What a blessing and honor it would be to be the chosen one."

"Our God in heaven does have only one Son and He will choose the right girl to be His mother." Jesus did not take his eyes off Joanna.

"I wonder how old she will be, Jesus—young like myself, or a bit older?"

If Jesus were embarrassed about their conversation, he did not show it, Joanna thought as his constant gaze held hers. "She was fifteen-years-old, Joanna." His statement took her by surprise.

"Was? Are you saying…God has already chosen her?" Joanna's voice trembled as she wondered how Jesus could possibly know this.

"Joanna, I am only going to say this one time; then we shall drop the subject and it will not be spoken of again." Jesus hugged her and stared into her eyes. "You must never speak a word of it to anyone, promise?"

"You can trust me to keep this, our special secret, till I die! I promise!" She sat up even closer to him, unable to keep still. "Tell me!"

"God, in the form of the Holy Spirit, came to the girl He had chosen and gave her His Son and at this very moment He is growing into a man, where in twelve more years he will go forth to do His Father's will for the three short years left of His life on earth. Then once again He will return to the Father in His kingdom forever!"

"Jesus, I will not ask you how you know this. I know you are truly gifted in all things concerning God!" Joanna felt numb at this revelation and had not noticed Jesus stand up and stretch out his hand to her.

"It is time I go help Father Joseph, Joanna. I must not be late."

"You are truly a loyal and devoted son, Jesus." Joanna took his offered hand and got to her feet. "You never fail to obey your father."

"Your words are correct, Joanna. I will always obey my Father's word in all things and do His will." At the end of the path, Jesus turned toward the carpenter's shop.

On another occasion, Jesus helped his brother get ready for his big day. "You seem a bit nervous, James."

"It is not every day one gets married, my brother." James glanced out at the cloudy sky for the fifth time. "And to have it rain on the day of your nuptials! What bad luck!"

"Calm yourself, brother, is not the day more than rain or even a cloud-covered sky?" Jesus patted his back. "This is a day of great joy and the beginning of a new life for you and Laura, filled with overflowing love!"

"I do love her, Jesus. This you of all people should know." James nervously fixed his long hair and glanced at Jesus through the cloudy mirror. "Truly she will make me happy as well as being a good wife."

"Yet your heart does not completely belong to this one, does it, James?"

James never understood how this one brother could always see his inner feelings as he listened to him continue. "There is one who has taken the main part of your heart."

"She does not love me, Jesus. She never has, nor will she ever. Her heart belongs to another; it always has." James turned to stare into Jesus' eyes. "Yet I fear the poor girl is destined never to have that same love returned to her by him."

"You speak of Joanna and you speak of me!" The penetrating eyes of Jesus held James in a trance. "Joanna will marry one day, brother—not to you, not to me, but she will be happy, as will you. Her marriage will be cut short, for death will rob her of her husband. Her sadness will end when she pays a visit to a friend in Judaea and falls in love with Herod's steward."

"Again you mystify me with your words, Jesus." James knew it was nearly time for his wedding. "Wish me luck, brother."

"May you be blessed with a long happy life with your bride, James, and may you have many sons and daughters." Jesus opened the door to the gloomy outside where the wedding was to be. As he looked up into the sky, he added, "And may God bless you with sunshine to start your new life together!"

With those words, the sun came out from behind the dark clouds and as blessed, James and Laura had a beautiful wedding, as well as a wonderful life together, surrounded by lots of children.

CHAPTER 20

A message came to the house of Joseph. Elisabeth, cousin to Hannah and Mary, had passed away. She had lived ten years longer than her husband, Zacharias. They both had reached a ripe old age, and Elisabeth lived to see her only son reach his twenty-first birthday.

Joseph's family made the long trip to the Judaea town to pay their last respects to the woman they had loved so dearly and to give John any comfort they could, for he was left with no close family.

When they arrived at the big airy house, the mourners were gathered inside, weeping over her death. Joseph's family looked around for any sign of John, but he was absent from the group. Inquiring about where he had gone, Jesus and his brothers set out in the garden to find their cousin. They found him perched on a tree limb, his eyes closed in prayer. Jesus held out his hand for his brothers to stop.

"Give John time to find comfort in the Heavenly Father."

After a few minutes, John opened his eyes and looked down to find Jesus and his brothers waiting for him below. He smiled and jumped down from the tree at their feet. "My dear cousins, you have arrived!" John reached out in brotherly love to hug each man. "I see you have found my hiding place."

"We thought you might be inside next to your dear departed mother, cousin John." James felt sadness for his cousin, for he was left alone with no parents, no brothers or sisters to share his sadness.

"All the weeping, I must confess, bothers me greatly." John's eyes kept going to Jesus. "Mother was old and very ill. The dear soul was more than ready for her suffering to stop. I believe the dear lady was living for me." His eyes raised up to heaven. "I knew I must be leaving soon, and I told the dear beautiful woman she could go and that one day we would be together again."

"And you shall be, John." Jesus touched him gently on his shoulder, never taking his eyes off his special cousin.

John felt at peace looking into Jesus' beautiful eyes, and he asked the other four brothers if he could have some time alone with him. Wanting to get away from these two men who had always been different from the rest of the family, Simon was all too glad to escort his brothers back to the house.

"Come, my brothers, let us give them time to talk in privacy." Simon touched John's face gently, then led the way to the house to report to his parents that John had been found. Remaining silent until the four brothers disappeared in the big house, John motioned to a bench nearby so they could speak.

"After the proper grieving period has passed, I leave for the wilderness to fast and pray. I must prepare the way and my purpose for living." Their eyes met in understanding. "I must prepare the way for you, Jesus. The prophets foretold my coming as well. I will be the one crying in the wilderness."

"The words you say are true, John. We both have a plan to fulfill." Jesus touched his hand. "In ten short years we shall meet again at the River Jordan."

"I feel my life will be cut short." John gazed at his hands, knowing his wilderness experience would be one of deep prayer asking for strength to stay strong and not be afraid. "When you appear to me at the Jordan, you will grow stronger and I…I will grow weaker."

"John, you will make the Father proud." Jesus could feel his own heart beating fast with fear for what lay ahead for them both. "I will have three short years to complete my Father's will. You and I will meet with an early death, both brutal. Yours will be swift, John, but mine will be long and full of suffering. Only by the grace of my Father making the time for my last breath shorter will I be rid of the terrible pain that will tear at my body."

"If the purpose we die for has a rightful reason and I doubt not God's holy plan, then the reward given to those we die for will be great!" John closed his eyes, the heavy weight of his mission becoming clear.

"You die because you have prepared the way for me, and I die so others may live." Jesus knew the question hidden in John's heart. "John, you are wondering why the scribes spoke of Elijah coming before the Lord, and yet here you are to do that very thing."

"It has been weighing heavily on my heart." John turned toward Jesus and took his hands. "Jesus, do not think me mad, but I have not seen you since you have become a grown man, complete with a beard. When I last saw you, you were twelve, when you came with your parents to Jerusalem for Passover."

"What are you trying to say, John? Does my face seem familiar to you?" Jesus knew why John had recognized his face.

"When I look upon you, into your eyes, it is as though I have done so a million times before!" John shook his head, his wild locks bouncing around. "Can you explain this to me?"

"Let us step back for a moment, John. You ask about Elijah." Jesus' eyes stared into those of his cousin. "When the angel Gabriel came to your father, he spoke many things concerning you. One thing Gabriel said was, 'And he shall go before Him in the spirit and power of Elijah, to make ready a people, prepared for the Lord."

"Does this mean that I…" John swallowed.

"You know my face because Elijah has seen it many times in heaven." Jesus took John's shoulders gently. "Yes, John, you have looked upon this face many times."

"Is it because Elijah went up in a chariot of fire and horses of fire by a whirlwind into heaven that he should return one day?" John felt relief to finally know the truth, even though the very idea disturbed him—to think he had lived before as the great prophet but have no memory of it.

"There was no body left behind to be buried; therefore, Elijah arrived in heaven in his own body, just as I will ascend, my body alive, risen from the grave." Jesus felt John's torment and had great compassion for him. "Brother John, be at peace! God, my Father, in His great wisdom has chosen you to prepare the way for my mission. Please know you will never walk the rough ways alone!"

Feeling the blessing of peace from Jesus, John felt tears in his eyes, just knowing who this was sitting next to him. He could feel the great love pouring out from Jesus for him and for his people.

"I am ready to do my part, as are you, lamb of God!" John knew what he must do and he was ready even to die for the Son of God!

CHAPTER 21

The day came that Joseph was ill with a fever. He had reached his fifty-eighth birthday earlier as spring blossoms filled the air with their fragrance. Jesus would be turning twenty-eight when winter came and he knew he would soon lose his earthly father, if but a short time.

Mary sat beside Joseph and gently wiped his brow with a cool damp cloth. Dipping it back into the water, Mary noticed it had grown warm. It would not be easy for her to leave her beloved husband to make a trip up the hill to the village well to draw some cold water from the deep bottom below.

"Joseph, my dearest, the water has grown warm, and there is no one home besides you, me and Jesus." She smiled into his tired eyes. "I will have Jesus come in and sit with you."

"I am here, Mother." Jesus stood listening in the doorway, knowing Father Joseph had called for him earlier. "Be about your duty, woman. I will not leave his side."

Mary bent to kiss her husband's warm lips, then hugged her son before dashing quickly from the room.

Joseph gave Jesus a weak smile and motioned for him to sit down. "My son, there are so many things I want to say before I go to sleep with my fathers."

"But you will sleep with them only for a little while, Father Joseph." Jesus gazed lovingly down at the man who had raised him as his own. He could feel his heart breaking. "Soon you will rise again and live forever."

"Yes, my son, on resurrection day," was his weak reply.

"My dear Father Joseph, do you remember what the angel Gabriel told you in your dream before I was born?" Jesus could see there were questions on his earthly father's face.

"Who told you this, Jesus—your mother?" Joseph thought back to that night, the day Mary had revealed to him she was with child, not by a man but by the Holy Spirit.

"I know because I was there, Father Joseph. I heard the words spoken to you." Jesus noticed the carpenter trembled from his words. He reached and pulled the cover up over his shoulders.

"Son, how? How could you have heard the angel and in a dream?" Joseph's heart was pounding heavily, wanting to hear what Jesus was about to reveal to him on his death bed. Yet Joseph was afraid, not for himself, but for his Mary and his son Jesus.

"Whatever my Father hears, I hear also." Jesus' voice became tender, "The Father and I are always one. No matter where I am, I am with Him and He is with me."

Joseph began to speak the words of Gabriel, "The angel said, 'Joseph, son of David, do not be afraid to take Mary as your wife! What she has conceived is conceived through the Holy Spirit, and she shall give birth to a son, whom you will call Jesus.'" Joseph took a deep painful breath. Then Jesus continued the angel's words as his fingers gently rubbed through his earthly father's wet hair.

"Meaning the Savior, for it is He who will save His people from their sins." Tears filled his blue-green eyes as he looked into Joseph's teary ones. "Just as it was spoken by the prophet: 'Behold, the virgin shall be with child and shall bring forth a son, and they shall call his name Immanuel, God with us.'"

"Jesus, forgive me," came Joseph's weak voice. "I guess I wanted you for my own son as the years passed away, mine and Mary's."

"I will always be your earthly son, Father Joseph." Jesus kissed his hot brow. "You raised me with a father's love, gifting me with skills for the art of wood and faithfully taking me to the temple for daily prayers. Now, tell me about the special gift your father gave you when you were twelve."

"There is no one left on this earth who knows about that gift, Jesus." Joseph's eyes lit up. "But then you would know because you saw. You were there somewhere watching."

"Your father had a vision dream as well about a certain flower." Jesus remembered the vision and the meaning behind it: a flower with four petals.

"Of course, you are right." Joseph smiled, remembering, "The family had just returned from Jerusalem, the Passover celebration. When we arrived home, Father pulled me aside and said that while in the Holy City, he had a dream in which an unusual flower appeared with four white pedals, shaped much like a cross. On their tips was a red mark and in the center what appeared to be a golden crown.

"There was a gardener in his dream showing him the flower, a very gentle soft-spoken man with kind eyes." Jesus recalled the dream. "Your father asked the man what sort of flower he held in his hand."

"When the gardener told my father the flower was a dogwood, Father said he remembered laughing as he visualized the magnificent dogwood tree standing tall and strong. It was a tree that never had flowers like smaller flowering fruit trees or the great tulip poplar. The dogwood's long branches never seemed to need any." Joseph had learned from his father all about the different trees and about the wood from each to build beautiful objects. Among all the trees, the dogwood was the strongest.

"It is a fact that the dogwood tree we see today is without a lovely four-petal flower"—Jesus' tense stare held his earthly father's attention—"but yet, the dream vision that your father had convinced him to carve out a copy of the unusual flower, find the right plants and flowers to stain it until it looked like the flower he had seen in his vision."

"When my father told me his vision and gave me the beautiful wooden flower, he said the mysterious gardener told him to give the flower to his son Joseph and it would be revealed to him the meaning of the four-petal flower that did not yet exist." Joseph stared down at his hands. "If only I still had it, I think you could tell me the meaning."

"Your only brother stole the flower from you and broke off its white petals because he was jealous. The fact that you would get such a lovely gift and not himself tore away at his heart." Jesus could tell Joseph was experiencing deep pain as he moved about under the cover, his face showing physical distress. Slowly he took Joseph's hands and watched his face relax, the pain completely gone. Your brother had no idea the real reason why you received the flower carving, nor would he know the one who would reveal the true meaning behind its cross-shaped petals."

"I was twenty-seven, the age you are now, when my father went to sleep with his fathers." Joseph was filled with deep sadness. "I never told him the special beautiful gift he had given me at twelve had been broken."

"Heli, your father, was a good man, a Godly man who walked in the way of the Eternal Father." Jesus helped Joseph sit up and slide to a sitting position. “The angel Gabriel came to your father while he slept inside the Holy City and told him that the four-petal flower would not appear until the Son of God is lifted up in the spring when the trees are green. Now, you say if you still had this flower, you believe I could reveal to you its meaning?”

“The one the angel spoke of who would reveal its meaning to me—I know, Jesus, ’tis you.” Joseph touched his son’s cheek lovingly. “It is written on your face. It shines within your beautiful eyes! Jesus, you are indeed the Son of God!”

Jesus smiled and held out his empty hands. “What do you see in my hands, Father Joseph?”

Joseph looked at the open palms and found them empty. Then he glanced up at his son’s loving face. “What you have in your hands, I cannot see”—he smiled—“but by faith, I know there is something precious lying there for me to witness.”

“You have a strong faith, Joseph.” Jesus closed his hands briefly, then spread them open. “Look again and the meaning will be revealed to you.”

Joseph dropped his attention back to the open palms. This time he was taken by surprise when he saw the beautiful carving his father had given him so many years before fully-restored.

“The flower! My father’s gift to me! Mine is not to question how, but my faith knows with God, all things are possible!”

“The Roman’s choice of wood with which to construct their crosses to execute those they find guilty of crimes is the strong majestic dogwood tree. Thus, the four petals which form a cross.” Jesus’ face was draped in great sadness. “In a few short years, the reason for my coming to earth will be complete.”

“My son, my beautiful child, what are you saying?” Joseph suddenly felt the almost-unbearable sadness he had ever felt, even more than what he had felt when his parents died. “You must die on a Roman…cross? To be…crucified? Surely your loving Father in heaven would not ask you to undergo this, Jesus?”

“To suffer and die on the cross, in the end, will be my decision alone, Father Joseph. It is the will of my Father, but the final choice will be mine to make.” “Jesus’ hand rested on Joseph’s trembling shoulder.

“Then you must not do this thing, Jesus!” Joseph pleaded. “You are sinless, blameless! Never have you done anything wrong, my son.”

"Much like the innocent lambs my people carry for sacrifice to take away their sins." A tear ran down his face, not for himself but for the hurt and pain he was witnessing in his earthly father's eyes. "I am the lamb of God, sent by the Almighty Himself to take away the sins of every man, woman and child upon the earth. It is for this reason I came to the earth. I will be led as a sheep to the altar to be slaughtered." Jesus took Joseph's hand. "To save my people, I must die. But rejoice! Be of a glad heart! I will rise up again on the third day! Father Joseph, you say you will go to sleep with your fathers until the resurrection day. Beloved, you may close your eyes in rest for a short time, for I tell you true, I AM THE RESURRECTION! Be at peace. I will come and take you to my heavenly home to live with me forever!"

"Death has no sting to me, my son!" Joseph finally looked relaxed, happy and ready. "What joy is the day when I look upon your face, my Savior!"

Jesus' smile was as bright as the rays of sun flickering through the open window. He held up the carving of the flower. "On the end of each petal there is marked a red spot, representing my blood where the nails went through my hands and feet and the crown of thorns placed firmly on my head."

"And yet in the center there appears to be a golden crown, pure and untouched by blood." Joseph's fingers ran over the center of the wooden flower.

"A golden crown, the symbol of a risen Lord!" Jesus said softly.

"So this flower has a purpose, my son?" Joseph took the flower. "This beautiful flower that does not exist represents your dying on that horrible cross, then rising from the grave, our true Messiah!"

"As of now, the dogwood tree stands tall and majestic with only green leaves to dress up its branches." Jesus took the wooden flower and held it up. "The day is coming when the once-great tree will lose its great height and its once-straight branches will droop in sorrow. On the anniversary of my death and resurrection, this beautiful flower will appear and bloom for as long as the earth moves."

"To whom shall I leave my gift, my son?" Joseph felt a great peace in his heart and was no longer afraid of death which he knew was near.

"The one who holds your heart, your beloved one." Jesus placed the special gift in Joseph's weak hands. "Mary has filled your days with joy, happiness and great love."

"My Mary, my precious Mary." A tear ran from his tired eyes. "For myself, I am ready to rest in death, but to leave Mary is not easy. And now to know my dearest love must face the certain path which will lead her to your cross."

"She will not be alone, Father Joseph." Jesus sensed his mother nearby. "Mary comes to give you her final goodbye, but only until she joins us in my Father's kingdom."

"And gladly will I join you both, my son, my Joseph." Mary leaned over and kissed her dying husband. "My heart is indeed heavy with sorrow, my dearest love, but you must not worry yourself for leaving me. Was not it only yesterday you were at my parents' door, holding my precious chest? Our life together has gone by far too quickly and I shall always cherish all our good memories. We will be together soon enough."

Mary reached back and took Jesus' hand when she felt Joseph slipping away. He opened his eyes and gazed into hers as he whispered, "I love you, Mary." His eyes closed in sleep.

Tears fell gently on his peaceful face as Mary lovingly kissed his lips, still warm. Taking a deep breath, she whispered, "I love you, Joseph, my wonderful love. Sweet peace."

CHAPTER 22

"Jesus, do you not know Joanna's feelings for you? The girl speaks of nothing more!" Samuel watched Jesus closely to see what he might be thinking or feeling. As always, Jesus remained calm and showed no emotion. "I am some four months younger than you, soon to reach my thirtieth birthday, same as you. I was a married man by my nineteenth birthday, and now I am a father of five children."

"And you think I should be considering marriage, Samuel?" Jesus' serious eyes glanced over at his good friend. "Your sister Joanna is a beautiful person and if my life were one of an ordinary Jew, it might well have been Joanna I would choose." He turned back to his woodwork while Samuel stared at him in wonder. "I told Father Joseph I would teach my woodworking skills to my brothers, so they can take over when I leave."

"So, you are still planning to leave Nazareth and everything and everyone you know behind and heart-broken?" Samuel could not imagine not having his best friend in his life, and he knew the news would leave his sister grieving his absence. "Jesus, are you going to speak to Joanna before you leave? She must hear it from you. Her heart is set on becoming your wife, my friend."

"I will speak to Joanna the reason for my leaving. After our talk, she will understand." Jesus reached over and patted Samuel's shoulder.

"I hope better than I." Samuel rose to his feet feeling unusually sad. "Should I send her over here to the carpenter's shop?"

"Tell Joanna to meet me in the meadow by the clear brook." Jesus removed his heavy apron and hug it over the workbench. "She will know well the place. It was where we met whenever we were together. It became our special place when sweet Joanna was just a small child, for almost twenty years."

"Same as our secret fishing spot." Samuel felt his emotions give way to tears and he tried to laugh to hide the feelings rolling around in his head. "I would ask you to be gentle with her, Jesus, but you are the most gentle, loving person I have ever known." Feeling misty again, Samuel turned without another word and dashed off down the street to his childhood home.

"There you are!" Joanna ran over to Jesus and looped her arms around his chest. "My heart is overflowing with happiness, my dear friend, ever since brother Samuel announced you wished to have a word with me at our favorite place!"

"Joanna," his voice came so soft, she could feel his great love surround her like a warm cloak. "I know what thoughts dance through your mind, dear Joanna. It is love and marriage you seek."

"And not just any love or marriage, Jesus!" She took his hand and looked down at their joined fingers. "Those who gossip would say that it is bold for a girl to take a man's hand in this manner. But what I feel for you, Jesus, I have felt since I first saw you, a ten-year-old boy, yet your words were far beyond your years."

"Joanna, if things were different, I could have loved you and taken you to wife." Jesus' passionate gaze held her full attention. "My path has been set and it cannot be altered, nor would I wish it to be."

"Are you saying…we will not be getting married?" Joanna felt the hot tears forming. "You are choosing to leave Nazareth? Leave…me?"

"I must do the will of my Father, Joanna. That is why I came into this world." His hand ran slowly over her dark locks. "I love you, Joanna, as I love all my people. You are very special to me, so believe me when I tell you there is another for you. You will fall in love and get married even before I start my full mission." Jesus' eyes held her tenderly.

"I leave soon to meet my cousin John at the River Jordan. Then I shall remain away for several months. I will return with friends to attend your special day—this I promise, my long-time friend."

"You have always spoken with great wisdom, Jesus. If you say there is one I will love, I cannot doubt your words." Joanna could see her reflection in his blue-green eyes and felt at peace. "I will love you first, above all, now and always, Jesus! No one can ever take your place in my heart!"

"Yes, my friend, forever!" Jesus reached down and picked a perfect wildflower, then handed it to her. "Wear this in your hair on your wedding day for me."

Joanna carefully clutched the lovely white flower and lifted it to her nose to smell the beautiful aroma. "I promise to press it to keep it straight and with luck, it will still look good."

"Remember your old friend Jesus when you pin it in your hair, your beautiful raven hair." His hand brushed over it as he smiled.

"Jesus, you said you must do the will of your father. Why would Joseph, long-gone, send you away on a mission? For what purpose?" Joanna held the flower with care as she gazed up at Jesus.

"Joanna, it is not Joseph, my earthly father that I refer to. It is my Heavenly Father, my God and your God!" He took her hand firmly and started down the path by the sparkling brook. "I must become a shepherd to lead my flock, my people." Jesus stopped to lift up her face. "You, Joanna, are one of my sweet lambs. You are pure and have a good heart."

Joanna looked up at him in wonder. "No wonder my hearts leaps for joy and love when I draw near to you, Jesus. There is no greater love than the love you offer." She swallowed as the reality of his words hit her with his truth. "Jesus…are you…?"

"Let your heart always be open, Joanna. Let the things you hear about me when I go forth to do His will enter your heart and mind with truth." His eyes held her in tenderness. "Remember the words by the prophets I taught you on our many walks together."

"When you go, Jesus, a part of me will go with you." Joanna hugged him tightly, knowing her times with him were gone forever. "When I recall those words you taught me, the ones you know so well, I will follow your journeys and let my heart and mind guide me to this truth you speak of."

Jesus gazed up and listened to a message only he could hear, then closed his eyes, squeezed Joanna's hand and smiled brightly. "Be off now, my friend." He bent down slowly and kissed her forehead. "You have a visitor arriving from the town of Judaea. He has traveled many miles here to meet you. My cousin John is his friend."

"Tell me, Jesus, my dear friend, is this the one you spoke of?" Joanna noticed the twinkle in those perfect eyes. "It is then! The man I am to fall in love with and marry. It will indeed make our meeting an awkward one for me."

"You must not keep him waiting, Joanna." Jesus touched her face. "Go now and remember, I will always love you, my precious lamb."

Stretching up on her tiptoes, she kissed his lips gently, then turned toward her house, leaving behind everything she loved and wanted.

Jesus watched her in silence as she disappeared around the corner. His finger touched his lips, Joanna's final farewell still warming his heart. He closed his eyes to block out the one he would never have and the special feelings he had for her. It was that part of his human heart that knew he did love Joanna but he had to let her go.

CHAPTER 23

John's voice rang out over the countryside to all those gathered along the river shore to hear the one proclaiming, "I am the voice of one crying in the wilderness! Prepare ye the way of the Lord, make His paths straight!"

John had been baptizing in the Jordan River for some time as he preached loudly the baptism for repentance for the remission of sins. The crowds stood in a long line, wading in the shallow river toward the Baptist, feeling their emotions come to life when their turn came and he would dip them under.

John's voice grew reverent as he looked off in deep thought, saying the words, not just for those standing close by, but for himself as well. "There is one coming, mightier and stronger than I. Indeed, I am not good enough to kneel down and undo his sandals." Dressed in camel's hair with a leather belt around his waist, John held up his arms and declared, "I baptize you with water, but He will baptize you with the Holy Spirit!"

Looking up on the river bank, John could see many Pharisees and Sadducees coming for baptism. He knew their true hearts as he raised his voice to them, "Who warned you, you serpent's brood, to escape the wrath to come? Go and do something good to show that you are really changed!"

The high-ranking men sneered at him, but he continued, "The ax already lies at the root of the tree and if the tree fails to produce good fruit"—John stretched out his arm toward them and pointed—"it will be cut down and thrown into the fire!" His eyes burned on the angry men who stared at him with hate. "He comes already to separate the wheat from the chaff, and very thoroughly will He clear his threshing floor! The wheat He will collect into the granary and the chaff"—John's eyes blazed on the self- righteous men—"he will burn with a fire that can never be put out!"

Suddenly John's eyes fell on the tall man walking through the water toward him, and Jesus' words flooded back to him and echoed through his head, "In ten short years we shall meet again at the river Jordan."

John grew quiet and felt humble at the sight of Jesus. Then Jesus was standing in front of him. His voice came soft as he said, "Baptize me, John."

"I need you to baptize me." John tried to kneel so he could be baptized by Jesus, but Jesus lifted him up and stepped into his arms. John trembled as he embraced him. "Surely you do not come to me, Jesus?"

Jesus gazed deeply into John's eyes as he replied, "It is right for us to meet all the law's demands." He touched John's arm gently. "Let it be so now, John."

John agreed to His baptism and laid Jesus back in the Jordan. When Jesus rose up out of the water, suddenly the heavens opened up and John could see the Spirit of God coming down like a dove, resting upon Jesus. A voice came out of heaven saying,

"This is my beloved Son, in whom I am well-pleased."

John also heard the voice as he hugged Jesus; then he watched him walk away, as the Spirit was leading him into the desert where he would fast and pray for forty days.

The Baptist looked at Jesus as the distance between them grew longer until he was out of sight. His attention was still fixed on the desert, stretching out with only the hot haze obstructing the land beyond. He spoke up with reverence, "Behold, the lamb of God!" Then he turned silently and went back to baptizing those watching.

With each passing day, the human part of Jesus had grown weaker with hunger as he struggled to move forward. Except for the water the angels had given him, he had fasted for forty days without so much as a crumb of bread or a small fig to fill his stomach. He lifted his weary head as he slowed to a stop. His nose had caught the smell of roasting smoke just up a rocky slope. The good aroma drove him to climb slowly up to the smell. His strength had fallen and the climb was rough, but Jesus finally reached the top. He quickly saw the source of the tempting aroma.

An old man sat by a fire where he had roasted a leg of lamb. He was enjoying the tender meat when he caught sight of Jesus. After drinking a rich red wine, he smiled up warmly, then spoke in a long, drawn-out voice, "Son, that was quite a long climb you made." The old man looked down and smiled at his weakness. "The day grows short and soon darkness will fall. I do so love the night, don't you?"

he continued before Jesus could respond. "You look hungry." He broke off a big piece of the juicy roasted lamb and held it out to the hungry man. "Take it and eat."

"No." Jesus gazed at the tempting food the old man continued to hold out.

"Are you sure? Surely your body needs nourishment. You look so…hungry."

Shaking his head no, Jesus said, "Do you think I would not recognize you, Lucifer, disguised like an old man?"

The devil threw down the roasted lamb and stood up sneering, "If you are the Son of God, turn these stones into bread!" Stooping over, Lucifer picked up a smooth round stone resembling a loaf of bread and handed it out toward him, "Well, Son of God, make this hard stone soft warm bread!"

Jesus stared at the evil angel and said calmly, "Man does not live by bread alone, but from every word that comes from God's lips!"

The devil forced an evil smile as he walked over to the high ledge Jesus had climbed up and looked down at the rocky bottom below. "Jesus, you made the long climb up in the form of your weak human body, but if you are the Son of God"—he kicked a loose rock off the side and it fell a long way down before it hit the floor bottom, then he rolled his eyes around on Jesus—"throw yourself down from here, for it is written, He shall give His angels charge concerning thee: and on their hands they shall bear you up, lest you dash your foot against a stone!"

"That is the scripture, Lucifer, and it speaks what is true." Jesus stood still as he locked eyes with Satan "And the scriptures also say, 'Thou shalt not tempt the Lord thy God!'"

The angry angel walked over and grasped Jesus' hand and pulled him to the edge. He waved his hand over the desert in front of them and great cities arose, adorned with gold and fine silver as far as the eye could see. Bending close to Jesus' face, he spoke, "Look at the vast riches in front of you!" Lucifer had produced the vision of all the kingdoms of the world and their magnificence. "Everything you see, I will give you. I will make you great, far greater pleasures can I give you than He. I will make you a king over everyone on this earth and without sacrifice. Yes, Jesus, I will give all this to you and love you as my son." He smiled cunningly.

"All that I require of you is one thing I must have in return. Then it will be yours if you fall down and worship me!"

"Away, Satan! Away with you now!" Jesus' voice rang out and echoed back across the desert hills. "The scripture says, 'Thou shall worship the Lord thy God, and Him only shalt thou serve!'" It would have done you well, Lucifer, if you had obeyed His command! You could still be living in the heaven you can never return to!" With that, Lucifer was gone.

"He never gives up." Jesus recognized the angel's voice and, looking around him, saw he was surrounded with many familiar faces from heaven. They held in their hands the bread to nourish his body and the words of wisdom to feed his soul.

CHAPTER 24

Jesus walked through the streets of Capernaum and made his way down to a lake connected to the Sea of Galilee. The people pressed upon him to hear the word of God. Seeing two fishing ships standing by the lake, Jesus looked around for the fishermen and saw them washing their nets. He climbed into one of the ships, which belonged to a man named Simon. He called out to the fishermen, but Simon was speaking loudly to his brother and at first did not notice or hear the man calling him inside his boat.

"Not a single fish caught this day, same as yesterday and the day before that! Is Jehovah trying to get me in trouble with the wife?" Simon slung the net around. "How is an honest man supposed to make a living when he cannot catch one stupid fish?"

Jesus called out again. This time, all the fishermen looked toward him.

"Now, just who the devil is that sitting in my boat?" Peter threw down the net, and Andrew grabbed his arm.

"I have seen that man. He is the one at the Jordan River I told you about, Simon!"

"Is he?" Simon stepped up next to his fishing boat and stared at the stranger. "You called me?"

"Would you climb aboard and thrust out a little from the land so I may speak to the crowd?" Jesus turned Simon's attention to the huge crowd of people who had gathered on the shore.

"They are here for you? Are you some sort of preacher?" Simon looked at the crowd of excited people, then turned back to face Jesus who had the most interesting eyes he had ever gazed upon. "Very well, we would not want them to swamp my boat."

With Andrew's help, Simon moved the big fishing boat out away from the people. As he toyed with his ropes, he listened to Jesus as he spoke to the anxious group. The words of wisdom coming from this stranger amazed the simple fisherman. As he spoke, Simon's heart leaped with a new enlightened spirit.

Suddenly Jesus stopped talking and looked intensely at the outspoken fisherman. "Simon, launch out into the deep and let down your nets for a draught."

Simon felt his hand tremble as he looked into this man's eyes. He suddenly felt very small and knew this man was someone to respect.

"Master, we have toiled all the night and have taken nothing. I am tired and hungry. I and my fellow fishermen need to rest and start afresh this night."

Jesus stared even deeper into the fisherman's eyes. Suddenly Simon felt he needed to obey this simple command. "Nevertheless, at thy word, I will let down the nets." He pulled his boat away from the shore and called to his friends, "James, could you and John throw our nets to us? We are headed back out."

With the nets secured, the brothers took the fishing boat back out and threw their nets over the side.

"It would be nice to bring in a few fish, so my dear wife would not find me a complete failure," Simon mumbled to his brother. Then he felt his hands being jerked, and his eyes grew wide in total amazement. They had caught so great a multitude of fish that the nets began to break from their weight. Cupping his hands around his mouth, Simon shouted to their partners watching from their ship.

"John, James, come, my brethren, and help us! There is enough catch for all of us!"

And they came and filled both boats. There were so many fish between them, they began to sink. When Simon saw what was happening, he fell down at Jesus' feet, keeping his eyes on the boat deck. "Depart from me, for I am a sinful man, O Lord!"

Simon, along with the other three fishermen, were astonished at the catches of fishes which they had taken, much more than they normally caught in a year's time.

"James and John, sons of Zebedee, Andrew and Simon, sons of Malchus, fear not!" Jesus placed his hands on Simon's shoulders. "You shall be called Peter, and from this day forth you, Andrew, James and John will be fishers of men."

Without a word, they brought their boats to the land. Peter called his father over. "Divide our catches between our families." And with those words, the four fishermen forsook all and followed Jesus.

CHAPTER 25

Jesus, along with the first six of his disciples, was sent word that the marriage in Cana of Galilee was going to take place in three days.

Entering into the wedding feast, Jesus found his mother, along with his four brothers and two sisters, had already arrived and were enjoying the festivities. All the guests stopped their talking to stare at the dusty group of men who had traveled a long way there.

Samuel recognized his best friend immediately and laughed with joy, "Jesus! You finally made it! I can see you came straight here, my friend." Despite the dust covering Jesus, Samuel hugged the man he had always admired. "Come, let me show you and your friends to the baths so you can refresh yourself from your long journey."

Samuel led the group down a long hallway. Jesus caught a glimpse of his mother as she waved his way, her beautiful smile warming his heart. He returned her smile before stepping through the bath chamber door.

"Have you a change of clothes to wear, my friends?" Samuel looked around at their small traveling bags. "I am sure I can find something in my things for each of you."

"We have brought a change of garment, Samuel." Jesus touched his arm lightly. "Your kindness has not gone unnoticed. We shall be dressed in ample time, my friend."

"Yes, of course." He waved a hand toward the water jugs and vases. "I leave you then to your baths."

"Joanna, such a beautiful bride you make." Jesus stood just outside her open door.

"Jesus! You came!" With quick footsteps she raced over and looped her arms around his neck. "But then you said you would come and I take you at your good word for all time!"

"Love looks good on you, dear friend." He held her at arms-length smiling. "Joshua will make you a good husband, Joanna, and give you two sons to cherish."

"And as always, you were right, Jesus." She took his hand. "I love him dearly, just as you said." She eyed him with curiosity. "Did you just say I would have two sons? What—no daughters to help their mother?"

"Daughters? No, not by Joshua, just the two boys." Jesus looked over her hair, hanging in pretty ringlets. "The flower—where is it?"

"The one you picked for me ages ago?" Joanna glanced down sadly. "I but this morning took it from its press, and it was so delicate I could not bring myself to pick it up for fear it would crumble to my touch."

"Fetch the flower to me, Joanna, and I will place it in its rightful place." There was so much trust in his blue-green eyes, she could not resist getting the box that held her beautiful keepsake and place it in Jesus' hand. The dry pedals sprang back to life, just by touching the master's hand. "You must never lose faith, my friend. Always remember—if you have faith, no matter how small, you will be granted that which you seek."

"Then by faith I will accept this thing I am witnessing"—Joanna smiled joyfully as Jesus placed the white flower in her hair—"and true faith in the one who turned a withered flower into a beautiful living bridal flower!"

"It is time, Joanna. My girl is getting married today." Jesus smiled a tender smile, but there was a hint of sadness on his handsome face. "Our paths will cross again."

"Yes, they must"—she held him tightly, her old feelings pouring back inside her—"for there is no one who can ever take your place in my heart. I love you, Jesus."

Everyone was enjoying the wedding feast. The bridegroom had the finest table setting any bride could ever dream of. Lots of rich food and cakes filled the serving boards. The wine was flowing until the wine steward walked up reluctantly and whispered in the host's ear, "My lord, we are running out of wine." He stood straight when the master of the house jumped to his feet and pulled the nervous man to the door. "I could have sworn there was plenty on hand, sir, but the guests kept arriving!"

"This is not good! The shops are closed by now surely!" The bridegroom looked around at the guests, unaware of the bleak situation as they held up their glasses for another refill. "What must we do? The celebration has only begun!"

Mary was passing by and overheard their conversation and spoke with Joshua's mother. She made her way quickly to his side. "Excuse me, Joshua, there may be an answer to your dilemma. Mary heard you discussing your problem and asks that you go back to your guests and she will see to your problem."

"My dear mother, unless Mary has brought wine with her from Nazareth, I hardly see how she can help with this problem!' Joshua moved about nervously, rubbing his fingers through his hair.

Mary stepped out of the shadows. "I cannot help you, Joshua, but Jesus, my son, can. I will see to it."

"But, my dear Mary, what do you expect Jesus to do that could possibly help this crisis?" He wrung his hands as sweat began to form on his brow.

"Why not give it a try, my son?" Joshua's mother took his arm. "What other option do you have?"

"None." The nervous bridegroom looked past Mary to the far corner of the big room where Jesus sat talking to the six strangers he had brought with him. "Go then, see what can be done."

Mary made her way across the room to where Jesus sat talking softly.

"Jesus, my son, they have no more wine. It has run out."

Jesus gazed up. "Woman, what have I to do with thee? Is that your concern or mine? My time has not yet come."

Mary knew the anxious bridegroom was depending on her as she held out her hand for Jesus to rise. Without hesitation, Jesus respected his mother's wishes and followed her to the wine cellar. Mary turned to the servants and motioned them over, "Whatever he says unto you, do it."

Jesus stood silently beside his mother as the servants came to him, eyes wide with questions. Jesus looked around and spotted six stone water pots, meant for the purifying of the Jews. Each pot held about twenty gallons. Jesus turned his attention back to the silent servants, waiting for their orders and wondering what this man would do.

"Fill the water pots with water." Jesus watched as they filled each pot to the brim. "Now draw out and take unto your master."

Taking big ladles, the men dipped the water into serving jars and carried them to their master. He lifted up his glass and stared with amazement when a rich red wine flowed from the wine jar. Lifting it to his lips, he tasted the wine made from water. The rich master did not know where the wine came from, though naturally the servants who had drawn out the water knew.

The man lifted his glass to the bridegroom, who had watched in wonder as wine came from the jar. Joshua lifted up his glass when a happy, very important guest called out, "Everyone I know puts his good wine out first and then when men have had plenty to drink, brings out the poor stuff. But you, Joshua, have kept back your good wine till now!" The master of the ceremonies held his glass higher as he proclaimed, "To the bridegroom and his lovely bride!"

Jesus stood back watching. He had just given his first sign in public, at Cana in Galilee, as he demonstrated his power. His disciples had witnessed the miracle and believed even more in him.

CHAPTER 26

Jesus, along with Peter, James, John, Andrew and James, the son of Alpheus, walked into the town's border. Being shorter and younger than the other disciples, this new James was nicknamed Little James. Blocking the street was one of the town's publicans, collecting taxes from those passing through.

"I see the tax collector is busy at his tax office." Peter was walking next to Jesus as he watched the man taking money and motioning the traveler to go by. "It would appear every town we visit has a place of toll to rob the innocent traveler."

Little James stopped quickly and stepped behind Jesus to hide himself from the man behind the toll table. Jesus sensed his feelings and turned to face him, "Are you troubled over this man, Little James?"

"Master, I know him well. I used to live in this town before my parents died. He is vulgar in his speech and does not care who he embarrasses. He has become a disgrace to his fine Jewish family." James peeked around Jesus to see the tax collector joking with his fellow worker. "He is my brother, Levi."

"Do you love your brother, James?" Jesus started walking toward the man named Levi.

"I tell you, Master, he is a sinner, a foul-mouthed tax collector!" James did not want Jesus exposed to his bad brother.

"James"—Jesus stopped to look in the young disciple's eyes—"do you love him?"

"Yes, Rabbi, despite his sinful ways, I still love him." Little James slipped behind Jesus to hide from Levi.

"Where the devil is Judas? He has the purse! Why we allow him to carry it is beyond me!" Peter felt Jesus watching him. "It's just...he always manages to get behind us when we really need him."

"Peter, you worry too much." Jesus patted his shoulder. "God will provide our needs; have faith." He stopped in front of the tax collector and Levi gazed up into the unusual eyes of the tall handsome man, then looked past him to see the other four men.

"I count five." Levi started adding up the amount of tax required with a few pennies extra for himself.

"There are six of us here, Matthew." Jesus glanced behind him where James stood shaking his head.

"You know my other given name?" Matthew stared at Jesus. "I am certain I would remember you if I had ever met you before, yet you seem to know me already."

"Your brother is our sixth man, Matthew," Jesus spoke softly. "Say hello to your brother, James."

"James?" Matthew laughed out. "Are you hiding from me? Is it your brother you are trying to ignore or the tax collector?"

"I am not hiding from anyone!" James stepped out from behind his master and teacher. "I just prefer walking in his footsteps."

"Land sakes, little brother!" Matthew laughed out again. "If you are staying in town, you are welcome to join me this night at the harlot's den! Half-price specials on Fridays and all the wine you can consume! I can hook you up with a good lay!"

Levi noticed no one in the group was laughing at his rude remarks. His attention was drawn back to the man with the incredible eyes who appeared to be their leader.

"What have you to declare, sir?" He felt sure this poor man would not have much to tax.

"Our love for you, Matthew," Jesus simply said.

"Your love?" Matthew could not pull his eyes away from the soft-spoken man. He managed to glance over at his brother, who was studying Matthew with skeptical intent. "And my brother James—does he love me as well?"

"He does"—Jesus placed his hand gently on the tax collector's arm—"but the One who loves you the most is disappointed in you, Matthew."

"And who might that be?" The tax collector could not control the emotions he suddenly was feeling.

"The One who loves you the most is our Heavenly Father." Jesus did not take his eyes off of Matthew. "He wants you to return to His ways. He wants your love, Matthew."

"Love?" Matthew spoke just above a whisper, "I cannot tax you for love, now can I?"

"Matthew, follow me." Jesus continued down the street, along with the five men traveling with him as Judas finally arrived with their purse to pay the taxes required, then raced off to catch up with Jesus' long steps.

The tax collector refused the tax payment and waved them by as he continued to stare after Jesus. Matthew called out to his helper, "Take over the toll booth."

"When shall you return, Levi?" The man took the seat behind the tax table as he waited for his reply.

"I will not be back. I quit!" Without another word, he followed Jesus who had made his way into the temple for the evening services.

The rabbi stood boldly in front and spoke loudly, "Evil abounds in our streets! Those who commit the worst kinds of sin—the prostitutes and the publicans—are among the most offensive!" His eyes fell on Levi with obvious dislike as others turned to see who had drawn their leader's attention. "When men or women with these low morals commit their sins, we, as righteous men, must cast them aside!"

"Not so!"

Jesus spoke softly, but in the quiet temple his words were heard clearly as those around him, including their outspoken Rabbi, stared at him. Ignoring the stranger's interruption, the leader continued his ravings, "Good Jews, their evil is to be washed away and you must never have anything to do with them! Their wickedness will rub off on you and corrupt your very soul! I say plainly, REJECT THEM!"

"No, my friends!" Jesus spoke out with authority.

"You are a stranger in our mist! What is your name and where are you from?" The rabbi's eyes were trained on Jesus, angry that he continued to interrupt his speech.

"My name is Jesus and I am from Nazareth." His eyes searched the faces in the cool temple.

"If you disagree with my teaching, Jesus of Nazareth, kindly explain the reason." The leader motioned for Jesus to come to the front.

Jesus walked up and looked out at the worshippers. He noticed Matthew had slipped in and was sitting near the back with his head down.

"Brothers, I put this question to you. Is there any man completely free of sin? You must not judge another man's sin, for you will be judged in the same manner by our God in heaven! If someone has done you a wrong and asks you to forgive his wrong, then, my brothers, forgive him."

"Are you telling these men of faith to forgive someone who has done them harm?" the leader called out from his seat.

"I am telling these men of faith to show love to one another, to do unto others as they would others do to them." Jesus gazed up toward heaven. "Our Heavenly Father hears all, He sees all, there is nothing that can be hidden from His sight. You must walk in His light! Hear His calling and open up your eyes to what is true!"

"Kind sir, you speak of walking, seeing and hearing as a means to find the Almighty." An old man stood slowly on shaky legs, his hand trembling with overuse. "Yet there are some here in this very temple who cannot walk or see or talk."

"You speak of your son, old Aaron?" Jesus had noticed the old man rolling the blind middle-aged man into the cool temple. "He has been disabled since birth?"

"Yes, but how…?" Old Aaron suddenly felt numb. "I have never heard my son call me father, nor has he been able to look upon his dear mother's face." A tear trickled down his weathered wrinkled cheeks. "All he can do is lie in his bed or sit in this rolling contraption and stare silently into darkness."

Peter leaned over and whispered to his brother, Andrew, "Why does the old man bother to bring his son to the temple? He cannot see or hear what is being said. I find no use in it!"

Andrew noticed Jesus looking back their way. "Do not look now, brother, but somehow, someway, Jesus heard your remarks."

Never taking his eyes off Peter, Jesus said to the old man to address Peter's very statement.

"Yet you continued to bring your son into the house of God." Jesus turned to face the sad man. "One may lose all his senses but the gift of faith lives within everyone. Your son's name is Paul?"

Aaron could only stare at the man with the beautiful penetrating eyes as Jesus cupped his palms over Paul's deaf ears.

"Paul, child of God, your ears are open to hear my voice." Slowly the man lifted his head and looked toward the voice that had brought him out of silence. Jesus gently touched his eyes as he said softly, "Your eyes are open because of your faith."

Paul blinked three times as he focused in on the tall man

standing in front of him. Everyone watching sat in silence and wonder, afraid to move and break this link between heaven and earth.

"Is your faith strong enough to walk, son?" Jesus held out his hand to him. "If so, walk to me."

"I…I have felt God breathe upon me in this place. I know it well. It is here I feel alive!" Paul's voice came strange to his ears and he wasn't sure how he could understand the words that came from his once-still lips. "Yes, Lord, I have faith!"

"Then put your trust in God and walk!" Jesus stretched out his hand a short distance away.

Never taking his eyes off Jesus, the man slowly stood up on shaky legs, his father and friends ready to catch him. Paul stared into Jesus' face as he slowly started to move toward Jesus' hand. When he found strength coming to his legs, he began to move faster until he finally reached Jesus, where he fell into his arms crying, "I can walk! I can see and hear!" With tears streaming down his face, Paul fastened his eyes on the one who held him so lovingly. "It was you…you who made me walk, talk and see!"

Astonished by the miracle they had just witnessed, the crowd, as well as his chosen disciples, stared in complete wonder. Everyone in the temple were amazed, and it held them speechless.

Jesus touched the man's trembling shoulders. "Lad, it is your faith that has made you well. Give your thanks to the Father of all creation. It was He who healed you."

Then Jesus turned and walked from the temple as the news began to spread about the man from Nazareth.

CHAPTER 27

"Lord, some of John's disciples are just outside this crowd and wish to speak to you." Philip had been sitting watch when the men walked up, obviously depressed.

"Show them in, Philip." Jesus had sat down to speak to the crowd that followed him. The men who followed John came over and dropped to their knees, exhausted from their long walk.

"Jesus, my master John has been imprisoned by Herod. He has suffered there for many weeks. He grows weaker in the damp surroundings and goes without food, fasting and praying for God to release him either from his bondage or from his tortured life."

"John," Jesus spoke his name softly. "His days are numbered and his spirit has fallen."

"He has sent a message to you to ask if you are the One who was to come or are we to look for someone else?"

Tears came to Jesus' eyes as he gave them his reply, "Go tell John what you see and hear, that the blind men are recovering their sight, cripples are walking, lepers are being healed, the deaf are hearing, the dead are being brought back to life and the good news is being given to those in need." Jesus stood up and placed his hands on the men's shoulders.

"Tell John to remember the day he baptized me in the Jordan and heard the voice of my father coming from the morning dove that flew on my shoulder when he lifted me up out of the water. Tell John to search his heart, for he knows. Happy is the man who never loses faith in me." Jesus watched John's disciples walked away.

He turned to the silent crowd who sat waiting. "What did you go out into the desert to look at—a reed, waving in the breeze?" Those listening shook their heads negative. "No? Then what was it you went out to see—a man dressed in fine clothes? But the men who wear fine clothes live in the courts of kings! But what did you really go to see—a prophet?" Jesus looked out at the curious faces. "Yes, I tell you a prophet and far more than a prophet! This is the man of whom the scriptures say, 'Behold, I send my messenger before thee." His blue-green eyes held their attention as he continued.

"Believe me, no one greater than John the Baptist has ever been born of all mankind, and yet a humble member of the kingdom of heaven is greater than he. From the days of John the Baptist until now, the kingdom of heaven has been taken by storm, and eager men are forcing their way into it. The law and all the prophets foretold it till the time of John and if you can believe it, John himself is Elijah who was to come before the kingdom." He stretched out his hand.

"The man who has ears to hear must use them!" Jesus noticed some Pharisees had walked up to listen to his words as he continued, "But how can I show what people of this generation are like? They are like children sitting in the marketplace calling out to their friends, 'We played at weddings for you, but you would not dance, and we played at funerals, and you would not cry!'"

His eyes fastened on the group of Pharisees as he continued to speak with authority, "For John came in the strictest austerity and people say, 'He is crazy!' Then the son of man came, enjoying life and the people say, 'Look, a drunkard and a glutton, the bosom friend of the tax collector and sinner!" Jesus turned his attention back on the eager crowd.

"Ah well, wisdom stands or falls by her own actions."

With one last look at the stony-face Pharisees, Jesus turned and walked away with his disciples.

CHAPTER 28

Jesus turned back toward Galilee, for he knew it was time to take his message to his hometown and he was longing to see his mother.

"You should get quite a welcome in Nazareth, Master." Peter wiped his hot brow as they walked under the mid-day sun. "The local hero come home at last."

"It will not be a joyful reunion, Peter." Jesus kept his attention focused straight ahead. "Some will receive my message with a glad heart, many other will despise me and think of me as only the carpenter's son who left at the age of thirty."

"Then why go, Lord? It sounds like a waste of time." Peter frowned. The thoughts of anyone despising Jesus filling him with offense. "They do not deserve the likes of you if they feel that way!"

"It is those who are lost I must reach out to, Peter." Jesus glanced his way. "Truly, if just one believes, then it will be worth the ridicule."

"Lord, why not wait a few years—five, fifteen, even twenty?" John had been listening to the conversation and thought of a good solution. "Perhaps time will soften their hearts and they will have heard of many more wonderful signs and wonders you shall perform."

"Time is something I do not have much left of, John." Everyone stopped walking at that bold statement and stared at Jesus, not sure what he meant. "Little children, you must not let your hearts be troubled. Even though I have only a little less than two years to complete this journey, the reason I have come will be accomplished, so we must not tarry. I must arrive back in heaven the way I left and became a seed planted in the virgin Mary. The only thing different will be my scars."

The disciples had no reply because they could not wrap their minds around his words. Jesus turned toward Nazareth, where they arrived on the Sabbath. As was his custom, Jesus led his men into the synagogue. After everyone had arrived and taken a seat, Jesus stood up in their midst to read.

The rabbi was in charge of the sacred scrolls and which scripture would be read, so he handed Jesus the book of the prophet Isaiah to read. Jesus opened the scroll and found the place.

"The Spirit of the Lord is upon me"—his finger followed along with the words, but his eyes were on his mother sitting on the edge of her seat in the balcony—"because He has anointed me to preach the gospel to the poor. He has sent me to heal the broken-hearted, to preach deliverance to the captives and recover sight to the blind, to set at liberty those who are bruised, to preach the acceptable year of the Lord."

He rolled up the scroll and gave it back to the rabbi, then sat back down. The eyes of everyone in the synagogue were fastened on him. Seeing he had everyone's attention, he began to speak, "This day is this scripture fulfilled in your hearing."

Everyone listening were amazed and wondered at the gracious, beautiful words that came from his lips. There was mumbling among the worshipers as they kept saying, "Is this not Joseph's son?"

Others glanced at Mary, who was looking at her son with great love. One man stood up and pointed up at the mother of Jesus and said, "And is he not the son of Mary, who sits among us in the same bench every Sabbath?"

"I expect you to quote this proverb to me, 'Cure yourself, doctor! Let us see you do in your own country all that we have heard that you did in Capernaum!'" Jesus looked around at faces that were familiar. "I assure you that no prophet is ever welcome in his own country."

Jesus stood up as he continued, "I am telling you a plain fact because in Elijah's time, when the heavens were shut up for three and a half years, there was a great famine throughout the whole country. There were plenty of widows in Israel, but Elijah was not sent to any of them, his own people. He was sent to Sarepta, to a widow in the country of Sidon.

"Also, there were a great many lepers in Israel, but the prophet Elisha did not heal one of them, not one—only Naaman, the Syrian."

Most of those in the synagogue who heard him were furiously angry. They sprang to their feet and like a mob, drove him out of town, yelling hateful words as they pulled him to a steep hill, intending to hurl him down to his death. Some of the mob pushed his disciples back so they could not defend him.

When they reached the cliff, they stopped and looked around them. They were astonished to find him gone. Jesus had vanished before their eyes and walked straight through the whole crowd and went on his way to see his mother.

"What was Jesus thinking coming here?" James, the brother of Jesus, helped his mother inside their house, away from the rioting crowd. "Never have I seen such an angry bunch of people! I hardly recognized any of town's citizens in that synagogue today! They were all consumed with hate!"

"And in the house of Jehovah!" Simon, another brother, looked from the window to see if they had been followed. "Do you think they will actually hurt Jesus?"

"His Father will not allow it, my son." Mary pulled off her outer cloak. "I am only glad your sisters were not there to witness such hate for their beloved brother."

"Jesus is such a good man and he does such wonders and miracles." Jo'se joined his mother on the double bench Joseph had built for their house years back. "Why can't they see him the way we do?"

A knock came on their door. Looking out, Simon recognized one of his brother's followers, opened the door and pulled him inside. With an anxious tone, Simon asked, "John, what do you know of Jesus?"

"I am not worried about the master. If angels do not help him, His Father will." John knelt down next to Mary and took her hands. "I have come to check on you, Mary. Watching friends and people you have always known turn into a mob, wanting to hurt your son, could not have been easy on you."

"John, it hurts me deeply." Mary touched his sweet face. "They do not know Jesus as we do. John, you are so kind to be concerned about me. It does my heart good to see my son has such a loving disciple."

"You are right, Mother. John is a loving, caring man." Everyone turned to see Jesus standing in the room. He just simply appeared.

"Jesus!" Mary's eyes lit up as she stood from the bench and looped her arms around him in a tight hug. "How I have longed to hold you in my arms again, my son."

"My visit must be short under the circumstances." After hugging all his brothers, Jesus joined his mother on the love seat, letting his fingers glide across the smooth wood. Closing his eyes, he could see Joseph, happily working alongside his oldest boy, days long gone but memories forever. Opening his eyes, he noticed everyone waiting and watching. "Tell me true, did anyone receive my message with an open heart?"

"I counted ten, Jesus." James looked away, feeling ashamed of the townspeople he used to look up to. "Those ten men received you into their hearts. The rest are blind!"

"I did not see my friend Samuel among the worshipers." Jesus noticed the fallen faces of his family. "Mother?"

"Son, sweet beautiful, loving son." Mary took his hand, sadness in her beautiful blue eyes. "Samuel has married the head rabbi's daughter. No longer is he married to your sister."

"The same rabbi who handed you the scroll and told you what to read! Samuel has turned his back on you, Jesus. Your good friend is a back-stabber!" Simon said angrily. "The spoiled wench stole his heart and now he follows his father-in-law's will like a street puppet!"

"Simon, say what you will about Samuel, but I say he regrets leaving your sister and his true loyalties are with Jesus." Mary hugged her son and spoke softly, "I know he still loves you, Jesus. I am certain he was not part of that crowd who tried to hurt you."

"Yes, Mother, you are right. Samuel was not among those who tried to push me from the cliff." Jesus took them by surprise. "As I was passing through them, I saw Samuel, standing alone by himself." Tears came into Jesus' penetrating eyes as he remembered seeing his very good friend, standing there, heart-broken. "Samuel was weeping, thinking the angry mob had succeeded in their evil deed."

"Did he not see you, Lord?" John stood silently listening.

"No, not at first. Then I appeared to him and he cried in my arms and called me Lord." Jesus looked up, sensing something only he could feel. "My other disciples are looking for me. I must be going. Do not be afraid, my dear ones. My Father has sent angels to guard you and this house until the anger lifts and Lucifer moves on."

"Son, when will I see you again?" Mary held him tightly, his leaving tearing at her very soul.

"There is much for me to do, Mother, and my time is running out." Jesus felt her tremble in his strong arms. Pulling away, but still holding on to her, their eyes locked. "I love you, Mother. You will be a part of my life forever." With those words of comfort and one last kiss, Jesus walked away.

John hugged Mary. "Do not worry about your son, Mary. We will watch after him and get him safely out of Nazareth. We are on our way to Capernaum. The master is well-received there." He turned to catch up with Jesus.

CHAPTER 29

Leaving Nazareth behind them, Jesus and his group of followers had been walking for some time down the dusty road of Galilee, going from town to town as they made their way to Capernaum. He stopped to teach in the local synagogues and to preach the gospel of the kingdom. While there, he healed all manner of sicknesses and disease among the people.

As they walked along, Peter kicked a rock lying in his way. He noticed it looked unusual so he stooped to pick it up. Peter rolled the stone around in his hand and noticed it glistened with sparkles, making it appear like a costly stone.

"What have you found, Peter?" Andrew glanced over at the stone as Peter held it up for a better look. Jesus and the other men walking nearby also looked to see what had fascinated the tough fisherman. Peter glanced at Andrew briefly, then turned back to admire the pretty stone.

"I'm not certain, brother, but my guess is some rich traveler lost it as he made his way to Nain." Peter noticed Jesus looking. "It could be sold and put into our dwindling purse."

Jesus held out his hand. "Costly? Mumm, could be." He turned the smooth stone around in his hand as his eyes lit up with mischief. "I recognize this stone, Peter. I know what it is. This rare stone, as you put it, is a droparite!"

"No kidding! A droparite?" Peter took the stone to admire it. "A real droparite!" he smiled broadly, proud he had been the one to spot it. "I have never heard of it, but that is why I did not recognize it!" Peter laughed. "What should we do with it? Trade it for food or sell it?"

"Well, since it is a droparite, Peter, we shall do just that!" Jesus smiled. "Just drop-a-right here; it is worthless!" Jesus laughed at Peter's expression of shock and dismay, then pointed to the rocky ledge along the road, where millions of the same common rocks lay.

Peter grunted and turned to his brother, "Well, at least Jesus has a sense of humor!" He threw down the stone and gave it a kick before walking away, mumbling, while the other men continued to laugh.

As they approached the next town, a great crowd waited, having learned Jesus had been spotted coming their way. Some had brought members of their family or friends who had all kinds of sicknesses. Among them were people who were possessed with devils.

One such young woman was named Mary, who had been brought down from Magdala, about thirty miles from Nazareth. Standing next to her was a familiar face Jesus had not seen in over a year. The possessed woman was held secure by a strong servant. Jesus made his way to them, healing those who stepped up, pleading for healing. He stopped and smiled down at his long-time friend. "Joanna, my sweet lamb," he spoke softly as he bent down to kiss her cheek. "I know your time with Joshua was short. Forgive me for not being there in person to comfort you, but my heart knew so I prayed that you might have complete healing."

"Jesus, I felt your presence with me and it helped me through my sadness and the days of Joshua's loss." Joanna smiled sweetly. "He did give me two sons, twins, to remember him always."

"The twins live with your mother in Nazareth." Jesus always knew. "You feel they are safer there."

"I love Chuza, my husband. He is a good man, and under different circumstances, he would make a wonderful father. He is forever giving to me for he permits me to come and go as I choose." Joanna whispered for safety's sake, "It is Herod I do not wish my sons to grow up around. Chuza serves as his head steward, so it is hard to avoid being in the king's presence once in a while."

"This young woman you brought—tell me about her." Jesus looked into the wild eyes of a once- beautiful girl, gone mad.

"Oh, Jesus, it is so tragic!" Joanna looked around at the girl, moving wildly in her servant's tight grip. "Her name is Mary. She is from Magdala, just outside of Cana. Joshua knew her before this madness hit her. He said she was a sweet giving person and walked in the ways of our Lord."

"It appears Satan has sent his demons inside her so he can claim her for his own and rob God of his beautiful child." Jesus waved the servant aside. "Release her and step away."

Mary's body jerked from the nearness of the tall man standing over her. A strange voice came from deep within her, "LET US ALONE, JESUS OF NAZARETH! HAVE YOU COME TO DESTROY US? WE KNOW WHO YOU ARE, THE HOLY ONE OF GOD!"

Jesus recognized the seven fallen angels turned into demons by Lucifer himself. He sensed their evil power, so strong that a human body was defenseless against them, but they were no match for the Son of God.

"Evil spirits, hold your peace and come out of this woman!" Jesus raised his voice, "LEAVE HER!"

The seven demons tore from her body and cried with a loud voice as they departed. Mary fell limp on the ground, weak and crying. Jesus knelt down by her side and lifted her up to see his face.

"Mary, they are gone from you now, child, never to return. Go on your way in peace."

"Jesus, my Lord, I have no one left to return to," Mary spoke softly. "May I come and follow you and do for you whatever you choose?"

"Mary," Jesus looked into her eyes, then up at Joanna, who stood watching, tears in her beautiful eyes.

"I too want to come with you, Jesus. Joshua left me well-off and my current husband gives me plenty." Joanna knelt down to join them. "Mary and I can serve your needs. Cook for you, prepare for your rest, you as well as your men. We shall have our own tent to stay in. We only wish to serve you, Jesus. Please, let us provide for you the things you need."

"Then you both are welcome, if you choose to make the long journeys with us." Jesus stood and helped the women to their feet. "Come, follow me."

"Master!" Peter came running out of breath. "News has just reached us! John the Baptist has been beheaded by Herod!"

The group of followers and Jesus sat listening as the disciples described what had happened to John.

"Whenever John saw Herod, he would warn him about being married to his brother's wife, Herodias. John would tell King Herod, 'It is not right for you to possess Philip's wife!' This made Herodias furious with John and she wanted him executed, but she did not have the power and Herod had deep respect for him, knowing he was a just and holy man. Herod protected John and used to listen to him. Herod would get profoundly disturbed by John's words, and yet, he enjoyed hearing him."

Another of John's disciples added, "Even after Herod had John arrested, he would go down to his cell to speak to him and listen to what he had to say. Then the day arrived for Herod to give himself a birthday party. His courtiers and some of his army commanders were invited. Many leading people in Galilee came to help him celebrate. His palace was filled and there was much wine for him and his guests."

A third man, who still had John's blood on his hands after removing the headless body of their brave leader from the palace for burial, then spoke, "Herodias' daughter came to the feast and danced at Herod's request. Watching her in his drunken state, Herod was delighted, as were his guests, by her seductive moves, directed to the king himself. Herod had had his eyes on the shapely teen, his own niece, for some time, so after the dance, he told her, 'Ask me anything you like and I will give it to you!' She looked at him temptingly. Then he swore to her, 'I will give you whatever you ask me, up to half of my kingdom!' The girl went to her mother and asked her, 'What shall I ask for, Mother?' Herodias smiled an evil smile as she whispered, 'The head of John the Baptist.'"

The first man spoke up, "The girl then rushed back to the king's presence and made her request in front of everyone." The disciple had tears in his eyes as he remembered her words. "She said, 'I want you to give me, this minute, the head of John the Baptist on a platter!' Herod rose to his feet. He could see his wife smiling from the doorway, and he was aghast at what he had done. But because of his oath made in the presence of all his guests who were watching him closely, he could not refuse her."

Again, the second man spoke through tears, "So Herod sent one of his guardsmen straightway to bring him John's head. Herod, distressed for having been tricked, went to his chamber where he heard the Baptist shout for the last time, 'HEROD, REPENT!' Then the sound of the ax came down loudly to Herod's ears as the executioner cut off John's head! They placed it on a silver platter and carried it up to give to the heartless girl who took it and handed it to her smiling mother!"

The disciple whose hand was covered with John's blood, whispered, "We took away his body and placed it in a tomb."

Jesus was heartbroken. After seeing the sad group of men off, he turned to go to the hillside to be alone, never knowing that a great multitude of people were following behind him.

CHAPTER 30

Jesus had earlier sent the disciples away two by two to deliver his message and heal in His name. They had been gone for some time when they all returned and reported to him every detail of what they had done and taught. Jesus still felt sad over the loss of his cousin John, so he spoke to his disciples before the group of people coming their way reached them,

"Come along with me to some quiet place by ourselves and rest for a little while." So the disciples took Jesus and went off in the boat to a quiet place to get away.

Many of the people from all the towns saw them go and recognized Jesus and the disciples so they hurried around the shore on foot to forestall the one they came all that way to see from leaving.

When Jesus disembarked, he saw the large crowd and his heart was touched with pity for them. They seemed to him like sheep without a shepherd. Jesus settled down on a rock to teach them about many things. As they day wore on, his disciples came to him and said,

"Master, we are out here in the countryside and it is getting late." Andrew glanced up at the sky. "See, the sun is low in the western sky."

"Let them go now, Lord, so they can buy themselves something to eat from the local farms and villages." Peter joined in with his brother and waited for Jesus to reply.

Jesus remained calm as he replied simply, "You give them something to eat."

The brothers looked at one another in confusion. Then Peter spoke, "There are more than 5,000 men here, not counting the thousands of women and children! You want us to go and spend ten dollars on bread? Is that how you want us to feed all these people?"

"Tell me, Peter, Andrew, what bread have you got here?" Jesus asked as they stood staring at him as though he had lost his mind. "Go and have a look around."

Peter and his brother began to walk among the people, finding no one had brought any food until a young boy tugged at Andrew's sleeve. He glanced down into the boy's big brown eyes.

"Son, I am busy right now. If you have a question about anything, ask your father!" Andrew started to walk away when the boy's hand grabbed him again.

"Please, sir, I overheard Jesus asking if you have bread." His young voice shook as he lifted up his basket. "I have five loaves here and two fish that my mother packed for me this morning."

"Mumm, only five loaves, two fish." Andrew jumped when Peter reached for the basket.

"Thank you, son, for your thoughtfulness." Peter gripped the handle as he patted the small head. "I know God will bless you."

The young boy smiled as he watched Peter take the basket of food meant for him and hand it to Jesus.

"This is all we could find, Lord, given by a small lad." Peter looked down at the small basket and thought, *Even if everyone just got a crumb, there would not be enough for this big group.* "What is this for such a big crowd?"

Jesus took the basket and ordered the people to sit in parties on the fresh grass. Everyone sat down in groups of fifty or one hundred. Jesus held up the five loaves and two fish to heaven. He gave thanks to God, then broke the loaves and gave it to his disciples to distribute to the crowd. Then Jesus divided the fish among them all. Everyone ate and were satisfied.

Jesus called the twelve over and asked them to collect the leftovers. There were twelve baskets full of pieces of bread and fish. The large group was speechless as they walked away after Jesus instructed the crowd to be on their way before nightfall.

Jesus had already made his disciples get aboard the boat and go on ahead to Bethsaida on the other side of the lake, so he could send the great crowd home. Jesus watched the last group go out of sight. Finally, he was alone, so he went off to the hillside to pray.

Jesus lifted his head from praying and saw it had grown late. He stood up and looked out on the lake. The boat was in the middle of the lake, all his men on board and he by himself on land.

Moving closer to the shore's edge, he saw them straining at the oars, for the wind was blowing dead against them.

"The wind is holding us back!" Peter paddled hard. "If we make it to the other side, it will be a miracle!"

"If Jesus were on board, we would have that miracle, Peter!" Andrew pushed his oar with all his might. "He took five loaves of bread and two fish and supplied food for everyone on that hillside!"

"Are we to go back for Jesus? There is no other boat to bring him and it will take him days to walk around this lake!" John tried to see where they had left hours before, but it had grown too dark.

"I suppose the master will wait until morning, then find a boatman to bring him across." Peter handed James the oars. "You row awhile; my arms are falling off!"

Jesus decided he would go out on the water, get next to the boat and walk beside it until it reached land. But some of the men saw him walking toward them in the moonlight on the water.

"Good Lord!" they screamed out, frightened by the apparition. "It is a ghost!" The men were all absolutely terrified.

Jesus called out in a quiet voice, "It is alright! It is I myself. Do not be afraid!"

Peter looked over the side of the boat to see Jesus standing on the water smiling. "Lord, if it is really you, can I come out to meet you?"

Jesus stretched out his hand. "Come to me, Peter! Walk out in faith and you shall not sink!"

Peter lowered the rope ladder and climbed down. When he reached the water, he stepped away slowly and started walking on the water, making for Jesus, who stood a little way from him. Suddenly the wind picked up and began to blow heavily against him, causing him to panic. The waves began to lap about his feet as his heart melted in fear. Peter was sinking! He could feel himself going under the water and although he was an excellent swimmer, his lack of self-control was making him scared. He was drowning! He came up, spitting out water as he shouted,

"Lord, save me!"

Jesus felt Peter's fear and rushed to his side. He quickly reached out his hand and caught him before he went back under. As Jesus held Peter up, their eyes met and Jesus said softly, "You of little faith! What made you lose your nerve like that? Could you not see you were indeed walking on the water when you stepped down with faith? Peter, did I not tell you, if you have faith the size of a grain of mustard seed, you shall say unto this mountain, 'Remove from this place and go to another place and it shall be moved!' Nothing shall be impossible for you to do if you have faith instead of unbelief!"

Then some of the disciples helped Jesus and Peter aboard the boat and quickly the wind dropped. Every man, being moved by what they had seen, came and knelt down before Jesus crying,

"You are indeed the Son of God!"

CHAPTER 31

Jesus and his twelve, along with the women who had joined them to give service and help pay their way by giving of their own money, stopped for the setting sun. After they had come from the coast of Caesarea Philippi, they quietly finished their simple meal of bread and cheese.

Gathering up the remains and the wooden bowls, the small group of women—Joanna, Mary Magdalene and Salome—took them to clean and to prepare the bedding for the men before going inside their own tent for the night. That left Jesus alone to speak with his disciples.

"The crowds grow bigger, Master." Little James stretched his arms as he moved closer to the small fire. "Never have I seen so much suffering."

"Yes, Rabbi, they surround us everywhere we go!" Matthew was sitting next to his brother. "Your fame is spreading throughout Galilee and Judaea, further still!"

"Tell me, whom do men say that I, the son of man, am?" Jesus looked around the circle of men.

"Some say you are John the Baptist, come back to life"—James glanced into Jesus' eyes—"some, Elijah."

"I have heard men say you are Jeremiah or one of the prophets," Thomas offered.

"And who do you say that I am, Thomas?" Jesus' eyes held him tenderly as the large disciple began to grow nervous.

"You…are a very good man. The best teacher I have ever heard." Thomas looked down at his trembling hands, ashamed of his answer.

"Who do you say that I am, Philip?" All the men could tell Jesus was hurt by the answer and the way they all felt.

"I know you are truly…a man of God." Philip's voice trembled as he looked into the sad face of Jesus. "The signs and wonders you preform can only come from one who is close to God."

Peter had been listening to their pitiful proclamations and, noticing the hurt written on the perfect face of Jesus, stood up quickly, his heart pounding in his chest.

"I know who you are!" Peter looked around at his fellow disciples. "I think every man here knows who you are! They are just afraid to say it aloud!"

"Then tell me, Peter, who do you say that I am?" Jesus looked up into the fisherman's wet eyes.

"You are the Christ! The Messiah! The Son of the living God!" Peter spoke boldly from his very soul.

Jesus closed his eyes, then stood up and placed his hands on Peter's shoulders. Looking deep into his eyes, Jesus declared,

"Blessed are you, Simon, son of Malchus, for flesh and blood hath not revealed this truth to you, but my Heavenly Father has revealed this truth to you." Jesus hugged Peter. "Now I tell you that you, Peter, are the rock, and it is on this rock that I am going to build my church, and the powers of death will never prevail against it!"

Jesus took a firm hold on Peter's arm. "I will give you the key of the Kingdom of Heaven and whatever you forbid on earth will be what is forbidden in heaven and whatever you permit on earth will be what is permitted in heaven!"

Jesus turned to face the silent group of men. "Beloved, you are to tell no man that I am the Christ while I remain alive on this earth."

"Jesus, do not think me terribly harsh, but to say you are truly the Son of God some would call blasphemy." Judas felt a bead of sweat run down his forehead from the looks he was receiving from his fellow disciples. "Some might think you believe this because it arises out of pride."

"Some, Judas? Or do you speak of yourself? Judas, is it hard to believe the things which you have seen and heard?" Jesus knew this man's heart and what he would do in his final days. "He who has eyes to see and ears to hear, may they know the truth."

"Do not get me wrong, Master. I know there is no other like you." Judas felt sick and wished he had kept his doubts to himself. "I too have dreams about being someone better. We are all born of women, are we not?"

"How well do you know the scriptures, Judas?" Jesus knew no words would change the road that lay ahead for Judas.

"I must admit my knowledge of the scriptures is poor." Judas glanced down, suddenly feeling ashamed.

Jesus looked around at all the anxious faces showing mixed

emotions. First Peter's bold declaration of the truth that lifted each man's spirit, then Judas, depressing them with questions of unbelief.

"Who among you know the scriptures and the books of Isaiah?"

"I am learned in the verses of the prophet Isaiah," John spoke up softly.

"Then will you quote from chapter 7, verse 14, chapter 35, parts 4, 5 and 6 and lastly Isaiah 9, verse 6." Jesus took his seat next to Judas and gathered up his hand in his. "Listen to the words the prophet spoke concerning God's Son. Let your ears hear, Judas. Let your heart be opened up to the truth."

John closed his eyes to block out those watching and listening as he recalled the scriptures Jesus asked him to quote. John remembered the chapters and verses from the prophet Isaiah and began to speak,

"Isaiah 7, verse 14 states: 'Therefore, the Lord himself shall give you a sign; behold, a virgin shall conceive and bear a son and shall call his name Immanuel.'" John then thought of the next three verses in chapter 35. "'Your God will come with vengeance, even God with a recompense; he will come and save you. Then the eyes of the blind shall be opened and the ears of the deaf shall be unstopped. Then shall the lame man leap as a deer and the tongues of the dumb sing.'"

John glanced up into the face of Jesus, and he knew this prophecy was indeed about him. He lifted up his voice to continue with chapter 9, verse 6: "'For unto us a child is born, unto us a son is given: the government shall be upon his shoulder: and his name shall be called'"–John locked eyes with his Savior, tears flowing down his face—"'he shall be called Wonderful, Counselor, the Mighty God, the Everlasting Father, the Prince of Peace!'"

John stood up on trembling legs and walked over to Jesus, then fell to his knees at Jesus' feet.

"Lord, forgive me for not speaking out like my brother, Peter, for I have believed in my heart that you are the Christ! I have felt this way ever since the wedding feast in Cana and because of the love that radiates from you. There are no words to describe the great love I feel for you, Jesus."

"John, my beloved disciple!" Jesus lifted up his fallen head. "In time, I will leave in your care my dear mother to watch after and to love, as you have loved me."

"It would be my honor to care for the mother of my Lord. How blessed is she to have been the chosen one of God." A glow of warm love reflected on the disciple's face. "She was the first to look into the face of God!"

"Not to take away from the beauty of it all, but this same pure girl had six more children, did she not?" Judas felt hated by everyone there, including Jesus, for doubting openly, so why stop there? he thought to himself, never knowing that Satan himself had already started working on his mind and soul.

Jesus felt Lucifer near and looked over at his smirking face which vanished from his sight when Jesus stood up and looked down on Judas, "You speak out of hurt, Judas, fears and doubts, crafted by the dragon. But I tell you true, Judas, my love for you is as great and true as it is for any man or woman here. Though you speak ill of my mother, if you must know, the saintly woman remained a virgin until my second birthday. With blessings from my father, her devoted husband, who waited with patience and love for her, was finally permitted to know the love of his heart. Their love produced six of their own children and gave me a full lively family to grow up with."

Jesus felt tears filling his eyes. "Judas, Judas, my heart is breaking—not from your unbelief, for that part of your heart could change. It is what cannot be altered that brings me great sadness."

"Jesus, never have I loved anyone like I do you." Judas could not control his own tears. "Forgive my doubts, Lord, my words, my actions. I do not know what comes over me."

"You are forgiven, Judas, for present things and things to come." Jesus hugged him and walked toward his tent, tired and mentally hurting.

CHAPTER 32

Six days before the Passover, Jesus went to Bethany to the home of Lazarus and his sisters, Martha and Mary. Earlier in the week, Jesus had sent John to Nazareth to bring Mary, his mother, to him. They had arrived shortly after Jesus and the other eleven disciples.

Seeing his mother enter, Jesus greeted her with a kiss. Without a word, he took his mother by the hand and led her out back to Lazarus' rose garden. There, Jesus found a secluded bench for them where they could sit. Mary ran her fingers over her son's wavy hair, then touched his handsome face.

"Son, my heart has been troubling me with thoughts about your safety." Mary held tightly to his strong hand. "There is something on your mind, son, something you wish to share with me."

"A woman who loves with a pure heart is wise beyond her years." Jesus forced a smile. "It grieves me deeply to have to share this with you, but I feel you must know, must be prepared for what is soon to happen."

"Simeon, an old man in the holy temple, many years ago when you were but a baby, spoke of a sword piercing my soul. Joseph and I had taken you, our little baby boy, there for the Jewish custom. So long ago, yet it seems like only yesterday when Simeon spoke those chilling words to me."

"Yes, I remember, Mother." As Mary's eyes grew wide with wonder, Jesus gently stroked her beautiful hair. "I felt you tremble from sudden fear as you pulled me close to your bosom."

Mary's heart was filled with worry as she took his face in her soft hands. "Jesus, must you go into Jerusalem this Passover? The Pharisees hate you and even more because the people love you."

"Mother, sweet loving mother, I must ride into Jerusalem on Passover, for it will be the beginning of the end. All that the prophets spoke of me will come to pass just as they have said." Jesus put his arm around his mother's trembling shoulders. "You must stay with Mary and Martha, Mary of Magdalene and Joanna. If you hear the shouting hosannas and praise rising up from the large crowd, you must not let your hopes rise."

"The people do love you, son," Mary spoke softly.

"Yes, they will be filled with love for me, call me their king." Jesus knew the words he must tell his mother would start that sword toward her very soul, but she must be prepared. "All those standing in the temple will hear their shouts. The Pharisees will start looking for a way to steal me away, but the time is set; they cannot alter it. In the end, they will turn the crowd against me, and their shouts of praise will turn into shouts of 'Crucify him!'"

Mary grabbed her heart, tears fell from her eyes, the very thought of her beautiful son being crucified filling her with anguish.

"My son, is there no other way?"

"Mother, it is for this reason I came into this world. The shepherd gives his life for his sheep. He becomes the perfect lamb, without blemish, and takes away the sins of the world! Every man, woman or child who believes in me will never die. I die so that anyone who believes in me will live forever! When I return to heaven, my disciples will start my church to win the souls of all true believers."

"Jesus, how hard it must be for your Almighty Father to ask you, His only son, to suffer and die on a cross for the children on earth." Mary held tightly to her son as he embraced her.

"In the end, Mother, it is my choice to make." Jesus knew he must go through this trial alone, even though 10,001 angels would be there, surrounding him on every side and flying above him. They would remain silent unless he called out for their help, at which time this army of angels would begin destroying the earth.

"My son, if you must die"—Mary could not control the flood of tears that raced down her cheeks—"I will be there for you, to give you what comfort I can and more love than I thought I could possibly feel! It is more than a mother's love, Jesus. You…you are my…Savior!"

Jesus lifted her up gently and wrapped his arms around her, tears falling from his own eyes, for he knew this could possibly be the last touch from his mother until he came to take her home to heaven.

Mary, Lazarus' sister, sat at her dresser and stared at her prize possession: a fancy sealed bottle of expensive perfume, weighing a pound. Her devoted brother had given it to her on her fourteenth birthday.

Minutes before, Mary had looked at the touching scene below her window in the rose garden. She knew the news Jesus shared in secret with his mother must have been something to do with his future. Mary felt in her own heart that something bad was going to happen to their beloved friend.

Mary thought back to the first time Jesus had visited them in Bethany, how she had sat at his feet listening to his beautiful stories and teachings. She laughed softly to herself as she remembered how Martha had gotten upset with her for leaving her to fix the meal and set the table, then took her complaint to Jesus. Mary giggled when she recalled his reply.

"Martha, you trouble yourself with many things, but Mary has chosen the one thing good."

Mary's giggles turned to sadness as she recalled the day Jesus came after their loving brother had been dead in the grave for four days. She and Martha had sent word to Jesus when Lazarus became ill in hopes he would come and heal his friend. Instead, Jesus had waited. She learned later from John, one of his twelve, that when the news reached Jesus' ears, he told them,

"This illness is not meant to end in death. It is going to bring glory to God, for it will show the glory of the Son of God."

John told her that after that, they waited two days longer. Then Jesus told them, "Let us go to Judaea."

The disciples argued against it, saying, "Master, only a few days ago the Jews were trying to stone you to death! Are you going to go back there now?"

Jesus replied, "There are twelve hours of daylight every day, are they not? If a man walks in the day time, he does not stumble, for he has the daylight to see by. But if he walks in the night, he stumbles because he cannot see where he is going. So pack your things quickly; we go." Before he started on his way, he paused, "Our friend Lazarus has fallen asleep, but I am going to wake him up."

Peter spoke up, "Lord, if Lazarus has fallen asleep, he will surely be alright. He is getting rest now."

Jesus spoke clearly, "Lazarus has died and I am glad that I was not there for your sakes, that you may learn to believe. And now, let us go to him."

Mary glanced at her reflection in her mirror. She remembered seeing Jesus and his disciples walking toward their house. She could still hear the mourners who stayed with them, weeping and lamenting. Her sister Martha had gone out to meet him while she chose to remain inside. From the open window, Mary could hear her sister sobbing out her words to Jesus, "If only you had been here, Lord, my brother would not have died! Yet, I know that even now, God will give you whatever you ask from Him."

"Your brother will rise again," Jesus spoke softly.

"I know." Martha wiped her swollen eyes. "I know that he will rise on resurrection day, the resurrection of us all!"

"I myself am the resurrection and the life," Jesus had told her. "The man who believes in me will live, even though he should die, and anyone who is alive and believes in me will never die! Do you believe me, Martha?"

"Yes, Lord!" Martha cried. "I do believe that you are the Christ, the Son of God! The one who was to come into the world!"

Mary could remember her sister running inside the house whispering to her, "The master is here and is asking to see you!"

Mary remembered how she had sprung to her feet and gone out to him, all the Jews following her and Martha to see what was making the sisters so excited. When she had reached Jesus, she looked up at him, then dropped to her knees in front of his feet. "If you had only been here, Lord, my brother would never have died!"

Then Mary remembered the great sadness reflected in Jesus' face after watching her unstoppable tears and all the Jewish friends weeping along beside her. In sorrow, Jesus asked, "Where have you put him?"

"Lord, come and see." The sisters took Jesus up to the tomb on a small hill above the house. Everyone watching was deeply moved as Jesus himself wept.

Mary recalled the words from the Jews, "Look how much he loved him. Could he not have kept this man from dying if he could open that blind man's eyes and make the cripple walk?"

Mary could tell Jesus had heard their words, for he was deeply moved as he walked up to the grave. There was a cave in the cliffs and a stone lay in front of it to seal it tightly from would-be thieves and passing animals looking for a free meal. Jesus spoke softly to the servants who had followed them, saying, "Take away the stone."

"But, Lord"—Martha touched his arm gently—"Lazarus has

been dead for four days. By now, he will be decaying!"

Jesus looked at the sisters. "Did I not tell you that if you believe, you would see the wonder of what God can do?"

After they took the stone away, Mary remembered Jesus raising his eyes up to heaven and speaking, "Father, there is no other mightier than you! You heal, you bring death, you make alive again! Thank you, my Father, for you have heard me! I know in my heart that you always hear me, but I said this for the sake of these people standing here, so that they may believe that you sent me!" Then Jesus turned his face to the open grave and spoke again, "My Father, breathe on this man, so he may live!" Then Jesus cried out, "LAZARUS, COME FORTH!"

Mary trembled when she recalled seeing her once-dead brother walking out of that cold tomb, his feet and hands bound with graveclothes and his face muffled with a handkerchief, then Jesus telling their servants to unbind him and let him go home.

Mary reached for her perfume. It was hers to keep or hers to give. Suddenly things did not hold any value to her. Jesus had taught her to lay her treasures up in heaven and she knew it meant doing good works to help others in need. Now her heart was set on helping her Savior by anointing his head and feet with her perfume.

Below, they all enjoyed a supper together, as Martha, with the aid of Joanna and Mary of Magdalene, served the large group of men, while Mary, the mother of Jesus, relaxed by her son.

Everyone had finished eating and were making small talk when Mary, Lazarus' sister, made her way quietly behind Jesus and removed his head wrap. She opened the expensive perfume, its fragrance filling the air in the large dining chamber, drawing everyone's attention to what she was doing.

Pouring about one-third of the warm liquid into her hands, she rubbed it gently over Jesus' head and through his hair, then walked in front of him and dropped to her knees. As she began to open the perfume bottle, Judas grabbed it out of her hand and burst out,

"What are you doing, wasting this expensive perfume, woman! Why on earth wasn't it sold? It is worth thirty dollars, which could have been given to the poor!"

"Are you so concerned about the poor, Judas?" Jesus knew Judas did not really care about the poor because he was in charge of the disciples' purse and sometimes would take money for himself.

Jesus stared at him. “Let her alone, let her keep anointing me, Judas. She is preparing me for the day of my burial.”

There was a gasp from everyone listening, a heart-sinking sadness that swept through each man and women there.

Jesus’ attention was still on Judas as he continued, “You have the poor with you always, but you will not always have me!” Jesus retrieved the perfume bottle from Judas’ trembling fingers and handed it back to Mary.

Mary pulled the head wrap from her hair and let it fall down to her waist. With loving care, she removed Jesus’ sandals, then divided the remaining two-thirds on each foot. Gathering her long black hair, she wiped the feet of Jesus as her tears fell gently down. She had given what she cherished most, but would gladly give her life for the man who would shortly die for her.

CHAPTER 33

All during the week, since Jesus had made his triumphant entrance into Jerusalem on the first day of the week, he had been teaching within the temple and the courtyards. He had called out the wrong-doings of the chief priest and the Pharisees. These religious leaders had tested Jesus and failed so they had a private meeting to discuss how they could trap him for publicly warning the people against them. He boldly stated,

"The Scribes and the Pharisees speak with authority, that of Moses! So you must do what they tell you and follow their instructions! But you must not imitate their lives! For they preach but do not practice. They pile up back-breaking burdens and lay them on other men's shoulders; yet they themselves will not raise a finger to move them!" Jesus glanced over at the well-dressed leaders staring angrily at him.

"Their whole lives are planned with an eye for effect. They increase the size of their phylacteries and the lengths of the tassels for their robes! They get the seats of honor at dinner parties and front places in the synagogues. They love to be greeted with respect in public places and have men call them 'Rabbi'. Don't you ever be called 'Rabbi.' You have only one teacher, and all of you are brothers." Jesus looked out over the group of listeners in front of him and noticed sons sitting next to fathers.

"And don't call any human being 'Father' for you have one Father and He is in heaven. You must not let people call you leaders. You have only one leader—Christ! The only superior person among you is the one who serves others. For every man who promotes himself will be humbled, and every man who learns to be humble will find promotions." Jesus turned his attention to the church leaders, who were watching him closely.

"But alas for you, Scribes and Pharisees, play actors! You scour sea and land to make a single convert and make him twice as ripe for destruction as you yourselves! Alas for you, Scribes and Pharisees, play actors! That you are! You lock up the doors of the Kingdom of Heaven in men's faces; you will not go in yourselves, neither will you allow those at the door to go inside!

"Alas for you, blind leaders! You say, 'If anyone swears by the temple, it amounts to nothing; but if he swears by the gold of the temple, he is bound by his oath.' You blind fools, which is more important—the gold or the temple which sanctifies the gold?

"You utter frauds, for you pay your tithe on mint, aniseed and cumin and neglect the things which carry far more weight in the law—justice, mercy and good faith! These are the things you should observe without neglecting the others. You call yourself leaders and yet you can't see an inch before your nose!

"What miserable frauds you are, you Scribes and Pharisees! You clean the outside of the cup while the inside is full of greed and self-indulgence. First wash the inside of the cup; then you can clean the outside!"

Everyone listened to Jesus as he kept speaking to the angry leaders, calling them out for their misguiding and self-pious behavior. Judas stood back in the shadows as he observed Jesus closely.

"Alas for you, you hypocritical Scribes and Pharisees! You appear like good men on the outside, but inside you are a mass of pretense and wickedness! Go ahead then and finish off what your ancestors tried to do! You serpents, you viper's brood, how do you think you are going to avoid being condemned to the rubbish heap?

"Listen to this: I am sending you prophets and wise and learned men. Some of these you will kill and crucify; others you will flog in your synagogues and hunt from town to town, your hands covered by all the innocent blood you spill! Yes, I tell you that all this will be laid at the doors of this generation!"

So the chief priest and the elders of the people assembled in the court of Caiaphas, the high priest, to discuss how they might get a hold of Jesus by some trick and kill him.

"It is far better for one man to die for our people than all of us perish." Caiaphas had discussed earlier that because the people were calling Jesus their king, Pilate would take offense because of King Caesar.

"Caiaphas is right! This man brings nothing but trouble!" Annas spoke up, "He claims to be their king!"

"Has he said so, your grace?" Nicodemus had arrived late because no one had told him about the meeting. "I have heard Jesus speaking and not so much as one time did he declare himself a king."

"Nicodemus, this is why we did not tell you about this meeting. Your views differ from ours." Caiaphas patted his shoulder. "And it is wise to remember that I, sir, am the high priest, the one who is closer to God!"

"Are you?" Nicodemus said softly. "I will have no part of this outrage! Jesus is a good man and does not deserve this treatment!" He turned to leave. "Beware what you do; this man is a man of God!"

After he left, they continued plotting, unaware that one of the twelve was outside listening. A diabolical plan had come into the mind of Judas Iscariot. He shook off his misgivings and stepped inside.

One of the chief priest's guards stopped him and asked for his name and what business he had with the assembled priest and scribes. After he answered, the guard took Judas to Caiaphas. "Lord Caiaphas, this is Judas Iscariot, one of Jesus' disciples. He wishes a word with you."

"What do you wish to talk to us about, Judas?" Caiaphas felt a sudden ray of hope as he looked at him.

"You are after Jesus, are you not?" He swallowed, knowing the entire assembly was watching him closely. "I can give you Jesus."

"Can you?" Caiaphas glanced at Annas, his father-in-law, and smiled, then turned back to the nervous man. "And why would you want to betray…" The high priest noticed the instant hurt look on Judas' face so he stepped back and thought, *And if you give us Jesus, what will you want in return?* Caiaphas recognized Judas as a man who was greedy and not to be trusted.

"What do you offer me?" Judas wanted them to give him a price; perhaps it would be more than what he was thinking of himself.

"We will gladly give you thirty pieces of silver, Judas, a rich collection of coins." The chief priest was handed a leather pouch that jingled when he tossed it up in front of the betrayer.

"Very well! I will find a suitable opportunity for you to take him when there is no crowd present."

They counted out the thirty silver coins and walked away, leaving Judas standing alone in the empty courtyard.

CHAPTER 34

The fifth day of the week arrived, along with the day of unleavened bread, on which the Passover lamb had to be sacrificed. Jesus called out to Peter and John, "Go and make preparations for us to eat the Passover meal."

"Where would you like us to do this, Master?" Peter asked.

"Go into the city. There will be a man carrying a jug of water. He will meet you in the street."

"Then what, Master." John glanced over at Peter who had his attention on Jerusalem.

"Follow him to the house he is going to, then say to the owner of the house, 'The master has this message for you. In which room may my disciples and I eat the Passover?' He will take you upstairs and show you a large room, furnished for our needs. Make all the preparations there."

"It is exactly as Jesus described, Peter!" John walked around the big airy room where a long table had been set up with thirteen places to sit.

"When I spotted the man carrying the jug of water, I could not imagine which house he would take us to." Peter had returned with the roast lamb, unleavened bread, cheese and wine for the Passover meal. He counted the spaces as he placed the food around the table. "There are exactly the right amount of space for us around this table!"

"I am sure Jesus knew that, somehow." John's eyes fell on a basin and a large towel, a jar of water sitting next to it. "Peter, why did you buy this water basin and big towel?" John poured some of the water into the round bowl. "Did the master ask you to get it?"

"John, you saw me arrive with the food. Did I have a water basin and towel with me? Seriously, John, I never got it so it must have already been here, just like the long table and the exact number of spaces for our group to sit." Peter placed the bowls and cups that were also there around the table. He and John watched the rest of the disciples come into the room. John leaned over to Peter and whispered,

"Jesus did say the room would be furnished with what we needed. Angels maybe?" John looked over at the door when Jesus walked in and went over to the basin of water.

"Thank you, John, for pouring the water in the basin. Have the men sit down and pull off their sandals."

Always the loving disciple, John followed Jesus' instructions without question. Peter, on the other hand, was watching as Jesus pulled off his tunic and wrapped the big towel around his hips, then got down on his knees and started washing each man's feet and wiping them dry.

When Jesus reached Peter, he knelt and placed the basin in front of him. Peter, still with his sandals on, pulled his feet away and said, his face red with embarrassment, "Lord, do you intend to wash my feet?"

"What I do, Peter, you do not realize now but you shall know hereafter." Jesus watched as Peter moved his feet further away, feeling it wrong for the Son of God to wash the feet of someone as undeserving as he.

"Lord, you shall never wash my feet!"

Jesus looked up into Peter's eyes and spoke softly, "Peter, if I do not wash your feet, you will have no part of me."

Peter set up quickly and removed his sandals, then placed his feet in the water basin.

"Lord, not only my feet, but also my hands and head!"

Jesus smiled as he washed Peter's feet. He removed the towel and dried them, then lay the towel aside and put back on his clothes as he looked at Peter, "He who is washed need not be washed anywhere else, just the feet need to be cleaned, for they have traveled through the dusty streets." Jesus thought about Judas and said, "You are not all clean."

The men looked at one another, confused by his last words, never knowing one of their own was betraying their master. He took his seat in the middle of his men and spoke,

"Do you realize what I have just done to you? You call me teacher and your Lord and you are quite right, for I am your teacher and your Lord." His gaze fell down over each man. "But if I, your teacher and Lord, have washed your feet, you must be ready to wash one another's feet. I have given you this as an example so that you may do as I have done. Believe me, the servant is not greater than his master, and the messenger is not greater than the man who sent him. Once you realize these things, you will find your happiness in doing them." Jesus knew these men, except one, would serve him, their master, as he would send them out to all men and all nations to tell of his life and his grace for all believers.

After the disciples found their places at the table, six on the left side and six on the right, Jesus stood up and lifted his eyes upward.

"Now is the Son of God glorified!" Then he turned his attention to the twelve. "With all my heart I have longed to eat this Passover meal with you before the time comes for me to suffer. Believe me when I tell you, I shall not eat the Passover again until all that it means is fulfilled in the Kingdom of God."

Then taking the loaf of bread, Jesus thanked God, broke it and gave it to them with these words, "This is my body which is given for you. Do this in remembrance of me." Then taking the cup of wine, he held it up and thanked God, then looked down both sides into each of the disciple's eyes. "Take this to drink and share it amongst yourselves. This cup is the new agreement made by my blood, which is shed for you and for many. Drink in remembrance of me."

After the first six had drunk it, they passed it back to Jesus, who handed it to Peter, sitting on his right as he declared, "I tell you this, I shall not drink any more wine until I drink it new with you in my Father's Kingdom!"

Jesus' heart was deeply troubled over Judas. He had known someone he had broken bread with would betray him, but up until now, he had never thought it would be one of his chosen. But then it was just like Lucifer to pick the one weakest and most easily tempted. Again, Jesus looked over each face sitting at the long table, sadness filling their eyes.

"My good friends, we have traveled many dusty roads together for three long years and we have seen and done many things. Throughout it all, I have loved each one of you dearly. But I must tell you in truth, this scripture will be fulfilled. 'He that eats my bread lifted up his heel against me.'"

"What does the prophecy mean, Lord?" Simon leaned forward.

"I know you, for you are the twelve I have chosen. Never did I think this prophecy would be about as close a friend as one of my own chosen." Jesus could tell they were still confused, so he spoke bluntly,

"Then I shall say it plainly. One of you is going to betray me."

The disciples stared at one another, completely mystified as to who he was talking about. Then they all started to question themselves, asking, "Master, is it I?" or "Surely you cannot mean me, Master!" Peter nodded to John and asked, "Tell us, John, whom does he mean?"

John looked up into the beautiful face of his Lord and saw it was filled with compassion. John rested his head over on Jesus' shoulder and spoke softly, "Lord, who is it?"

Jesus closed his eyes and could plainly see the face of Judas Iscariot. When he opened his eyes, he looked directly at Judas and said, "It is the one I am going to give this piece of bread to, after I have dipped it in the dish of broth." After breaking off the piece of bread, Jesus handed it toward Judas, who was looking down at his hands, his heart pounding with the knowledge of what he was about to do to the one man he loved most in the entire world. Jesus thought as he observed the disciple who would betray him, *What will my people believe, Judas? That my Father deliberately chose you as my betrayer? My Father is a God of love and mercy. He would never destroy the hopes of eternity for any man, woman or child. Would my people believe that I would say it was the devil that made you betray me and if so, could not I have driven the devil from you like I had done for others? Judas, you do not have a demon inside you; you just chose to listen to him instead of me. Like the other eleven disciples who believe in me, you struggled with the truth. You witnessed the same miracles and were given the same teachings for three years.*

It was the gift of choice, given to all men and angels, that brought about Judas' actions, not the will of the Father, not the will of the Son of the Father, but the choice Judas made. He chose treasures on earth, like gold, silver and money instead of placing his faith in Jesus and winning lost sheep for the glory of God. Judas could have remained a true disciple, but he chose betrayal.

"Remember, my people, I had many trusted friends with whom I have shared bread."

Jesus dipped the bread in the dish of broth in front of Judas and gave it to him. With tears in his eyes, Judas took the bread from Jesus, knowing he was indeed guilty. Taking a small bite, Satan entered into his heart. Looking sadly at Judas, Jesus said, "Be quick about your business."

Judas rose quickly, still holding the piece of bread, and went out the door into the dark of night.

No one else at the table knew why Jesus told Judas that. They assumed since Judas was in charge of the purse, Jesus had sent him to buy other things they needed or to give something to the poor.

Jesus' heart was breaking, for soon he would be leaving these loyal friends, his family and his dear loving mother. With great sadness, he said, "My beloved friends, only for a little time am I with you. Where I am going, you cannot come."

"Let me come with you now, Lord!" Peter looked up hopefully.

"You will come later, Peter." Jesus could not help but smile at the fisherman's anxious face.

"But why can't I come now? I will die for you!" Peter's heart was filled with love for Jesus.

"Will you, Peter? Will you die for me?" Jesus could feel Peter's great love for him.

Peter's eyes lit up as he declared, "I will! I will!" He sat up joyfully.

Jesus gently took his shoulders. "Peter, Peter, this I tell you in truth, before the cock crows twice, you will deny me three times."

Peter stood slowly and backed away, sudden fear gripping him. "Lord, even though I might not die for you, I would never deny you!"

With tears in his eyes, Jesus looked down and closed them, knowing the hurt Peter would face when he saw those very words come true. Calmly Jesus said, "In my Father's house there are many mansions. If it were not true, I would have told you. I go to prepare a place for you, and if I go, I shall return to take you with me."

"Master, please speak to us plainly without proverbs." Thomas looked confused by his words. "How are we to know where you are going?"

"I am the way, the truth and the light! No one, not one, comes to the Father, but by me, believing in me!"

Jesus' hands shook as he placed them on the table for support. "This night I will be arrested and taken in for a mock trial. I will be convicted, beaten and hung upon a Roman cross to die."

"Lord?" was all they could say through their heartache and sudden overwhelming sadness. Jesus looked into every face as he spoke,

"Be at peace, my children, for on the first day of the week, I will arise and live again! Have I not told you so before? And because I live, you too shall live!" Jesus pulled his wrap around him to ward off the night chill and walked toward the door. "I am going to the garden to pray."

Andrew jumped up and grabbed his arm. "Master, must you go out tonight? It is far too dangerous for you out there!"

"The grain of wheat is very small, Andrew." Jesus touched him gently. "If it is planted in the ground, there it will die. Many will grow, many will live because of it." Jesus knew the parable was about himself, His dying and being buried, so that many who believe in Him would live and not die.

Before leaving, Jesus turned one last time to his loyal disciples and spoke calmly, "So, now comes the end of what they wrote about me in prophecy."

CHAPTER 35

Out on the Mount of Olives, Jesus went to his usual place, the one where he often prayed. His disciples followed him and sat down, tired not only from the long day but also from their mental state, worrying about Jesus. He looked down on them, their eyes heavy with fatigue.

"Pray that you may not have to face temptation. The soul is willing, but the body is weak." Jesus turned and went off alone, a stone's throw away, where he fell down on his knees to pray.

"My Father, this thing you ask of me, to suffer and die in pain on that cross, has filled me with great anguish and sorrow! Father, if…if there is another way, take this cup away from me!" Jesus' heart was brimming with fear "I…do not wish to drink this deadly cup!" He lifted his face to heaven. "But, my Father, it is not my will, but Your will that must be done. My heart knows this!"

Getting up on shaky legs, Jesus walked over to where his disciples were and found them all sleeping.

"Peter, James, John? Could you not stay awake one hour with me?"

Leaving them asleep, he walked back to the same spot and fell down. Looking up, he saw a heavenly angel standing beside him to give him strength and help him follow through with what he had to do.

Jesus was in agony and prayed even more intensely, sweat falling from him like great drops of blood streaming to the ground.

"Father…Father…if you cannot take this cup away from me, unless I drink it, then let their hate tie me down! Let them chastise me! Crucify me!!!" Jesus buried his head in his hands and wept. Slowly, he lifted his head and looked up into the open doors of heaven. A calm radiance lit his face as he said softly, "It is for this reason I came into the world. I will drink your cup, my Father! Thy will be done!"

Jesus got up and walked back to find his disciples still sleeping through sheer grief.

"Why are you still sleeping?" He spoke to them as they tried to open their heavy eyes, "You must get up and go on praying that you may not have to face temptation."

Suddenly they could hear the sound of a crowd approaching, led by Judas himself. He stopped when he reached Jesus, leaned in and kissed him on the cheek.

"Judas, would you betray me, the Son of man, with a kiss?" Jesus gazed deeply into his traitor's eyes, and suddenly Judas felt remorse for his actions.

The disciples, seeing what was happening, cried out, "JUDAS! Lord, shall we use our swords?"

Peter grabbed a sword and slashed at the high priest's servant, cutting off his right ear. The young man grabbed it, screaming in fear and pain, as Jesus turned to Peter and the other disciples and stated loudly,

"That will do! He who lives by the sword will die by the sword! Put them away!" Then Jesus touched the servant's ear and it was immediately healed. The young man who had been healed stared at the man they had come to arrest as Jesus spoke to the chief priest, the temple officers and elders who had walked up to Gethsemane after him.

"So you have come with your swords and staves as if I were a bandit. Day after day I was with you in the temple and you never laid a finger on me, but this is your hour and the power of darkness is yours!"

As they arrested Jesus and were marching him off to the high priest's house, the young servant watched the men who had been with Jesus run in all directions just as it was told, "My sheep will be scattered." Then he noticed one had remained behind, the one who had cut off his ear. This one had slipped off behind those taking his master and was following them.

One of the remaining temple guards took the servant by the arm and said sharply, "What are you waiting for? Caiaphas might need you!"

"I think it might have been wrong to take that man, hands bound like a thief." The servant felt his ear. "He must be a man of God."

"Magic! That's all it was, you fool!" The stony-face soldier sneered and walked away with the others who trailed behind.

Malchus, the young servant, stopped when they reached the high priest's home. He made his way quickly down the street to where Nicodemus was staying and knocked on the door. A servant opened it and stared into the high priest's servant's eyes.

"It is late! What is your reason for this intrusion?"

"I need a word with Lord Nicodemus at once! It is of a grave matter!" he pleaded. "They have arrested the man from Galilee!"

"Jesus?" Nicodemus pushed his servant to one side. "Tell me, where have they taken Jesus, son?"

"To the house of my master, Lord Caiaphas." Fear shone on his young face. "I think this Jesus is in danger! The high priest hates him!"

"Come, let us go at once! We must not tarry!" He grabbed his overcoat and followed alongside the young man, asking him questions as they walked. "Tell me, son, why are you telling me this? Are you not afraid of Caiaphas, that he will find out? He can be dangerous to those who go against him."

"This man, this Jesus, he is not an ordinary man, as I think you already know, Lord Nicodemus." The young man kept his eyes ahead. "Some of the priests, elders and temple guards arrested him in the Garden of Gethsemane, the Mount of Olives, where I overheard this man called Judas say they would find him praying. This Judas was one of Jesus' twelve who led them to him. We went up by torch light, for they waited for dark to come.

"They would!" Nicodemus knew there would not be any of his friends there to help him. "They are afraid of what the people who rally around Jesus might do if they saw them take him."

"You ask me why I came to tell you these things." The man pulled his head cover off and pointed at his right ear. "One of Jesus' men drew his sword and slashed off my right ear."

Nicodemus examined the ear closely and it appeared to be perfect. "Son, there is no sign of it being cut off."

"That is because Jesus touched it and restored my ear like new!" Tears filled his eyes. "One of the guards told me it was magic that he used. But he did not feel the terrible pain, the sudden loss of hearing from that ear or"—Malchus held out his blood-stained hand—"feel the ear hanging with warm blood flowing out into my hand."

"Jesus has performed many miracles, son. He has made blind men see, deaf men hear, crippled men walk, the dumb speak and even driven out devils and demons from innocent victims and"—

Nicodemus' eyes went up to the night sky as he spoke softly with reverence—"brought the dead back to life!"

"I knew he must be a man of God!" Malchus stopped and stared up at the high priest's large house. "Lord Nicodemus, we are here. I cannot go in with you. I must use the back entrance." He took the kind Pharisee's hand. "Please do what you can to help him."

"Son, it saddens my heart to know the prophet's words so well." Nicodemus had genuine tears in his eyes. "I will speak for him, but in the end, Jesus will be the sacrificial lamb, the one who will take away the sins of this world, if you believe."

"In him?" the servant whispered. "I truly believe, Lord Nicodemus, and if I get caught and die, then it is because I love him. I truly love Jesus!"

Nicodemus hugged the young man and walked through the wide double doors to the high priest.

CHAPTER 36

Before Nicodemus arrived, Caiaphas and his followers had brought in phony witnesses to testify against Jesus. Nicodemus walked up to the high priest after he saw what they were doing.

"Lord Caiaphas, what is the meaning of this? Having a trial in the dead of night! Why was I not informed about this meeting?" Nicodemus looked around at the assembled men. "Is my good friend Joseph of Arimathea here and Benjamin …? No, I thought not!"

"Lord Nicodemus, we did not have time to get the word out to everyone on the council." Caiaphas forced a faux smile. "And the reason for having it at night is to avoid a riot!"

"I see all the council members who think like you are in attendance, but Joseph is far closer than a good many of these men!" Nicodemus knew the high priest was setting Jesus up by false accusations.

"Nicodemus, I must ask you to sit down and restrain from asking any more questions or you can leave!" Caiaphas motioned for one of his guards to come forward. "Will you sit down or must I have you thrown out?"

"This is wrong, Lord Caiaphas!" Nicodemus took a seat and his eyes met Jesus'. He remembered not long ago going to Jesus to talk with him. The conversation they'd had flooded back into his mind.

"Master, we realize that you are a teacher who has come from God," Nicodemus had stated to the man from Galilee. "Obviously, no one could do the miracles that you do unless God were with him."

Jesus then responded, "Believe me, a man cannot even see the Kingdom of God without being born again."

"How can a man who is getting old possibly be born again?" The kind Pharisee had searched Jesus' eyes. "How can he go back into his mother's womb and be born a second time?"

Jesus had touched his arm gently as he spoke softly, "I assure you that unless a man is born from water and from spirit, he cannot enter the Kingdom of God. Flesh gives you birth to flesh and spirit gives you birth to spirit; you must not be surprised that I told you that all of you must be born again." Jesus waved his hand up in the air.

"The wind blows where it likes. You can hear the sound of it, but you have no idea where it comes from and where it goes. Nor can I tell you how a man is born by the wind of spirit."

Nicodemus remembered being confused by Jesus' words as he blurted out, "How on earth can things like this happen?"

"So you are a teacher of Israel, and you do not recognize such things?" Jesus had gazed deeply into his eyes. "I assure you that we are talking about something we really know and we are witnessing to something we have actually observed, yet men like you will not accept our evidence.

"So if I have spoken to you about things which happen on this earth and you will not believe me, what chance is there that you will believe me if I tell you about what happens in heaven? No one has ever been up to heaven except the Son of man who came down from heaven. The Son of man must be lifted up above the heads of men, so that any man who believes in him may have eternal life! You must understand that God has not sent his son into the world to pass sentence upon it, but to save it through him."

Jesus touched the face of Nicodemus. "Does not my friend recognize me?"

Then Nicodemus could see clearly the blue-green eyes of the young twelve-year-old boy who had touched his heart over twenty years ago. Tears rolled down his cheeks as he tried to speak,

"The young boy whose presence I have longed for. How could I not recognize the one I have been waiting for these many years! You said I, along with my friend Joseph, would see you again. You knew!" He wiped his eyes, brimming with new tears. "Jesus, will I be judged for not recognizing the Son of God when he was standing right in front of me?"

"My dear friend Nicodemus, any man who believes in Him is not judged at all. It is the one who will not believe who already stands condemned because he will not believe in the character of God's Son. This is the judgment, that light has entered the world but men prefer darkness to light because their deeds are evil. Anyone who does wrong hates the light and keeps away from it, for fear that his deeds may be exposed."

Nicodemus looked at those condemning Jesus and knew they fit that description. Then he remembered Jesus' final words to him on that night,

"Anybody who is living by truth, my friend, will come to the light to make plain that all he has done has been done through God."

Then Nicodemus recalled his words, "Oh, Jesus, my Lord, my Savior, if only I could save you from the pain you must endure." Nicodemus had fought to hold his tears in when he heard Caiaphas speaking,

"Some have said they heard you say, 'I will destroy this temple that has been built by human hands and in three days I will build another without human aid.' What have you to say to this evidence?"

Jesus remained silent and offered no reply. Nicodemus was trying to piece together what Jesus had meant by that declaration. Then he saw the high priest get in Jesus' face and say loudly,

"Jesus of Nazareth, I am asking you, by the Living God Himself, tell me, ARE YOU THE CHRIST? ARE YOU THE SON OF GOD?"

The voice of Jesus came softly, yet strong, as he declared, "I AM! YES! You will see, all of you, the Son of Man sitting at the right hand of power coming in the clouds of heaven!"

With that, the high priest tore his robe dramatically as he cried, "Why do we need witnesses? You heard the blasphemy!" Caiaphas turned to Nicodemus and smirked, "What is your opinion now?"

Nicodemus was not aware that Caiaphas had spoken to him. All he could see and feel was the most incredible love he had ever known. In that instant, he knew what Jesus meant about destroying the temple and building it back in three days. He would be crucified and die and on the third day, he would arise again by the hand of the Almighty God." *Jesus is the Temple!*

CHAPTER 37

Peter waited outside the high priest's courtyard. He was not allowed to enter. He could smell the smoke from the warming fire just inside the walled courtyard and he could hear the people talking about the man brought to Caiaphas to stand trial. Peter had grown cold, standing out in the night air. Smelling the smoke, he wished he could settle down by the fire and wait for news of Jesus.

Someone patted Peter on the back and spoke softly and politely, "You must be cold waiting out here by the gate. My name is Malchus; I work here." Peter did not recognize the one whose ear he had only moments earlier slashed. Malchus opened the gate and waved the guard to stand back.

"This man is a friend of mine. He needs only to sit by the fire for a while."

"Very good, Malchus." The guard spoke dryly and motioned with his head for Peter to come inside. "Enter!"

Peter walked behind the kind stranger. "Thank you, Malchus, for your kindness. Why are you doing this? You do not even know me."

"I know you are a friend of his; that is enough for me. You are truly blessed to be one of his chosen." The firelight brushed across the young man's face; then Peter recognized him. With that, Malchus walked back inside the big house.

Peter was still looking his way when the guard who had let him inside came over to warm himself. He looked hard at the stranger he had just let through the gate.

"You were with the Nazarene, with Jesus!"

Peter looked around at all the questioning eyes. "I do not understand. I don't know what you are talking about!" He scrambled to his feet when he noticed the angry faces watching. In the distance, a cock crowed.

A maid of the high priest came outside and saw Peter by the fire warming himself as he tried to stand in the shadows. She walked over next to him and looked up at him.

"This man is one of them. Listen to his speech, see his clothes!"

"No, you are wrong, madam!" Peter was growing afraid of the crowd and walked out into the gateway. The group followed slowly behind him and he hoped they would not question him again.

Inside the high priest's house, Caiaphas, Annas and a few head elders had brought Jesus outside to take to Pilate. They did not notice the anxious crowd questioning Peter, but Jesus looked at the fisherman.

One of the bystanders walked up next to Peter and grabbed his shoulder.

"You certainly are one of them! Why, you are a Galilean!"

"Damn you! I swear I am telling you the truth! I do not know the man you are talking about!" Just as the words escaped his mouth, Peter looked up on the steps to see Jesus looking right into his eyes and immediately the cock crowed for the second time. Back in Peter's mind came the words of Jesus.

"Before the cock crows twice, you will deny me three times."

Peter backed out of the courtyard and onto the dark street. He broke down and wept.

John made his way quickly to the home of Lazarus to get Mary. He knew she would want to be there for her son at his hour that was to come. She hurriedly grabbed a wrap and pulled out one of her most cherished possessions, the swaddling clothes she had put on her newborn baby boy.

Daylight was breaking through the clear morning sky when John and the small group of women set out toward Jerusalem. Lazarus remained behind at his home; he had been warned that Caiaphas had threatened his life as well as Jesus'. Caiaphas had let it be known that if people saw Lazarus, knowing he had died and now was alive, more people would turn to Jesus. Caiaphas needed the crowd to be against Jesus and stand with his own great wisdom, as their leader, the high priest of them all.

John and the group of women found out on their arrival that Jesus had stood before Pilate, who found no fault in him and had sent him to Herod, who only mocked Jesus and demanded the Nazarene give him a sign or show him a miracle. Herod had already killed one man of God, John the Baptist. He would not risk the hate of the people a second time over this man, so he sent him back to Pilate.

John took Mary, Jesus' mother, Mary Magdalene and Joanna to

the iron fence surrounding Pilate's large courtyard. Pilate stood on the top marble step, looking around at the large crowd that had gathered around the courtyard. He looked down at Jesus, standing silently, his eyes cast on the stone courtyard below his feet. Pilate could tell this man was weary and innocent of any wrongdoing. He spoke softly to Jesus,

"Are you the King of the Jews?"

"You say that I am" was his soft reply.

Then the chief priest stepped up and began making accusations against Jesus, so Pilate turned his back to Jesus and, glancing over his shoulder at him, asked, "Have you nothing to say? Listen to their accusations against you."

But, to Pilate's astonishment, Jesus made no further answer.

Pilate's wife, who had secretly gone to listen to Jesus and believed in him, called her husband over. "Pilate, have nothing to do with this just man. I had a dream last night concerning your part in his innocent death. I beg you, husband, do not put his death on your hands."

"Then what do you suggest I do, wife? Can you not see the angry crowd crying for blood?" Pilate felt torn.

"Is there not a custom to release a prisoner during their Jewish festival time—any prisoner they choose?" Her eyes looked at him hopefully.

"I see what you are referring to." Pilate touched her gently on the face. "I will bring out one of those rioters who committed murder in a recent outbreak, a man called Barabbas."

Pilate knew the chief priest had handed Jesus over to him through sheer malice so he announced that he would release one prisoner—either Barabbas, a murderer, or Jesus, their king. The priest had worked up the crowd to yell for Barabbas' release so he was set free, and Pilate's problem remained. Those who had shouted for Jesus to be released had been drowned out by the angry mob screaming for Barabbas.

Pilate glanced back at his wife and saw her in tears. He turned his attention to the shouting mob and his voice rang out, "Then what am I to do with this man?" He waved his hand at Jesus.

They shouted back even louder, "CRUCIFY HIM!"

But Pilate replied, "Why? What crime has he committed?"

Again, the voices rose to a roar and again drowned out those calling for him to save Jesus.

"CRUCIFY HIM!" they continued.

"Would you have me crucify your king?" Pilate shouted.

Jesus heard a familiar loud voice in the crowd shout, "We have no king but Caesar!" Lucifer sneered as the crowd joined in shouting,

"We have no king but Caesar!"

"You hypocrites! You hate us more than him!" Pilate spoke loudly as he tried to block out his new headache. He motioned for a servant and asked that a wash basin be brought to him. He plunged his hands down in the water and yelled out, "I wash my hands of this man's innocent blood!"

"Then let his blood be on us and our children!" screamed a woman from the angry mob as they repeated her hate-filled words. The only one smiling was Lucifer.

Pilate ordered Jesus to be flogged with thirty-nine lashes, then handed him over to be crucified.

Mary fainted into John's arms after watching her beautiful son beaten and dragged away by Roman soldiers.

Pilate noticed the sad young man standing next to the outspoken high priest. He whispered for the guard to bring him over to him.

"There is something I wish for you to do for me, young man," Pilate motioned for an older man wearing an apron. He listened a brief moment, then rushed off. "My wood carver is making a sign to hang on the cross above the head of Jesus. I want you, someone who cares for him, to take it and hand it to my head soldier. Tell him that Pilate ordered him to nail it there."

"What will it say, sir?" Malchus felt his heart breaking and had not noticed his master walk up next to him.

"The sign states plainly"—Pilate stared at Caiaphas—"'Jesus of Nazareth, the King of the Jews.'"

Caiaphas stepped up in anger. "Write not 'King of the Jews'! Instead write that he said, 'I am King of the Jews'!"

But Pilate replied smoothly, "What I have written, I have written." With that, he walked away from the high priest with Caiaphas' servant.

Then the soldiers of Governor Pilate took Jesus into the common hall, where they gathered around him. Laughing, they stripped him and put on him a scarlet robe.

"Now, we need a crown for this…king!" one man laughed and with thick leather gloves, they plaited a crown out of thorns and mashed it down on his head.

Feeling the sharp thorns dig deep into his head and brow, Jesus moaned in pain as the soldiers continued to laugh and shoved a reed into his right hand. Then they mockingly bowed down on one knee saying,

"Hail, King of the Jews!"

They took turns spitting on him as one grabbed the reed and began beating him on the head with it, laughing all the harder as he cried out from the thorns digging in deeper after each blow. After they had mocked him repeatedly, they took off the fine robe and put his own clothes back on him, then led him away to be crucified.

Pilate watched from his highest portal. Standing just inside the open entrance, he could see Golgotha, the deadly hill, known as the place of a skull. Pilate knew his soldiers would be arriving there soon with Jesus. His mind drifted back to the time when Jesus had been first brought before him. He had asked Jesus the same question that he asked just a short while ago. The words echoed through his head.

"Tell me Jesus, are you the king of the Jews?"

Jesus had looked Pilate in the eyes as he answered, "Do you say this thing yourself, or did others tell it to you about me?"

Pilate remembered laughing as he said, "Am I a Jew? Your own nation and the chief priest have delivered you to me. What have you done?"

Jesus had remained calm as he answered, "My Kingdom is not of this world. If my Kingdom were of this world, then my servants would fight that I should not be delivered to the Jews, but my Kingdom is not here."

Pilate was captivated by Jesus' unusual eyes as he asked, "Are you a king then?"

Jesus answered, "You say that I am a king. To this end was I born, and for this cause I came into the world, that I should bear witness unto the truth. Everyone that is of the truth hears my voice."

"Truth?" Pilate looked thoughtful. "What is truth?" Then he remembered the high priest speaking, "We have a law, and by our laws he ought to die because he claims to be the Son of God!"

After hearing that, Pilate was even more afraid as he asked the prisoner, "Jesus, where are you from?"

Jesus had remained silent as Pilate walked up next to him.

"Please, speak to me. Don't you know that I have the power to crucify you or the power to release you? What do you want, Jesus? Tell me! Why do you not speak when I hold your life in my hands? Do not you realize you could die soon?"

Once again, Jesus trained his eyes on Pilate. "You would have no power at all against me if it were not given to you from above! Everything that is happening has been planned and you cannot change it! Therefore, he that delivered me to you has the greatest sin!"

Pilate's attention was drawn back to the deadly hill where he could see movement. He spoke softly to himself, "Jesus of Nazareth, are you the Son of God? Are you truly the Christ?"

CHAPTER 38

The streets were lined with many mourners as Jesus pulled the heavy cross made of solid dogwood down the narrow path. He dropped it many times because he was so tired and weak from a great loss of blood from the beating. Each time Jesus would drop the cross, the soldier walking behind him would order him to pick it up and continue walking.

At one point when Jesus dropped the heavy cross, he was unable to find the strength to lift it again. After several attempts from the angry soldier to force him back on his feet, the soldier turned and pulled out a man who had been standing with the crowd, wondering who this man was who had drawn so much attention.

The tall man had dark skin and was from Cyrene in Africa. Simon had just returned from the fields when he noticed the commotion and went to see for himself what had excited so many people.

"You there, pick up that cross and help carry it up to the hill!" the soldier ordered. Everyone knew that if you disobeyed a Roman soldier, you could wind up carrying your own cross up to Golgotha.

After lifting the heavy cross off Jesus' shoulder, Simon held out his hand to help him stand. Jesus smiled weakly into the dark eyes staring down at him, "Bless you, Simon," Jesus said softly and Simon was amazed that this man, a total stranger, knew his name. The man from Cyrene could not understand the beautiful feeling he had felt when he gazed into those blue-green eyes filled with the most incredible love he had ever known. Simon gladly bore most of the weight the rest of the way to Golgotha.

With the back of his hand, the Roman soldier knocked Simon out of the way and had his men drag the cross the rest of the way as Jesus stumbled behind them. When they reached the hill, they dropped the heavy cross and four men lifted Jesus onto it. It was about nine o'clock in the morning when they nailed him to the cross and placed the sign Pilate had sent over his head. They lifted up the cross in place where it slid into the waiting hole, permanently placed in the ground for executions.

The jar of the heavy cross going into place sent incredibly agonizing pain throughout Jesus' body. He moaned in pain as he squeezed his eyes shut.

"Father, forgive them; they do not know what they are doing."

Below him watching it all was his mother, her very heart and soul in extreme anguish. John stood by her side, his heart breaking in two as he held Mary up. On her other side stood his life-long friend, Joanna. Next to Joanna was Mary of Magdalene and other women who loved him. They all were weeping uncontrollably.

Jesus looked down and saw them. He felt compassion for each one for he could feel their great sorrow.

On each side of Jesus, they crucified a bandit who yelled abuse at him. As the people passed below him, they would jeer at Jesus, shaking their heads in mockery, saying things like,

"Hey, you! You could destroy the temple and build it up again in three days. Why not come down from the cross and save yourself?"

"He trusted in God; let God deliver him now!"

Even the chief priest and scribes came out to make fun of him saying, "He saved others; he cannot save himself! If only this Christ, the King of Israel, would come down now from the cross, we should see and believe!"

One of the bandits suddenly felt something in his heart for this man and looked across at the other bandit who shouted out to Jesus, "Save yourself and us!"

"We deserve what we are receiving for our deeds, but this man has done nothing wrong." The changed man turned to Jesus, tears in his eyes. "Jesus, remember me when you come to your kingdom."

Jesus looked over at the tear-stained face of the bandit and said, "I tell you true, today you will be with me in Paradise."

The bandit closed his eyes, feeling love and peace for the first time in his life.

Jesus saw his mother, who was looking back, tears flowing down her beautiful face. He saw the swaddling clothes clutched tightly against her chest. Jesus felt his own tears coming into his eyes as he recalled happy memories growing up with this loving, giving woman and Joseph, his earthly father. Jesus called out to her,

"Mother."

Mary walked up to the foot of the cross and reached up to touch his feet.

"You had such perfect little feet when you were born." She tried to smile as she remembered, "I would rub them and you...you would...laugh." Tears again as she looked up into his beautiful eyes, "Jesus, my son, my beautiful little boy."

"Mother, you know how much I love you. Know this, in three days I will look with life into your eyes." Jesus looked down at John who was walking up to help Mary. "Mother, behold your son." Mary glanced at John who was watching Jesus as he looked back at him and said, "Behold your mother."

"I will take good care of your mother, Lord." John took her a few steps back when the sky began to grow dark. It was midday when Jesus looked up into the sky and said,

"My God, my God, why have you forgotten me?"

Some bystanders whispered, "Listen, he is calling for Elijah!" Others said, "No, he is calling up to God!"

Darkness covered the land when Jesus spoke softly, "It is finished." His mind drifted. "I have completed my purpose for coming down to earth, my Father." It was almost three o'clock when his last words came, "Father, into Your hands I commend my spirit." Jesus' head fell limply to the right, his hair blowing out gently in the heavy wind that suddenly arose. There was a loud ripping sound as the huge temple curtain was split in two from top to bottom. Jesus' sacrifice for mankind opened up heaven for all the children on earth, all who would confess their sins and believe in Jesus.

When the head centurion, who stood in front of Jesus, saw how he died, he said solemnly,

"Surely this man was certainly the Son of God!"

The heartrending sobs and cries below the cross were felt by all standing nearby, while overhead, in front, behind and on both sides, unseen by the people, were 10,001 angels, watching in silence, where they had been waiting for one word of command from the lips of Jesus to them. Should that have happened, the angels would have taken him down off the cross and destroyed the earth. Jesus chose to save those who believe in him, so he suffered alone for all believers. My Lord, what a Savior!

Evening came on the sixth day of the week and because it was the day before the sabbath, Joseph went boldly to Pilate to ask for the body of Jesus. Pilate was surprised that he was already dead and sent for a centurion. "Has this Jesus been dead long?"

"Yes, your grace. The man died around three o'clock this afternoon," the centurion answered. Pilate remembered the sky turning dark and a strange storm coming about that time. "Sir, we pierced him in the side with a spear to be sure he was dead so we would not have to break his legs before the Jewish sabbath. It was most unusual, sir. When we pierced him, first blood flowed out, then water, pure clean water!"

Pilate dismissed the soldier and gave Joseph the body of Jesus.

When Joseph arrived at Golgotha, he saw Jesus' body had been taken down and his mother was cradling him in her arms, weeping loudly. His heart was breaking watching the mother who had rushed inside the temple to get her twelve-year-old son some twenty-one years before. Joseph heard a familiar voice behind him and knew his friend Nicodemus had arrived to help him with the burial preparations. "We will give the dear woman all the time she needs to say goodbye."

"But only goodbye for a short time, my old friend." Joseph looked sadly at the grieving mother. "It must be hard to lose such a special son."

John noticed the two friendly Pharisees waiting and whispered to Mary, "Dear lady, some friends have come to take Jesus and prepare him for burial. The Sabbath grows near."

Mary's sad wet eyes turned to see the two men waiting, holding new linen and spices. "You have come after my son," Mary spoke between sniffles. "Where will you lay him?"

"I have a new tomb hewn out of solid rock." Joseph took her hand. "It was mine, but I want to lay your beloved son inside. You may come with us if you like and see where he will be laid to rest."

"Then take him. I think I will say my goodbyes here. I shouldn't wish to see my little boy wrapped in burial clothes." Mary bent down and kissed his face one last time as the Son of man, for the next time she saw Jesus, he would be her King, her Savior, the Son of the Living God!

"Goodnight, my dear boy." Mary caressed his body, her heart breaking. "Sleep in peace, until your Heavenly Father awakens you into His light on the first day of the week."

Mary of Magdalene, Joanna and Mary, the mother of Jose,

followed the men to see where Jesus would be laid. When the two men came out of the tomb, Roman soldiers stood ready to roll a very heavy stone in front of the entrance.

Earlier Caiaphas had demanded Pilate to have the tomb secured well and have a guard posted to keep watch, afraid the followers of Jesus would steal his body away and say he had arisen from the dead.

To get the high priest out of his hair, Pilate agreed.

CHAPTER 39

It was turning daylight when Andrew rode into Capernaum. He found Peter sitting in their old fishing boat, his face staring up at the rising sun over the Sea of Galilee. Andrew walked up to the water's edge and called out to his brother. Peter looked up sadly and waved as he climbed down from the ship.

"I thought I might find you here, brother." Andrew spoke softly as he placed his hand on Peter's shoulder. "Did it help to come home to your wife and familiar surroundings?"

"I thought it would," Peter mumbled. "I sought comfort in my wife's arms. When that did not help the ache in my heart, I cast out alone to fish. I have changed, Andrew. I'm not the same man I was when I left here three years ago."

Andrew nodded in agreement as he let Peter pour out his heart to him.

"Do not get me wrong, Andrew. I still love my wife, but...I love Jesus more." Peter had tears in his eyes. "He called me his rock. He said he would build his church on me. I...I let him down, Andrew. I denied my Lord, just as he predicted."

"Peter, don't you know how much Jesus loves you?' Andrew looped his arm around his brother's shoulders. "Surely, you must know he forgave you even before you denied him."

"That is the one thing I keep seeing, Andrew." Peter glanced out at the peaceful sea as he recalled locking eyes with Jesus after he had denied him a third time and the cock had crowed a second time. "Jesus had love written all over his face, and I just knew he understood what I was feeling. It was as though I could hear his beautiful voice say, 'It will be alright, Peter. I forgive you.'"

"I have come to take you back to Jerusalem, Peter." Andrew took hold of his brother's arm. "The others wait for us in the upper room where we shared Passover with our Lord. We must return this day! There will be no rest for us until we reach Jerusalem."

"Forgive me, brother, but to walk the long distance to Jerusalem will take far longer than a day." Peter suddenly had regrets about leaving Jerusalem in the first place. "Well, we can never make it back in time! I messed up again!"

"No, not by walking; you are right." Andrew smiled and turned Peter around to see two fine horses he had tied to a rail. "Our good friend, Lazarus, has loaned us a quicker way to travel, but we must hurry."

"Then we go at once!" Peter walked over toward the horses. "I always thought I was the strong one out of our lot." Peter climbed into the saddle. "How wrong could I have been?"

"Peter, you are the strong one, remember—Jesus' rock!" Andrew settled on the fine stallion. "You will lead us to build the church Jesus spoke of. After our Lord has arisen, he will instruct us what we to do."

It was late when the two brothers walked into the candle-lit room. The other nine were already there, along with the group of women who had accompanied them on their journeys. Mary, Jesus' mother, was also among the group that waited for the return of Jesus. John welcomed the brothers in greetings,

"Peter, Andrew! You made it before dawn breaks on the first day of the week. Let us warm up some food for you both. You must be starving after the long trip here."

Two of the women had overheard and went to prepare two warm bowls of stew, fresh bread and wine. They placed it on the small table where the brothers sat. Philip and Simon walked over to join them.

"We have news of Judas."

"I figured Judas got paid well by that high priest and left to enjoy his new-found wealth!" Peter frowned at the mention of the traitor's name.

"Peter, we all feel bad about what Judas did, but he suffered greatly because of his actions." John's heart always held compassion for others. "Judas was one of us, Peter. Despite what he did, even Judas had love in his heart for Jesus."

"John, how can you say Judas had love in his heart for Jesus when he sold him to Caiaphas and led them to the Mount of Olives and Jesus?" Peter laid his spoon down loudly, feeling the urge to hit something, preferably Judas' face. He stared into Philip's eyes. "You said you have news of the traitor! What, for heaven's sake, so I may eat my supper in peace?"

"A young man brought us news about Judas," Philip continued

calmly. "He said he was there when Caiaphas gave him the thirty pieces of silver coins. The young man also said he had been a witness that night in the garden when Judas betrayed Jesus with a kiss!" Philip noticed that Peter had sat up, clearly being more interested in what was being said. "He also said he was there when Judas returned to his master, Lord Caiaphas, hurt and confused, crying to the cold and uncaring Annas and Caiaphas that they had tricked him. Judas was under the impression they wanted Jesus to protect him from future actions toward them, but never to hurt him. Then the young man said Judas pulled out the silver coins and slung them at the high priest's feet and ran from the house, weeping."

Simon picked up the story, "The temple guards found Judas' body hanging from a tree limb beyond the home of Caiaphas. It was that young man who asked for the body of Judas to bury him. He said he felt compelled to do this because he knew Judas had been one of the twelve."

John touched Peter's trembling arm. "That young man asked about you, Peter. He said he also witnessed what had happened in his master's courtyard. He told us he had noticed the exchange of looks between you and Jesus and how you had fled in anguish and grief."

"It was Malchus, Caiaphas' servant, who lost his ear by my hand, my sword"—Peter buried his face in his hands—"the same man whose ear Jesus healed, and who learned to believe in Jesus, the same as us."

"When we begin our missionary journeys, we will be looking for faithful believers to spread the good news!" John smiled. "But for now, daylight is nearing and the hope of our Lord's resurrection!"

Just before dawn, inside the cold dark tomb flashed a brilliant light, unseen by the soldiers keeping watch on the outside. The large stone had sealed up the opening completely, blocking the entrance.

Jesus opened his eyes and looked up at the two familiar faces standing reverently over him. His smile was brilliant as they lifted him up.

"Gabriel and Michael, what welcome sights, trusting faces my Father sent to awaken me from death to life! Much friendlier than the fallen angels I just encountered in the pits of hell, who were not pleased to see me. I brought out many deserving souls who now wait for me just this side of heaven's veil."

"Yes, Lord! While your body rested in death, you did make a visit to some old friends." Gabriel smiled as he pictured Jesus' spirit descending to retrieve those waiting his arrival.

"The demons backed away from my presence, knowing they had no authority over me there. I am the Lord God, no matter where I dwell. My people had to be set free and brought up from the pit." Jesus stretched his arms, releasing the linens that had wrapped him up. "Many will see the dead rise this day and walk."

"Yes, Lord!" Michael bowed down. "I will roll the stone away, for the first rays of sun are rising in the eastern sky."

When the stone began to move with a mighty force, the Roman guards jumped back, startled. They quickly covered their eyes with their hands to block out the bright light radiating from within the tomb.

Shaking, the four men backed away out of uncertain fear. When they saw the form of three men, two very tall dressed in shining white robes, appear at the tomb's entrance, the four soldiers were even more perplexed. Their attention was drawn to the man standing in the middle and their minds were racing with questions, but they seemed to be frozen in place. As they looked at Jesus, they all thought, *Was this not the same man we mocked on Friday before we led him away to be crucified?*

Then all four soldiers fell on their knees as if in a deep trance. When they finally snapped out of it, the three mysterious men were gone and they were alone, staring at the open empty tomb.

The men looked at one another, confused about what had just happened. "Did…did you see that heavy stone roll away all by itself?" One of the soldiers swallowed, still nervous about the strange event they had witnessed. "It took four strong men to roll that into place."

"The man standing in the middle"—a younger guard looked nervously around the wide-eyed group—"it was he! The same man we nailed to the cross!"

"Yes, it was he, but we…all saw him dead, pierced in his side with a spear to make sure!" An older soldier looked wild-eyed. "What will become of us? Pilate will surely kill us! He will say we fell asleep on duty! He will say his men kidnapped him while we were sleeping!" He shook at the thought of standing before Pilate.

"Pilate will surely line us up and have us executed!"

"Not necessarily. He tried to get this Jesus released, remember?" the fourth man spoke up. "I say we go to Pilate and ask for an audience with him. He saw something different in Jesus that drove him to defend him. Anyway, what can we lose? Rather Pilate than that high priest. He would condemn us without a trial."

"Or pay us off to keep quiet! Make up their own version of what happened and tell their people the disciples of Jesus stole his body away to make it look like he had truly arisen from the grave." The older man had no trust or fondness for the Jewish leaders.

"Maybe Pilate can help me understand why my heart beat with joy when I saw Jesus of Nazareth walk out of that death tomb alive!" The youngest guard looked up to heaven, tears filling his brown eyes.

In the upper room, Mary Magdalene, Joanna and Mary, the mother of James, prepared their spices to take to the tomb so they could rub them on the body of their beloved Lord. Just as the sun was rising over the hills, the small group of women made their way to the tomb of Joseph. Joanna asked as they walked along the rocky path, "Who is going to roll the stone back from the doorway of the tomb for us?"

"Maybe we can convince the guards to help us." Mary Magdalene clutched the spices in her hand.

The women stopped suddenly when they saw the heavy stone had already been moved away and there were no soldiers guarding the tomb. Mary stepped forward while Joanna and Mary hung back, frozen in fear. Peeking inside, Mary saw the two angels in dazzling white garments, sitting on the death table, one at the head and the other at the foot, the same place where the body of Jesus had lain. The angel spoke to her, "Why are you crying?"

"Because they have taken away my Lord, and I don't know where they have put him!" Mary backed out nervously and looked around helplessly at the other two women after witnessing the stone bed empty.

"Mary, have they taken Jesus away?" Joanna cried as Mary Magdalene looked anxiously around until she spotted what appeared to be a gardener a stone's throw away.

"My friends, wait here. I will ask the man working here if he saw anything." Mary made quick steps to the man, whose face was well-hidden by his head wrap.

"Forgive me, sir, but did you see anyone take his body from the open tomb?" She burst into sobs. "Please..."

"Why are you crying? Who are you looking for?" the man asked her.

"My Lord! Please tell me where they took my Lord and...I will take him away!" Mary cried.

"Mary," came his soft reply. Suddenly she recognized Jesus and a smile of total joy escaped her lips as she sang, "My Lord, you are alive!" Mary reached her hands out to him. "My master!"

"No!" Jesus said warmly as he held out his arms to stop her. "Do not hold me now. I have not yet gone up to my Father. Go and tell my brothers that I am going up to my Father and your Father, to my God and your God." As Jesus smiled, his eyes radiated with love. "Mary, go and tell my brothers also to go to Galilee and they shall see me there."

Jesus vanished and Mary ran to get the other women so she could report back to Peter and the other disciples about having seen and spoken to Jesus.

The Roman guards had been waiting outside Pilate's office, nervously pacing the stone floors when his secretary called them inside. The four men stood tall in front of the governor, ready to tell their story. Pilate motioned for them to speak. The older soldier was the first to give an account as to what really happened, despite how preposterous it was going to sound.

"We relieved the first four guards around midnight. We were alert and well-aware the stillness of the night could bring unwanted visitors, humans or animals."

"Around five-o'clock in the morning, the heavy stone sealing off the entrance to the tomb suddenly started moving! It rolled away, as if by an earthquake!" The tall guard remembered, jumping back. "It was like a giant ghost rolled the stone out of its way."

"The bright light coming from within the dark tomb lit up the entire ground in front of us!" The third man shook, remembering. "Never have I seen a more brilliant light."

"Then he appeared in the entrance—the one who was dead—and two angelic visions were standing on either side." The youngest man felt tears coming he could not control. “Forgive my weakness, your grace, but it was Jesus of Nazareth, come back to life!”

Instead of getting an angry remark from their leader, the small group of soldiers noticed the governor had a faraway look on his face, as he remembered the words of Jesus, “Tear down this temple and I will rebuild it in three days.” Pilate rubbed his chin and mumbled to himself, “I wonder….”

“This Jesus did say he was the Son of God!” The young guard spoke up, as he remembered the testimony of the high priest against Jesus.

“My kingdom is not of this world,” Pilate added as he walked over and looked up towards Golgotha. “You men can go back to your duties.” Their commander turned to face them. “Keep these things to yourself. Caiaphas need not know the truth!” Pilate walked away to tell his devoted wife the good news he was sure she was waiting to hear.

CHAPTER 40

Mary was filled with excitement when she flung wide the upper room door and ran in, crying out

"He is alive! Jesus has risen!" Mary grabbed John with excitement "Go and see John! The tomb is empty!" she raced across the room and threw her arms around Peter, her voice ringing with happiness. "I saw him Peter! I saw our Lord! He wants all of the brothers to go to Galilee where you shall see him!"

"I am going to the tomb at once!" John dashed out, Peter close behind him. They ran a little faster the closer they got, staying together. John, feeling the need to go faster, raced ahead, reaching the tomb first. He stopped just outside, stooped down and saw the linen clothes lying on the stone table.

Hard on his heels, Peter went straight inside the tomb. First, he noticed that the linen clothes were lying on one end and the handkerchief used to cover the face of Jesus was not lying with the other linens but rolled up by itself, lying a little way apart. Then two angels appeared in the tomb, dressed in dazzling white gowns. They seem to speak in unison the words the two disciples had been longing to hear.

"Why seek ye the living among the dead? The Lord is not here! He has risen!"

John hearing the angel's message, finally came inside with Peter and looked around and saw what had happened there. When the breath of life came back into Jesus, the radiance from his face caused the handkerchief to swore off. With closer observation, they could see the scorched cloth caused by the tremendous flash of heavenly light. John and Peter finally locked eyes, the truth had been revealed and the words Jesus had spoken to them had come to pass. Jesus had indeed arisen!

Overcome with joy, Peter and John started laughing and hugging one another as they walked from the tomb. Peter slapped his friend's back, still laughing.

"Come John, let us tell our brothers the good news Mary spoke of is real! Jesus has risen! Let us go to Galilee at once and wait there for our master! HE IS ALIVE!"

"Mary, I will see you safely home to Nazareth before meeting up with my brothers." John picked up his small bundle "When you finish packing your things, I will come back to get you."

"Bless you John. I can see why my son loves you so." Mary's smile was radiant, the news of Jesus being alive filling her with overwhelming joy. "Go tell your friends goodbye. I shall not be long." She watched John walk out of the large room, leaving her alone with her thoughts and things. Mary continued to pack her few personal items. She gently folded Jesus' swaddling clothes and laid them on top. It was one of her special treasures she would placed back in the chest Joseph had given her when they became engaged.

"Mother, my baby clothes are so special to you. Did they give you comfort when I hung on the cross?" Mary closed her eyes, and smiled. She turned and gazed up into his beautiful eyes.

"Jesus, my son! Your swaddling clothes hold such happy memories for me and they have given me comfort many, lonely night." Mary started to step toward Jesus, the need to hold her son in her arms, until he held up his hand for her to stop.

"Dear mother, I too long to hold you as I know you do me, but you must not touch me until I return from seeing my Father." He watched her tenderly "I knew I must look into your eyes before going up. They were the first I saw when I came into this world and I have long to see them many times. Do you remember while I hung on that cross I told you I would look into your eyes on the third day?"

"Yes Jesus, I can still hear your words clearly. You said, 'On the third day, I will look at you with life in my eyes!" tears flooded down Mary's face "Could you give your Father a message from me, son?"

"Gladly mother, but he is your Father too." Jesus stood calmly, filled with love and patience.

"Them tell our Father I send a warm thank you, blessed one, for allowing me, a simple, humble girl, to bare His beautiful son. To watch as a small sweet baby, to see grow up, always perfect and becoming the man, he was intended to become, our Savior." Mary could not take her eyes off his handsome face as she continued. "Never have I seen another son look so much like his Father as you do, Jesus."

"We are one, mother. I shall give Father your beautiful greeting, dearest one." Tears swelled in the perfect eyes of Jesus. "I shall thank Him as well that you were the chosen one we picked to be my mother from a very short list. Mary, my beloved mother, I love you deeply."

"And I love you, my son, above all!" Mary's smile seemed to radiate the big room "Will I see you soon, dear one?"

"I will return for a while before I go up to stay in heaven with the Father, until I return in Glory!" Jesus held out his hand in peace and love as he said "I go now. I will come to you in Nazareth soon." With that, he was gone, while at the same moment John came back to get Mary so they could start back home to Nazareth.

Some of the disciples found a large place to meet and decided it safer to lock the doors, for fear of the Jews. Two of the men had arrived last, for they went by the village called Emmaus, about seven miles from Jerusalem. They began telling the other disciples in the room about seeing Jesus.

"We were on our way to Emmaus, talking about everything that had just happened back in Jerusalem. While we were absorbed in our serious talk and discussion, Jesus himself approached and walked along with us, but for some reason, we did not recognize him." Simon shook his head, still baffled as to why he looked like a stranger.

"Simon is right, it was most unusual. It is as though something prevented us from recognizing his face." The one called Cleopas remembered the words he had spoken to them. "He asked us what was the discussion about while we walked. I remember saying to him, you must be the only stranger in Jerusalem who has not heard all the things that have happen there recently."

Simon picked up the story "Then he asked, what things? We told him about how Jesus of Nazareth, a holy man, was handed over by the chief priest and rulers for execution, and was crucified."

"Then we told the stranger it was going on the third day, some of our womenfolk had disturbed us profoundly when they came in, joyfully proclaiming the good news. Three women had gone out to the tomb at dawn and could not find the body of Jesus. One had spoken to an angel and still upset, she went to whom she thought was a gardener, and found out he was Jesus himself!" Cleopas looked around at the interested listeners. “I told the stranger two of our friends ran straight to the tomb and saw everything the three women had described to us!”

“This is when he got our attention.” Simon said, wide eyed “He stated, aren’t you failing to understand, and slow to believe in all that the prophets have said? Was it not inevitable that Christ should suffer like that and so find His Glory?”

“Then beginning with Moses and all the prophets, he explained to us everything in the scriptures that referred to Himself.” Cleopas was thoughtful as he continued “When we neared the village, we ask him to stay with us. It was indoors, while sitting at the table, he took the loaf, gave thanks, broke it and past it to us…”

“Then our eyes were opened wide and we knew him!” Simon looked into the face of each man present “Brothers, it was Jesus! He vanished from our sight!”

“That night, we both discussed how our hearts were glowing inside while he was with us on the road and when he made the scriptures so plain to us.” Cleopas laughed with joy “That is when we got to our feet and without delay, came to find you all together, with the good news! The Lord is really risen! He is alive! Jesus is alive!”

Suddenly, standing right in the middle of the group, was Jesus.

“Peace be with you!” he proclaimed, then he stretched out his hands to show them where the nails had been driven through. Then he lifted up the hem of his robe to reveal the nail holes in his feet and continued to lift his robe to show them the fresh slash where the sword was driven through.

When they saw the Lord standing in their mist and showing them the scars he had suffered, they were overjoyed to finally see him. Jesus’ smile glowed with love as he spoke.

“Yes, I say, Peace be with you, my brothers! Just as the Father sent me, so I am going to send you.” Then Jesus breathed on them, saying “You will receive the Holy Spirit, the third one in our Trinity, on Pentecost! If you forgive any man’s sin, they are forgiven, and if you hold them unforgiven, they are unforgiven.”

Thomas had not been with the group when Jesus came to them. The other disciples kept telling him about seeing the Lord, but he had replied solemnly

"Unless I see him myself, his hands and feet having been nailed through and his side so I can put my hand in the scar, I will never believe!" Still, after many years have past since he made that bold statement, he will be labeled: DOUBTING THOMAS!

Just a week later, when the disciples were indoors again, Thomas was with them. As before, the doors were locked shut, but Jesus appeared and once more stood in the center of the group.

"Peace be with you!" was his familiar greeting. His attention went solely on Thomas, who looked back in distress "Do you doubt what you can see, Thomas? Put your finger here, on my hands, look at the holes in my feet, then take your hand and put it in my side. Thomas, you must not doubt, but believe."

Thomas fell down on his knees in front of Jesus, crying "My Lord and my God!"

Jesus reached out and touched his shoulder gently "It is because you have seen me that you believe!" Jesus' looked out at unseen faces, known only to him, into another time, yet to be born. And with tenderness he said softly "Happy are those who have never seen me and yet have believed in me! My blessing will be with them for believing!"

Jesus stayed with the disciples and gave them many signs and taught them what they must do after receiving the Holy Spirit. He gave them so many more teachings and signs that are not recorded in the Holy Bible. What was chosen to be written about Jesus of Nazareth, tells of our Lord and Savior, so that you and many more may believe that Jesus is the Christ, the Son of God, and in that faith of believing, you may have life as His disciple.

The disciples used many of their teachings from Jesus, as their guide in the right direction to start His church and bring the good news to all the earth. This is still our mission today, to tell those we meet about Jesus and the great salvation he has made possible for everyone born on this earth. To except His grace and sacrifice, we must confess our sins and believe in the one true Savior, Jesus Christ, the Son of God!

CHAPTER 41

Joanna had invited all the woman who had traveled with Jesus and his disciples to her home. They all felt a sense of loss for what to do now that Jesus had become their risen Lord and no longer needed their services. They questioned among themselves, would they still be needed to help carry on Christ ministry or was their help no longer required.

"My dear women, your help is always needed!" suddenly, Jesus was standing in front of them. "After I go home to live with my Father, my brothers will receive the Holy Spirit and their message will start here in Jerusalem. Then they must go out, proclaiming the good news to all nations. They will need your aid and support just as you lovingly gave me on our journeys together. It will be at this time, you too, will receive the Holy Spirit, I and the Father with you always!"

"Master, we feel blessed that you would come to tell us this wonderful news yourself!" Mary of Magdalene stepped forward and kneeled at his feet, letting her fingers run over the nail holes as tears fell from her eyes "I will serve you Lord the rest of my days!"

Jesus reached out and lifted her up into his arms. "I love you, Mary."

Then the other women came forward and fell on their knees, saying similar words spoken by Mary of Magdalene and like he had done for Mary, Jesus lifted each woman in his arms and said the beautiful words to them. Calling each name, he said I love you.

Before dismissing the women, he blessed them and said "In ten days, come to the country side outside of Bethany. I will be ascending to Heaven and I want each of you there."

After the group left, Joanna had lovingly had her turn at Jesus' feet. Now, she stood back, remembering how she practically asked Jesus, the Son of God, to be her husband. Was that morally wrong, she wondered. Jesus turned from seeing the other women out and smiled at his blushing friend. He had read her intimate thoughts.

"Joanna, wanting me to become your husband was no sin child. You just did not fully understand why you had such incredible love for me." Jesus took her hand "I think you know the reason now."

"Yes, now I know you are so much more than a man, Jesus." Joanna gazed into his beautiful eyes "I loved you far better than I did my parents, my brother, my children, either of my dear husbands. At first, I could not understand why I loved you so much more than anyone or anything else. Then, after being with you, hearing your words, seeing your miracles, watching you being beaten and suffering on that horrible cross, I knew. Jesus, you are the Christ, the Messiah, the Son of God and my Savior!"

"Come here little lamb and give your shepherd a hug." Jesus laughed "Now my sweet friend can tell me why she still holds on to that dried up white flower I gave her by our brook?"

"You know I kept it?" Joanna looked down and smiled "To be honest Jesus, and you would know if I weren't, it was the one thing you gave me and at our special place."

"Bring it to me Joanna." Jesus walked over to her window and looked down in the court yard.

She hurried over to the window and opened the small wooden box that held her precious keepsake.

"Here it is, safe and sound."

Jesus held out his hand "Give it to me Joanna."

Carefully she lifted the delegate flower from safe keeping and placed it carefully in Jesus' palm.

"I cannot help but noticed your flower garden below has been neglected."

Joanna glanced down at the grown- up garden she had always enjoyed keeping extra pretty, but being away for so long had took its toll. It had fallen into bad shape. Feeling guilty, she gave Jesus a weak smile.

"It would appear I put my priorities in something of a greater value."

"And your loving sacrifices have not gone unnoticed, but" Jesus looked at the dried- up flower in his hand "You really don't need to keep this dried up flower anymore. You have a far greater gift from me now, Joanna."

"I...do?" Joanna looked down sadly at her special memory gift she had cherished for so long.

"The gift of life, eternal life!" his gaze held hers "The flower Joanna? It is yours, it is up to you."

"What better gift can I receive than eternal life!" Joanna smiled brightly "Jesus, I give the flower back to you. Do with it as you please."

Smiling, Jesus closed his hand into a tight fist. The crackling sound of the dried flower mashing to small pieces. He opened his palm and blew the pieces out into the air.

"Your treasures are in Heaven Joanna." Jesus winked at her "The dead pedals have fallen back into the earth, and livened up your sad garden."

Joanna recognized the old twinkle in his blue-green eyes as she looked down to find her garden alive with lots of white flowers.

"What a blessing it is for those who have seen the risen Christ." Nicodemus gazed out his window to the hill where the cross stood. "Did we not feel his power and his great wisdom?"

"Even as a child of twelve, my friend." Joseph joined his long-time friend at the large window over- looking Golgotha. "To be alive to see the Messiah is a wonderful gift Nicodemus."

"A most precious gift, indeed." He smiled "I know our words could not have saved Jesus from the cross. Did not the holy scriptures say as much?"

"They did my good friend, Nicodemus." The two Pharisees turned to find Jesus had suddenly appeared to them. "It was the reason I came into this world." Jesus smiled at the other man, who's tears were gliding down his cheeks. "Dear Joseph, thank you for your loving kindness in letting me borrow your tomb." He touched his trembling shoulder "It shall be the resting place for your earthy body, but your beautiful soul will find a spiritual body when you dwell in my kingdom."

"That is what you meant by being born again!" Nicodemus had joyful tears, finally putting meaning behind the words of Jesus. "I was baptized by John, God rest his soul, in the River Jordon and my belief in you will allow me to be born again, in a new body!"

"You have indeed been baptized by water." Jesus hugged him "Now, you will be baptized by the Holy Spirit!"

"Lord, on the day you arose, there were reports of men, long dead, up and walking about." Joseph had heard many nervous citizens bringing this news to the cancel meetings. The scriptures also speak of these things occurring."

"Tis true Lord, and what about poor John, beheaded by Herod?" Nicodemus had wondered about those who had died before the resurrection.

"When I arose on the first day of the week, I had to ascend into heaven to my Father before anyone living have physical contact with me." Jesus loved his two friends, so he answered their questions "The day I ascended, John, my cousin, was also by my side, as was father Joseph and Judas."

"Judas?" Nicodemus and Joseph said in unison, shocked that he would be saved after betraying Jesus. Nicodemus stepped forward, to voice his opinion.

"Excuse me, my Lord, but Judas betrayed you to the enemy!"

"And, did not the scriptures foretell this as well?" Jesus said with passion "When Judas saw what Caiaphas had in store for me, he repented. For in his heart, Judas loved me and he knew the truth in the end. His words were, while he stood shaking and weeping on that tree limb, 'Forgive me Lord. I…I know now Jesus, you are the Son of God!" then he fell to his death."

Nicodemus looked down, feeling ashamed.

"My Lord, forgive me for judging when I had no right. What of those like Caiaphas and Annas? What will be their eternal fate? If I may ask?"

"They did not listen to me. They still have the chance to hear and see my disciples after the Holy Spirit as fallen upon them, but I fear their fate is sealed. All will see me coming in the clouds of glory and sitting at the right hand of the Father, but not all will be at my right side when I judge the world." Jesus looked out sadly, hating to lose one soul. Then he told Nicodemus and Joseph when and where he would be ascending back up into heaven and he wanted them both to be present,

Gladly both men accepted, happy that they could witness the ascension of their Savior.

CHAPTER 42

Mary had been sitting in the garden bench under her drooping dogwood tree, remembering her last visit with Jesus. How she wanted to hold him but could not because he had to go up to heaven first. Mary had heard about his many visits to his disciples since his return, but she knew Jesus was preparing his apostles for their hard work ahead.

While Mary's mind was preoccupied with her wondering thoughts, she had not noticed the tall handsome man who came up behind her. He gently stroked her hair as he spoke softly.

"My mother has the most beautiful hair I have ever seen and the smell of it will remain with me when I return to my kingdom.

Mary closed her eyes and smiled, knowing at last Jesus would visit with her. She turned and gazed up into his smiling face.

"Jesus, how long have you been standing back there?"

"Long enough to know my dear mother thinks I have gone to everyone but her, since my return." Jesus joined her on the bench and kissed her. "She is a wise woman and knows I have many instructions to give my brothers before I return to the Father."

"Will you be leaving us soon, Jesus?" sadness filled her blue eyes as she touched his face tenderly, "To live without seeing your face or hearing your sweet voice will not come easy."

"I need you to be a comfort to my brothers, woman. Theirs will be a hard road. There will be much demanded of them. Peter especially will need your constant support and reassurance. You are a strong woman, this I know." Jesus looped his arms around her neck in a loving hug. "I know I can count on you, mother."

"I will be there for them, son." Mary laid her head on his strong shoulder "Will you be seeing your brothers and sisters before you leave us? They love you so."

"And I love them dearly. They are a part of you and father Joseph and they are my earthy family. We grew up together." Jesus stood up and helped her stand "You can relax mother. I have already paid each one of my brothers and sisters a visit."

"Your love is so pure and perfect, my son." Mary clutched his hand tightly. "Jesus, you know I loved my parents dearly, my children with Joseph were all so special, and Joseph, my Joseph, my heart was his from the moment I laid eyes on that handsome face and his smell of new wood." Mary caressed his face "Jesus, my son, I hold you the highest in my heart. Never have I loved anyone like I do you. My precious boy."

"And did not the scriptures say: You shall love the Lord thy God with all thy heart! With all your soul, mind and strength!" Jesus kissed her forehead "Mother, the Father and the Son are one, as is the Holy Spirit, who I leave with you. I will always be by your side."

"That is a comfort to know son, but…I wish I could go with you!" Mary felt the tears coming and she knew she could never stop them.

"You shall have a long- life mother, before you join me and your one true love, Joseph." Jesus laughed softly, seeing the question written on her face "Yes mother, I took Joseph up with me. He is alive and very happy building a mansion for you and him."

"Joseph is building a mansion? In heaven? For us?" she smiled when Jesus nodded yes. "Jesus, could you tell me how old I will be when I die, just so I will know?" Mary knew her son was sure to know the answer.

"You are right mother! I know, but I will never tell you!" he laughed "You will be counting the days and marking the years off! Just like a small child does when it's time for their birthday."

"Then I will be there to see you before you go back? Surely your disciples want have those last moments to themselves. Not one of them could love you as much as I!" Mary patted his shoulder playfully.

"Nine days from now, outside of Bethany and bring my swaddling clothes." Jesus chuckled.

"I will not ask why you are teasing me, son." Mary reached up and kissed his cheek "Couldn't you give me one little hint how old I will be when I take my last breath on earth?"

"Mother?" Jesus shook his head and looked up at the once tall, majestic Dogwood tree, then down at where they had been sitting. "This old tree cast a deep shadow on your bench. It is really shady."

Mary noticed how Jesus had pulled her away from the subject on her mind. She finally gave a soft laugh.

"Yes, it does stay shady and that is why I come outside to sit here when it gets to hot to be inside." She touched his face tenderly "Very well, no more talk about my age. Do you have time to break some bread with me before you leave?"

"I would never turn down a chance to eat some homemade bread you made, Mother. Got any stew to go with it?" Jesus took her hand, smiling "The angels used cinnamon in their stew!" he noticed his mother giving him a 'how do you know' look. "I was there, remember?" Patting her hand, they walked inside to enjoy Mary's cooking.

CHAPTER 43

Jesus' last forty day on this earth was spent seeking out many different people. Some old friends, some new groups of disciples who had began to preach in his name and nations yet to be discovered. He could be in many places, no matter the distance, within seconds. He is, after all, the Son of God. Nothing is impossible with him.

Jesus' last personal visit was at the home of his dear friends Lazarus, Mary and Martha.

"Walk with me, my friends. It is just a short way into the country side." He led them to a green valley surrounded by rolling hills. They saw the familiar faces of Peter, James. John, Andrew, James the less, Thomas, Phillip, Nathanael, Bartholomew, Matthew and Thaddeus, eleven of the original disciples. They were all waiting in the open green field.

Besides the disciples, there were the women who had devoted their time to Jesus' cause, many other friends and Jesus' earthly brothers and sisters. Clutching Jesus' swaddling clothes, Mary stood out front, her attention strictly on her son.

With his last three friends joining the group, Jesus climbed up a small hill to address those he had known and been with for thirty-three years. Those he held a special love in his heart for.

"It is with mix feelings I leave you, my dear friends and family." Jesus' eyes scanned the faces he loved so dearly. "With sadness that I won't be here to guide you personally or…" he looked at Mary "or feel you in my arms for a long time. The joy that fills my heart is knowing you soon will be receiving the Holy Spirit, to guide your paths, fill you with words you never thought possible. I leave you knowing you will be taken care of." Tears filled Jesus' eyes as he continued "Please know, I am with you, even though you cannot see me." He held out his arms

"Go now, my brothers and sisters, my mother and friends, and teach all nations about me, making it your first care to love one another. To be great, you must humble yourself. To be big, you must be the smallest in the group. Your faith in me will win many souls!

Many lost sheep will be found and brought to the shepherd.

Your sacrifices will not come easy. Many will hate you because you are mine, but your reward is far greater in heaven!

Remember what I told you Peter! Now I say it to all of you, feed my sheep! Feed them with words of salvation, the only way to the Father is by me! No one can receive eternal life by their own good merits. All you have to do is believe in me! Believe that I died on that cross to take your sins away for all eternity."

Jesus' eyes fell on Mary, his mother, as his body began to rise up into the sky. He stretched out his hand toward her.

"I sit at the right hand of God, my Father! There is a stool below my feet, sweet mother, it will be your seat."

Mary's lips moved in a soft whisper as her tears fell.

"I love you, son."

"I love you, Mother!" Jesus smiled with total love written on his radiant face as he lifted his arms upward and in his right hand, he clutched his swaddling clothes, one precious memory to keep for his mother's arrival, home with him.

Mary gazed up into the afternoon sky, hoping to see one more glimpse of her son, who had vanished in the clouds. Even as her son Simon gently touched her arm, her eyes did not stray from the last spot she saw Jesus.

"Mother, he is gone, Jesus is gone." Simon spoke sadly, his own heart breaking at the thoughts of never seeing his beloved brother again on earth.

"You go on ahead, son. Take your brothers and sisters to prepare for our journey back to Nazareth." Mary did not look away as she spoke "I will be along shortly. I need just a few more minutes."

"We will be ready and waiting at the home of Lazarus, mother." Simon motioned for his sisters and brothers to follow him.

John had watched and waited for Simon to speak to his mother before walking over. He knelt down beside her and fixed his eyes upward.

"We shall all miss the master, mother Mary. My heart is aching to see and hear him already, but we must stay strong. It is our time to spread the good news to all the nations."

Mary looked over at the loving disciple and spoke softly

"The Holy Spirit, my son spoke of, will fill you with great

wisdom and power, John. He will give you the gift of healing and speaking in many languages. Jesus said, as he was going up in the clouds, 'Lo, I am with you always, even unto the ends of the earth'."

John glanced over into her peaceful blue eyes and smiled.

"We shall need you, mother Mary. You are the closest person we have to Jesus. You are a big part of our Lord."

"My son has asked me to be there for each one of you, his beloved disciples." Mary touched his face with motherly love. "My door and heart will always be open to all of you."

"You are truly a blessing, mother Mary." John stood up and held out his hand to her "I will see you safely home to Nazareth."

"You are most thoughtful, John." She took his hand and stood "But my sons will be with me. You need not bother yourself. You have a family of your own in need of your presence."

"It would be no bother, dear lady. More like an honor." John brushed off his robe "I promised Jesus I would look after you as I would my own mother. Besides, Nazareth is on my way to Capernaum."

"Then I gladly except your company on the road." Mary glanced back, remembering her last glimpse of Jesus. "John, did you see the cloth my son was holding in his right hand as he ascended?"

"Yes, and it looked very familiar." John could see the small bundle in Jesus' hand as he disappeared in the clouds. "do you know what it was?"

"It was my most cherished treasure, John, the swaddling clothes he wore as a baby in Bethlehem." Mary closed her eyes, remembering holding her tiny special baby boy with the incredible blue-green eyes, just like his heavenly Father. "Jesus took them up for me, John."

"A man is born into this world with nothing material and when he dies, he returns with nothing material, except a new eternal body, adorned with a heavenly robe." John was thoughtful as he continued "With man, to take a personal treasure up is impossible, but with God, all things are possible. There is nothing He cannot do! Jesus holds a special love for you, mother Mary!"

"Did I tell you the last time I was with Jesus?" Mary thought back to the garden and Jesus stroking her hair. "I ask him how old I would be when I closed my eyes in death. He said he knew but would not tell me because, like a child counting the days before their next birthday, I would be counting my life away." She laughed as she remembered his teasing smile.

"I then ask him for a small hint. Jesus gave me that 'what am I going to do with you mother' look and simply replied 'Mother?'. Then my sneaky son turned his attention to the dogwood tree Joseph had planted right after we were married and started talking about shade."

John laughed softly, recalling Jesus' sense of humor.

"Your son was not always serious, Mary. Once, poor Peter thought he had found a priceless stone and it turned out to be a droparite. Jesus told Peter that's what it was and he was excited until the master told him to do just that, drop-a-rite here! Looking around the road bank, Jesus pointed out thousands of the common rock."

John took Mary's hand "About the shad remark, I recall Jesus spoke in parables, stories with a meaning. We were slow to figure out many or most of them and he would have to explain the meaning behind the parable to us." John's eyes went up to the clouds "I think there were times he would grow aggravated with us when we ask him for the meaning."

"My son had to pack a lot of information inside you for the short time he had left." Mary began to walk as she continued. "I think we should go home now, John." As they walked toward the home of Lazarus, Mary smiled up at the loving disciple "John, do you think Jesus had a hint for me from the shade tree?"

"Knowing our Lord, I would say yes." John laughed "Let it run over through your mind, and when the time is right, he will reveal it's hidden meaning."

CHAPTER 44

It had been almost a year since Jesus, Mary's dear son, had suffered on the cross and shortly after ascended into heaven. Her slim fingers opened the chest joseph had given her so many years ago. Yet, it seen like only yesterday when he stood smiling in her open doorway holding her most treasured gift from him.

Mary's hand gently rubbed over the hearts and birds on the lid, remembering how her Joseph had lovingly made the chest just for her. Oh, how she missed him, her beloved Joseph.

As she began to lift out the contents inside, which she had done many times before, a tear ran down her face, still beautiful despite the passing years.

"Mother, I once wondered why you only kept those things, those memories of Jesus, inside your favorite chest." Simon laid a loving hand on her slim shoulder. "Before I came to know who my brother really was, I was a bit jealous over the special way you felt for him. I thought you loved Jesus far better than the rest of your children."

"Simon, my dear son, my heart is filled with love for you, as it is for all my children." Mary reached up and touched his face gently. "You are a part of my dear Joseph and he was the one true love of my heart."

Mary looked down and picked up a small robe and cap, remembering how Jesus had worn it to Jerusalem on his first Passover.

"And yet, the love I feel for Jesus is so much more than just the love of a mother to her son."

"I realize that now, mother, for I feel the same way toward him." Simon pulled a stool up next to Mary's small bench. "I care deeply for my brothers and sisters, and the love I have for you and father, long gone, is overflowing. Jesus is so much more than a brother. He is the Son of God!"

"Simon is right, mother. You are truly blessed above every woman ever born on God's beautiful earth!" Leah had join them around the cherished chest. Her hand reached in and pulled out a wooden flower. She gazed at it in wonder, then smiled down at her mother. "I know this fine carving must be a gift from father or Jesus."

"It is from neither, my dear. It was Joseph's father who carved this beautiful flower, restored by Jesus, after having a dream about it." Mary took the delicate flower from her daughter and held it up in her palm. "He was told by an angel in his dream to carve it and give to his twelve- year- old son, Joseph."

"Did grandfather tell father what sort of flower it was?" Simon looked at the unusual flower with four pedals.

"Joseph's father told him it was a dogwood flower." Mary handed the flower to Simon for a closer look.

"Dogwood? Isn't that a Dogwood tree in the back of the house, Mother?" Leah could vision how the strong massive tree out back suddenly started to droop after Jesus died on that cross, but it had no flowers, just green leaves.

"Your father planted that tree for me on our wedding night." Mary's mind flashed back to a happier time. Joseph standing in the doorway, smiling brightly, dirt covering his hands and knees. She could still hear the excitement in his voice 'come and see our wedding tree, dear Mary!' The sweet memory of Joseph taking her by the hand and leading her outside, in the dark, to the garden behind their house. Seeing the glow on Joseph's face from the moonlight as he pointed at the six-foot Dogwood tree. It had been early spring and the small green leaves had only begun to grow on its branches.

"That is when your father told me about his father's vision of the flower which has never been created." Mary smiled to herself as she remembered Jesus' words about the meaning behind the flower. "Heli, your grandfather, had told Joseph that it would be revealed, the meaning of the flower that did not exist yet. Before your father closed his eyes in death, this revelation was revealed to him."

"It was Jesus who told father the meaning he had waited for, all those years." Simon handed the heavenly flower back to his mother "Can you share the meaning with us?"

"Gather your brothers and sister, you two, and meet me in the garden, near the Dogwood tree." Mary stood up and put on a light wrap to ward off the spring chill.

Mary and her grown children stood staring at the tree, drooping even more as it seemed to have swanked several feet, as if in shame.

But it was the beautiful white flowers that took their breath away.

"Mother, the flowers are exactly like the wooden flower grandfather Heli made father all those years ago!' Leah stepped forward for a closer look. "Four equal pedals, shaped like..."

"A cross!" Mary pulled a branch down so everyone could see the flower better. The cross that Jesus pulled through the crowded streets of Jerusalem, then painfully nailed to, was made from a Dogwood tree. The pedals represent the cross. The red on the tip of each pedal is the blood shed from his feet, his hands and his head, where the crown of thorns were crushed down." A tear ran down Mary's face. Knowing that once again, the words Jesus had spoken had come true.

"Mother, the bright golden center must be our risen Savior!" Simon had tears of his own, as did the entire family standing in the garden. "Jesus was so much more than a loving brother to us, my dear family, Jesus is our Lord and Savior!"

"And are we not blessed as well?" Leah sang out "To have spent our growing up years together as a family!" her eyes lit up with joy "I can remember my long walks with Jesus and how happy my heart was whenever he would speak!"

"And mine!" James hugged his sister "He seem to have an endless supply of stories, each one with a meaning."

"Jesus called them parables, and each one taught us an important lesson!" Simon smiled as he recalled those happy times spent with Jesus. "Oh, to hear his voice again."

"You will Simon, my son. We all will hear Jesus speak to us again!" Mary placed the wooden flower inside her pocket and pulled her wrap tighter. "There is still a hint of winter in the spring wind. Let us return to the house."

The boys kissed their mother and walked toward the carpenter work shop to begin their daily job. Leah and her sister followed their mother back to her room so she could store the wooden flower away.

Leah's attention took in the items still left inside the chest. Something was missing. Something Leah remembered well, for it was her mother's most treasured memory of Jesus.

"Mother, have you taken out the swaddling clothes you had on Jesus in Bethlehem? They were your favorite!"

"They are waiting for me in a safer place, Leah." Mary replaced all the items and closed the lid slowly.

"Safer than your most precious chest?" Leah followed her mother over to the window where Mary had stop to gaze up into the clear blue sky.

"My son took his swaddling clothes to heaven with him and has laid them on the stool below his feet, where he sits at the right side of his Father."

"Mother, we come into this world with nothing material and go back the same way.' Leah watched her mother carefully "Yet, you say, Jesus took his swaddling clothes to heaven with him?"

"John reminded me of that very thing daughter, but he added, with God all things are possible!" Mary reached over to kiss her daughter's cheek "Jesus knew how much I treasured those little baby clothes he had worn." Mary's thoughts drifted back to when she held Jesus for the first time, smelt the sweetness of his breath near her face. "Jesus was such a sweet tiny baby, and yet, he was the Son of God. Leah, there are somethings you will always remember and I can remember everything about that night in Bethlehem. I can still smell the fresh straw in the manger. Hear the soft sounds of the cow, sheep and our precious little donkey. I can still see Joseph smiling down at Jesus with more love than I could describe." Tears came into her blue eyes as she recalled the powerful, emotional feelings that had come into her heart.

"Leah, when I looked down at that perfect little face, I was looking at the face of God!"

CHAPTER 45

Mary walked slowly to her bedroom. The house was once again quiet after her big family left from celebrating her 80th birthday. She had given everyone extra kisses and hugs. Her adult children, grandchildren, and great-grandchildren.

Mary reached inside her wardrobe and pulled out her old worn blue gown. It had been Joseph's favorite. Even with the passing years, the gown still fit her perfect.

"It still hangs nicely on me, Joseph, but the body inside has changed a bit." She laughed softly, remembering how her Joseph's eyes sparkled when she climbed into their bed wearing it.

Slowly, Mary walked over to the wooden chest Joseph had given her when they became engaged. She slowly ran her frail hand over the beautiful carving. Tears came into her blue eyes as she could vision Joseph's smiling face standing in her doorway, holding the loving gift. How they had love one another and were so happy, never knowing that God had a special gift of His own for them that would change their lives and the world forever.

"Joseph, my darling, how I miss you still. Holding me in your strong embrace, smelling the sawdust on your clothes, your warm lips kissing me." Mary carried the chest and sat it on her bed, the side where Joseph slept next to her.

She laid down next to it and place a hand lovingly over the chest as tears ran down her face. How much longer, she thought, before I see Joseph, before I see my beautiful son?

Mary could hear the wind blowing and got up to look from her window into the moonlit sky. She could easily make out the Dogwood tree in the bright moonlight, it's silhouette casting a shadow, that resembled noonday shade, over the bench Joseph had built for them. Her thoughts went back to her last visit from Jesus and how he had teased her when she had asked him how old she would be when she died. She remembered asking him a second time for just a hint of what her age would be when she joined them.

"That boy started talking about that tree! He said, 'this old tree cast a deep shadow on your bench, it's really shady!"

Mary stopped suddenly, her attention on the moon casting a deep shadow over the bench.

"Jesus spoke in parables! Mum…a hint…it's really shady. It's really…" Mary practically jumped up, her eyes bright as she said loudly "It's really 80! Jesus was telling me, in his own way! Will it be tonight?" she laughed happily and she walked to get back in bed.

Try as she might, Mary could not stay awake. She fell into a peaceful slumber. About midnight, Mary heard a familiar voice calling her.

"Mary, sweet child, wake up."

Mary tried to open her eyes as she thought

"Could it be mother?"

"Can't you hear your mother, baby girl? Open your eyes!"

Mary opened her eyes to see both her parents standing over her smiling. As they stepped back. Joseph stepped up, a look of love filling his eyes.

"Mary, my beautiful Mary!"

"Joseph, my dearest love! Is It really you! Please tell me I'm not just dreaming." Mary took a deep breath when he bent down and kissed her.

Then Mary saw him. Jesus reached down and touched her frail hand.

"Mother" as soon as her hand joined his, it became young again. He lifted her up "We have come to take you home."

"I truly am alive at last!" Mary rejoiced and turned to look down at her body, sleeping in death. There was a beautiful smile on her lips. One of her hands was lifted up, the one that took Jesus' hand. Her other hand still rested lovingly over the cherished chest.

"Goodbye beautiful memories. I have got them all inside my heart!" Mary took one of Jesus' hands and one of Joseph's as they turned to leave.

Jesus faced them forward as he glanced back at Mary's life long guardian angel, nodded toward the chest and winked.

Gathering the chest in his arms and placing Mary's cold hand on Joseph's pillow, the angel flew off behind the family of Christ!

www.ingramcontent.com/pod-product-compliance
Lightning Source LLC
Chambersburg PA
CBHW060438180626
46817CB00007B/2876

* 9 7 8 1 6 3 0 6 6 4 8 9 3 *